The Vanishing Physicist

(A third case for Commissario Beppe Stancato)

Richard Walmsley

By the same author:
The three novels in the Puglia series
Dancing to the Pizzica
The Demise of Judge Grassi
Leonardo's Problem with Molecules
+
Long Shorts
(A collection of unusual and humorous stories)
+
(The first and second novels in the Commissario Beppe Stancato series set in Abruzzo)
The Case of the Sleeping Beauty
A Close Encounter with Mushrooms

Book cover design by
Natalia Dalkiewicz

natalia.dalkiewicz@gmail.com

Published by nonno-riccardo publications
richard_s_walmsley@hotmail.com

Author's Preface

There was a real 'vanishing physicist' in Italy; his name was Ettore Majorana. He disappeared in mysterious circumstances on March 25 1938 whilst travelling from Palermo to Naples. To this day, nobody has ever solved the mystery. Ettore Majorana also studied neutrino masses – in fact, he had the Majorana Fermions named after him.

My 'vanishing physicist'- called Donato Pisano - works in the Gran Sasso mountain laboratory in Abruzzo. His real life counterpart announced one day in February 2011 that neutrinos shot from the CERN laboratories in Geneva had reached the Gran Sasso laboratory at faster than the speed of light. Repeated checks by him and his team still turned up the same 'impossible' result.

Later on in 2011, the chief scientist was forced to resign, announcing to the scientific world that it was a 'faulty connection' in their atomic clocks which had caused the erroneous result. He now works in another advanced physics laboratory in Switzerland and, to my knowledge, has never absolutely denied the results of his original experiment. That is the factually based background to this novel. The rest of the novel is, of course, a product of my imagination. My fictitious physicist suffered a worse fate – as you will gather when you read the story.

My thanks to the usual team of readers who have read and checked the story chapter by chapter: Professoressa Rina Culora, who lives near Lake Garda and teaches English as a foreign language. Karina Graham lives in France. I taught her 'A' Level French, eons ago. She also teaches English as a foreign language in local schools. Dottore Beppe Tristano, the inspiration for the main character in my last three novels, is a telecommunications expert from Torino. And last but not least, Rod Davis, who is one of the 'survivors' of the Liverpool rock group, The Quarrymen.

I would also like to mention an Italian physicist called Carlo Rovelli, who has recently published a fascinating book explaining the mysteries of Time – entitled 'L'ordine del tempo.' (Adelphi, Milano, 2017) You will discover the role this book has played as you read this novel.

My grateful thanks to a sixteen year old student called Natalia Dalkiewicz – who conceived and executed the book cover design as if by magic.

RW August 2017

PROLOGO

(A conversation which takes place in the Montenero underground physics laboratory in the heart of the Gran Sasso mountain range in Abruzzo – Year 2011)

That is absolutely impossible, *professore.* Our quantum atomic clocks must be out of sync with the ones at CERN. There is no other plausible explanation.

I've checked and rechecked the data and the apparatus a hundred times, Gianni. The neutrinos arrived here well before they should have done. Look – I've got the figures here.

Let me see them, *professore...* No, it's totally impossible. According to your calculations, the neutrinos covered the distance of 732 kilometres between CERN and our laboratory and arrived here 60.70 nanoseconds faster than they should have done.

Yes, Gianni, they did just that.

But you know as well as I do, *professore,* your result would mean they travelled faster than the speed of light.

Appunto! That is precisely my conclusion – improbable as it may seem at first sight.

Just supposing for one brief instant that your calculations are correct – and our atomic clocks are not playing up - I presume you are aware of what the consequences would be?

Yes, of course! What do you take me for? It means that Einstein and every scientist from Dirac to Feynman have got it wrong. We would have to rewrite the history of physics. We might even have to accept the existence of a multiverse or, even worse, include God within an explanation of creation. Our notions of time would be a total illusion. Need I go on, Gianni?

More to the point, *professore,* it would mean every accumulated bit of knowledge we have gained in over a century of scientific discovery would be called into question. And we are talking about the knowledge that has given us atomic power, the computer, the web... Everything we rely on would be overturned in one cataclysmic collapse of credibility.

It has happened before, you know, Gianni. Galileo did it. Sir Isaac Newton did it. So did Einstein, for a while. Now it is our turn to overthrow accepted wisdom.

It would never be allowed to happen, *professore* – even if what you say were proved to be true. But you *know*, in your heart of hearts, that Einstein was right. His theory of relativity – indeed the whole physical structure of the universe as we know it - depends on the fact that nothing *measurable* can exceed the speed of light.

And YOU know, Gianni, if the Big Bang theory is correct, that the expansion of the universe happened immeasurably faster than the speed of light. There are mysteries in creation that we have simply not yet fathomed...

D'accordo, professore – Donato. But we have to be practical. If we want our laboratories to survive financially, now is simply not the time to rock the boat. If you persist, the boat will sink to the bottom of the sea – with all of us on board.

*But which is more important to mankind, Gianni - our own personal interests or the scientific truth about our universe? I know which of those paths **I** would opt for...*

1: A politically undesirable result...

(A phone call made to the home of Agent Cosimo Moretto of the DASR (Directorate of Advanced Scientific Research - somewhere near Boston USA – May 8th 2011)

- DASR – Agent Cosimo Moretto speaking.

- Ciao. This is Agente Giada Costa – calling from L'Aquila in Abruzzo - In Italy, you know.

- Yes, thank you, Agent Costa. I am perfectly aware of who you are *and* whereabouts in the universe you are located. You know what time it is over here, I presume?

- Quite early in the morning, I guess. Sorry, I've been over here so long that I tend to forget about the time difference. But this IS important, Agente Moretto. I prefer disturbing your breakfast rather than being hauled over the coals later on for not informing you promptly.

- OK, OK. But I haven't even got to the coffee stage yet. I've still got a towel wrapped round my middle. But, so be it, Agent Costa – Giada. Give me a minute to get a dressing-gown on – I'd be embarrassed talking shop with a lady while I'm still half naked.

Agente Giada Costa suppressed the vaguely unpleasant images of the semi-naked, flabby individual which sprang to mind and concentrated her thoughts on the details of the explanation she was about to impart to her 'controller' in the USA. There was a lapse of a good five minutes during which she had to listen to the varied domestic sounds emanating from the other end of the dedicated telephone line. She could hear the familiar sound of a *moka* coffee pot being unscrewed and filled with ground coffee before being placed over a lighted gas ring. Then there followed the more discreet sound of a laptop being opened and keys being tapped. Giada assumed that her *capo* was going through the process of bringing up her details on his screen, thereby giving the lie to the impression he had wished to create earlier that he had recognised her instantly. So what the hell, she thought. She had had nothing of great interest to report for nearly two years from her 'undercover' post in this region of central Italy. The last time she had been obliged to submit a full analysis of anything had been as a result of the 2009 earthquake in L'Aquila. After that event, she had been told to concentrate on the underground physics laboratory buried beneath the Gran Sasso mountain range. She had become weary of pretending to show an interest whenever the good people of Abruzzo laboriously explained to her that the mountain range was nicknamed 'The Sleeping Beauty' because from a distance it resembled a supine young lady with long hair; the likeness was

9

obvious to anyone with a modicum of imagination, she considered.

It was *she* who should be nicknamed *The Sleeping Beauty,* she reckoned. It had been a relatively easy step to become intimately acquainted with one of the resident scientists, who spent his life engaged in trying to detect some practically massless particle called a neutrino. Quite incomprehensible! Her training had been in geology – not physics.

At the outset of their relationship, their pillow talk had, of necessity, often revolved round the subject of this elusive particle. She had been informed that millions of these neutrinos swept through her body in a constant stream every second of her life.

"So why are they so difficult to detect if they are so abundant?" she had naïvely asked Gianni.

"Simply because they are so minute they can pass through any matter they meet – even mountains – without reacting with whatever they pass through. It's only on the rare occasion when they collide with other particles that we are aware of their existence."

"So why do you bother to catch them at all?" she had asked.

"So we can understand them – and therefore understand the universe better. We watch out for them passing through a tank of pure water buried deep under the mountains."

"So they are like tiny bubbles, are they?" she had asked.

"No, but they cause a little 'puff' of energy when one of them decides to collide with another particle - and that's how we know they exist."

Despite the scientist's passion for tiny particles - and to Giada's astonishment - the relationship with Gianni had steadily developed and become sexually rewarding. He managed to be good company when he succeeded in setting his professional life to one side. They had explored hundreds of hidden corners of Abruzzo and Giada was left with the impression that there were thousands of other secrets still to be revealed. And 'the Eternal City' was only a couple of hours' drive away.

What amazed her most about her scientist-partner was the fact that his brain must be phenomenal. On the outside, he looked and behaved like an ordinary mortal. He enjoyed his food and waxed eloquent about the quality of *Abruzzesi* wines – almost in the same breath as trying to explain to her how a tau neutrino could transmute into 'other-flavoured' neutrinos, such as a muon neutrino. Or that they would even disappear completely for several nanoseconds at a time. When he had begun explaining about *dark matter* in the universe, Giada had begged him to stop.

But she prayed constantly that she could continue to be 'the sleeping partner' in this enchanted region of Italy. She had no desire to return to America in any foreseeable future despite her third generation Sicilian family being well-established on a farm just beyond the reach of civilisation somewhere in the State of Washington. She had formed a deep attachment to her motherland – and especially to this particular part of it. Now she could hear her interlocutor giving a polite cough as he finally deigned to pick up the receiver.

"Don't let your coffee get cold, Agent Moretto," said Giada pointedly before her official boss began speaking.

"I shan't – you can be sure of that!" was the sharp reply. "Now, tell me what is on your mind, Agent Costa."

"Last time we spoke, you intimated that I should investigate the Montenero physics laboratory – and that is just what I did. I was fortunate enough to make the acquaintance of the second-in-command at the laboratory. We have met up on a number of occasions since I got to know him. He has been very forthcoming..."

"I understand that to mean you have a sexual relationship going with this guy?" Agent Moretto interjected. From the insinuating tone of her *capo's* voice, Giada Costa had no difficulty imagining the hint of a leer on his face.

"That is quite irrelevant to what I am telling you, *Agente* Moretto."

"I take that to be a *'yes'*," he added.

"Yesterday, during our meeting," she continued without a pause, not wishing to give her controller the satisfaction of knowing he had caught her out, "he told me something potentially lethal…"

"Name?" snapped *Agente* Moretto.

"Giada Costa," she replied deliberately. "I thought we had established my identity."

"Don't waste my time, Giada. I mean the name of this physicist."

Giada felt reluctant to give him the name but realised all too well that a refusal would merely confirm his suspicions.

"*Professore* G. Marconi," she answered, "I believe the 'G' stands for Gianni. He used to teach at Bologna University."

"No lightweight, then, if he comes from Europe's oldest university…"

Giada ignored the comment – assuming that her overlord merely wanted to show off his trivial pursuit skills. Agent Moretto took a slurp of coffee before speaking again.

"Well, eh… Agent Costa… Giada - tell me what you have discovered."

"Well, I'm sure you are *au fait* with the joint experiment carried out by CERN and the Montenero laboratory over the last few months…"

Cosimo Moretto made an affirmative grunt so Giada did not go into the details of the neutrino experiment. If he hadn't been following scientific events in Italy, then he could make up for his omission in his own time. Giada would save her breath.

"Apparently, everything seemed to be totally routine until the professor in charge of the projects – his name is Donato Pisano – claimed that the neutrinos had travelled between Geneva and Abruzzo at faster than the speed of light..."

Giada paused to let the implication of her words sink in. There was a brief silence, during which time Giada tried to imagine the expression on her controller's face.

Giada jumped out of her skin when Agent Moretto let out a course guffaw which jarred on her nerves.

"The nutty professor!" he added scornfully. "Is *that* the only reason you rang me up this morning, Agent Costa?"

Giada felt a tide of irritation rising from within, which she was not going to be at great pains to stifle.

"Whether I happen to believe the professor is 'nutty' or a pure genius is neither here nor there, *Agente* Moretto. The point is that he is going round telling the scientific community that his neutrinos have just disproved Albert Einstein's mantra that nothing measurable can exceed the speed of light. He is claiming to have performed the experiment many times – with the same impossible result. He has even published an article in *Il Mondo Scientifico* in which he states repeatedly that we should no longer consider the speed of light to be a universal constant. Admittedly, the article was written in Italian, so only a limited number of the scientific community will have understood the full implications of..."

"You were right to call me, *Agente* Costa. I congratulate you on being so on the ball. I apologise if I seemed a shade dismissive just now. This situation could become a serious issue if it is allowed to get out of hand."

"Can I go now, Agent Moretto?" asked Giada since there had been a protracted silence from her boss.

"Sorry, I was thinking. Listen, I shall get in touch with the people who might have to deal with our rogue professor and I'll Skype you back later on this afternoon. *Our* afternoon, I mean."

"*Accidente!*" thought Giada. She had been invited out to dinner at the home of one of Gianni's fellow scientists that evening. That would mean she would have to invent an excuse to mollify her partner. If he ever suspected her of duplicity, she was lost. Besides which, she was too fond of him to want to lose him. Maybe she could get round it.

"I'm supposed to be going out with *Professore* Marconi this evening, Cosimo. It might not be a diplomatic move at this stage to stand him up."

Giada held her breath – but the ruse seemed to have worked.

"OK. I'll get back to you via Skype by 5 o'clock this afternoon – your time. And make doubly sure you've got that gadget we supplied you with plugged in, Agent Costa."

"Thanks for being so understanding, Cosimo," she said, feeling nauseated by the wheedling, sycophantic tone of her own voice.

* * *

Giada was dressed and ready to be picked up by Gianni Marconi. She had washed and dried her hair well before five o'clock. The computer was on and she had brought up the Skype page. By 5.30 that afternoon, there had been no call from her controller. She had to wait until half past seven before the familiar Skype ringing tone sounded out through the spacious flat. From the bathroom, she could only just make out the sound, which always seemed able to blend in perfectly with the usual domestic noises in the background. She had been applying lipstick and was conscious that she had probably left a smudge above her upper lip. How instantly badly applied lipstick could turn a respectable-looking woman into a tramp, she thought angrily. She unconsciously wiped her mouth with a tissue as she ran to answer the call.

To her further discomfort, she had to stifle the sarcastic words that were on the tip of her tongue when she saw not just Cosimo Moretto on the screen but a man and a woman flanking her controller. They were not smiling faces.

Giada Costa had seen such faces before. Her inner being recoiled and a stab of fear passed through her body. Those two faces spelt out the letters CIA – or something similar. The woman seemed to read the expression on her face and managed to assume a reassuring smile, which only marginally lessened Giada's discomfort. The man continued to fix Giada with an unblinking stare – as if he intended to let her know at the very outset that there was no chance he would ever entertain softer feelings. He was dark-skinned and swarthy. His appearance reminded Giada of a mafia boss from *Cosa Nostra* who had recently been depicted on a *Rai Uno* drama about the activities of one of the Sicilian clans. Not a great deal of difference between a mafia boss and a secret agent, thought Giada with a shiver. Her controller, Cosimo Moretto, was looking uncomfortable, wedged between these two heavyweight officials.

"May I introduce you to two of our colleagues, Agent Costa? Agents Monica Vitale and Attilio Lombardi," he stammered.

The epithet 'Attila the Hun' crossed Giada's mind; an appropriately sinister name.

"They both belong to a branch of the DASR which investigates false scientific claims..." said Cosimo Moretto – his voice trailing off unconvincingly. "They are travelling to Italy tomorrow to help us sort out your problem. You'll be pleased to know that the information you supplied has been taken up at the highest level."

"Are they coming to L'Aquila, *capo?*"

"Yeah," interjected Attila-the-Hun.

"Indirectly, yes," continued Agent Moretto nervously.

"How do you mean, *capo* – indirectly?"

"They will be arriving at Fiumicino Airport tomorrow afternoon. You are going to pick them up. I've just sent you their flight arrival details."

Giada's heart sank. A pall settled over the pleasant prospect of an evening out with Gianni. When her scientist companion arrived at quarter past eight, he felt puzzled by the unaccustomed look of anxiety on her face.

"Non ti preoccupare, Giada. Our hosts are charming people and are looking forward to meeting you," she was assured.

She looked wildly at her companion, debating whether she should come clean as to her covert role in his life. Now was simply *not* the appropriate moment.

Her tranquil life in Abruzzo was under threat from forces over which she had scant control. How irksome that she had brought this crisis about of her own volition through her over-zealous sense of duty.

"Che palle!" she muttered under her breath. Her boss, Cosimo Moretto, had certainly not taken her report lightly. The

involvement of what she suspected was some undercover organisation had left her dumbfounded - and scared. Her leaking of some obscure scientific revelation about a totally invisible and harmless particle had somehow taken on an alarming political significance. Why hadn't she just let sleeping dogs lie?

2: *Fatherhood and other challenges...*

Sonia Leardi's belly was still distended after giving birth to their second child.

"Isn't it time your new baby arrived, Sonia?" their well-meaning but elderly neighbour had asked sympathetically. Sonia had walked out into the afternoon sunshine in her parents' garden in Atri during a rare moment when her two-day-old son and his big sister were both sleeping.

"I had a baby boy the day before yesterday, Dorotea," she replied smoothly.

"I'm sorry – I didn't realise..."

"It's alright. We didn't announce my departure to the hospital from the rooftops. It *was* almost midnight."

"What are you going to call him?" asked the persistent neighbour.

"Oh, it's early days yet, Dorotea. We're still thinking about that," replied Sonia silkily as she deliberately walked further into the garden. She had come outside to gain a few minutes much needed peace.

Sonia had given birth to a baby girl fifteen months previously with what had appeared to her husband, *Commissario* Beppe Stancato, to have been accomplished with relative ease. The birth of their son seemed to have been totally effortless. Indeed, Beppe had commented that he had been the one to feel drained after the nervous strain of getting her to the hospital on time along the darkened roads on the way to the hospital in Penne.

"We women have to take these things in our stride, *commissario*," Sonia had commented drily. She was privately thinking that two children would probably mark the end of the Stancato line of succession – at least for the present generation.

The only problem seemed to be the decision which had to be made as to what they would call their second born. The issue over the choice of name for their daughter had rumbled on for several contentious days – and had actively engaged the extended family. Beppe's mother from Calabria had been anxious for the little girl to be called Imelda – her own name. She had been far more concerned, at the time, that her grand-daughter's soul was in danger from having been conceived out of wedlock – despite reassurances from no less a personage than the Archbishop of Pescara that God would look kindly on Beppe and Sonia's first born. Beppe suspected that his mother wanted their daughter to be baptised with the name Imelda – a 14th Century Spanish saint – in the hope that such a gesture would mitigate the premature nature of the little girl's conception.

"Mamma – it's a lovely name," Beppe had told her. "And it suits you down to the ground. But I can't quite see that it is a suitable name for a little girl born in the twenty-first century."

The ensuing hysterics on the other end of the line had to be diplomatically dealt with by Sonia, who always had more

21

patience than her husband when it came to dealing with her deeply traditional mother-in-law.

"Maybe Imelda could be her middle name," Sonia had suggested soothingly.

"*Stai scherzando!*" muttered Beppe under his breath in the background. "*Piuttosto la morte!*"   (You must be joking : Over my dead body)

In the end, a compromise had been reached. The little girl was baptised Veronica Isabella, thus at least retaining the initial "I", in the vain hope it would placate Beppe's mother.

"We'll have to appeal to our daughter to adopt the name Imelda whenever we visit my mother in Calabria – as soon as she has developed the powers of speech," said Beppe.

"You mean teach her to deceive her grandmother," replied Sonia in a tone of mock moral indignation.

"No – we'll be teaching her how to be socially diplomatic," replied Beppe evenly.

After a brief but intimate discussion, Beppe and Sonia decided not to throw open the debate as to the choice of their baby son's name. They decided upon Lorenzo and didn't bother with a middle name.

"Much less complicated, *amore,*" Sonia agreed. Thus Veronica and Lorenzo Stancato joined the human race with little more than a year's gap between them.

As Beppe reluctantly took leave of his little family, he consoled himself with the thought that Sonia had the constant support of her mother and father, whose large country house they shared. Beppe's two days' official paternity leave had come to an end in what seemed as brief a time as it took to down a cup of espresso coffee.

In the car heading towards Pescara and the police headquarters in Via Pesaro, Beppe Stancato had time to meditate upon the transformation to his and Sonia's intimate world. It was still intimate, he decided, but the intimacy now encompassed four living beings. Children added a whole new dimension to the notion of married life. And the change was absolute and irreversible.

It was not the sleepless nights, the insatiable desire for food, nor even the constant need to attend to their physical cleanliness that troubled him. He accepted these aspects of fatherhood philosophically enough – and shared the burden with Sonia whenever he was at home. The metamorphosis manifested itself at some deeper level; it was as if all the earlier passion and energy devoted to shoring up the physical and emotional intimacy of his and Sonia's relationship had resolved itself simply into the means to achieve the goal of bringing children into this world. Every waking moment of their lives had become centred firstly around Veronica and, as of two days ago, their new born son - who had simply compounded the already awesome task before them.

He smiled at the unbidden thought which sprang to mind that God had designed men's and women's desires in such a way as to guarantee the human race's future. Despite everything, he felt an overwhelming sense of achievement that he now had two children – whilst acknowledging the obvious truth that it was the woman in his life who was bearing the brunt of their joint venture.

What kind of people would Veronica and - he had to search momentarily for the new name which had been created – Lorenzo turn out to be? Happy? Clever? Just normal kids? Rebellious teenagers? Loved by their mother and father, certainly. He remained moved that, amidst all the upheaval, some of his moments of profoundest joy were inspired by the sight of the winning smile on the face of his daughter – of late accompanied by a gurgle of laughter and a display of newly grown teeth. Little steps forward.

His thoughts turned to that other group of human beings in his charge – waiting for his return at the *Questura.* How straightforward his responsibilities towards them seemed by comparison.

Life at the police headquarters had been routine for several months. He was mindful of his promise to Sonia after his close encounter with the mushroom poisoner, Damiano D'Angelo, to observe every precept of the code of police behaviour to ensure his own safety. Such situations had in truth barely arisen. He was of a frame of mind in which he hoped this routine existence would continue indefinitely. A vain hope, he feared as he parked his car outside the *Questura* on that mild, sunny day in late spring.

* * *

The two undercover agents, Monica Vitale and Attilio Lombardi, had arrived at the Montenero laboratory under their own steam. They had given scant notice of their arrival, having telephoned only one hour prior to their visit. *Professore* Donato Pisano's secretary had argued in vain that her boss needed twenty-four hours' notice before he could agree to see anyone.

"We might well be flying back to the States by this time tomorrow morning, *Signora...?*"

"Petrarco... *Il professore* cannot just stop what he is doing to see visitors. It is quite impossible..."

"Tell him we have authority from the President of the Directorate of Advanced Scientific Research in Boston. Your boss is not going to take kindly to his personal secretary turning away two such important visitors on a mere administrative whim."

The secretary felt cowed by the man's aggressive tones. His Italian was perfect although he spoke with a heavy American accent. The harsh voice continued:

"If the professor is busy when we arrive, we shall wait until he can see us, *signorina.* But be quite sure of one thing - we shall be there by 11 o'clock."

The man had hung up without another word. She had been obliged to go in person along the length of the tunnel-like laboratory in search of her *capo.* Feeling embarrassed at her failure to deter the visitors, she explained her dilemma to the chief scientist. Donato Pisano had looked her in the face and told her she had done the right thing.

"I've been half expecting a visit like this," he told her kindly. "No point in putting it off, is there? *Grazie,* Eva."

Eva, the secretary, noticed that the colour there usually was in his face had drained away. This was going to prove the moment in his life in which he might well have to summon up the courage to back his faith in his own convictions.

* * *

The bad taste in Giada's mouth persisted well after the day she had driven to Fiumicino Airport to pick up the two agents and driven them back to L'Aquila with hardly a word exchanged between them during the two-and-a-half hour ride. It was already evening by the time she pulled up outside a back-street hotel in Abruzzo's mountain capital city.

"Nothing ostentatious please, Giada," the female agent, Monica Vitale, had stipulated during the journey across the mountains.

"So be it!" thought Giada maliciously as she stopped in front of the *Bella Vista* hotel, which had been desperately trying to keep afloat financially since the earthquake in 2009. The 'beautiful view' was there to be seen as long as one ignored the collapsed pile of masonry opposite the hotel, which used to be home to several families. At the sight of the surroundings, the unpleasant agent, Attilio Lombardi, tutted in disapproval, thereby giving Giada a momentary feeling of inner satisfaction.

"You can pick us up tomorrow morning at 8 o'clock," Attilio had instructed her.

"What if I have other commitments tomorrow morning?" she snapped at him.

"They will have to be postponed, *signorina,*" was the taut reply.

"We should be able to dispense with your services before too long, Giada," interjected Monica Vitale in a more kindly tone of voice. "It's just until we know our way around the area."

Giada had left the American agents at the hotel reception. The owners, a tired looking couple, had given Giada a grateful smile for putting custom their way. Giada had been informed that she would be expected to find a hire car for the two agents the following day.

"Not from one of the international car rental places," Attilio had warned. "Find some small local individual with a spare car to rent out. I'm sure your local knowledge can stretch to that!"

"Sarcastic bastard!" thought Giada as she drove off under the darkening sky. If she could find someone willing to hire out a car with defective brakes, that would fit the bill admirably. As soon as she arrived at her flat, she looked at her *cellulare* and noticed that Gianni had phoned her three times. Now she would have to make up some plausible explanation as to why she had not answered his calls all day long.

"Che palle!" she muttered – not for the first time in the last twenty-four hours.

* * *

Giada had not dared to arrive at the hotel *Bella Vista* the following morning more than fifteen minutes after the appointed hour. The lateness was enough to ensure that the sour expression on Attila-the-Hun's face was firmly back in place.

Her lame excuse to Gianni that she had had to travel to Fiumicino to pick up some old friends of her parents who had arrived without warning seemed to be accepted. Gianni himself had been very tied up with his professor, Donato Pisano.

"I've been attempting to dissuade him from going global with his faster-than-light fantasies, Giada. In the end, we agreed to recheck out equipment yet again. That took most of yesterday until late in the afternoon. I didn't want you to think I was ignoring you..."

Giada had breathed an inner sigh of relief. Gianni was far too preoccupied with his own problems to ask too many questions as to how *she* had spent the previous day. Her excuse would, she hoped, cover her necessary absence for the next couple of days too.

"Have you managed to dissuade your *capo* from going public, Gianni?"

"No, I fear not. Our atomic clocks seem to be measuring time as accurately as ever – so Donato is even more convinced than ever that he's right. It's very alarming, in point of fact. At least, I have persuaded him to delay his revelations for another week while we work out the implications of his so-called discovery."

"I presume you still don't believe his claims, Gianni," stated Giada.

"Of course not, Giada! He simply *can't* be right. But at least we have breathing space for a few days."

Giada had no wish to disillusion him. She thought that a whole week's reprieve was very unlikely in the circumstances. Thanks to *her* interference...

"Where to?" Giada asked the two agents who had emerged from the hotel where they had been waiting for her arrival. Agent Attilio had been looking at his Rolex every ten seconds with mounting irritation.

"She'll be here in a minute, Attilio. Give her a chance..."

"She's obviously acquired an Italian notion of punctuality during her protracted time over here," he said with a sneer. "She needs a spell back in the States!"

"Where would you like to go first, *agenti?*" Giada asked again, sensing with some satisfaction the evident tension in the air.

"We would like you to drive us to the laboratory, *Agente* Costa," snapped Attilio. "So we can find our own way there in future."

"After that, maybe we could pick up a car from somewhere, Giada," added Agent Monica Vitale in a kindlier tone of voice. "That way we shan't be so dependent on you."

"And it must be a car with a Satnav on board," added Attilio aggressively. "Otherwise, we shan't be able to dispense with your extensive local knowledge..."

Monica Vitale laid a conciliatory hand on her colleague's shoulder from the back seat.

"I'm sure Agent Costa understands what's at stake, Attilio," said Monica Vitale, unusually speaking in English.

Giada, who always addressed the American agents in Italian, had decided not to let on that she was bilingual in English. Maybe she might glean some scrap of information from them in an unguarded moment.

The road to the Montenero underground laboratory was well sign-posted. The agents would find their way there easily enough. Giada headed back towards a village called Collecorvino on the way to Pescara. She knew a taxi driver called Gregorio, who also had a couple of cars he occasionally rented out. She had phoned him up late the previous evening to forewarn him of their visit.

Gregorio recognised Giada and gave her a brief smile as he shook her by the hand. He was short and stout in stature. He had an unkempt moustache and the shabby clothes of a peasant-farmer, all of which gave him a sadly neglected air. He shook hands with the two American agents – without a smile. Attila-the-Hun was visibly unimpressed by the prospect of doing business with Giada's choice of car hire agent. He sneered at the choice between a white Citroën C3 and a silver-grey FIAT Punto.

"They had better be reliable, *Signor...?*"

"...Mazzaferri, *signore,*" stated the taxi-driver-cum-car-hire-agent with some reluctance. "They are only three years old and are both very low mileage cars."

Attilio turned to Monica Vitale and spoke in undertones to his fellow agent in English with a mid-American accent:

31

"Well, at least this guy won't have bothered to fit GPS tracking devices on to a couple of old wrecks like this. I guess this'll have to do!"

Giada's ears were alert. So *that* was the reason why they hadn't wanted to go to one of the big car rental companies! They didn't want anyone to be in a position to trace their whereabouts. Giada felt her decision not to reveal that she spoke English had already proved to be a shrewd move. She deliberately maintained a blank expression on her face while she stared into the mid-distance. Attilio made a generous cash down payment, which provoked a simultaneous look of pleasure and suspicion on the face of the taxi driver. Attilio had picked the grey FIAT Punto as being the marginally less conspicuous of the two vehicles. Gregorio had to transfer the one and only portable satnav device available from the Citroën to the FIAT.

Attila-the-Hun dismissively told Giada that she could go about her own business, whereas it was left to Agent Monica Vitale to thank Giada for her time and apologise for disrupting her routine.

"When we need you again, we'll be in touch, Giada."

Giada drove off after being minimally polite to Agent Attilio Lombardi and thanking the taxi driver for being so helpful.

She hoped that was the end of her involvement with the two American agents – but severely doubted that she would get off so lightly.

3: An end to inactivity in Via Pesaro...

It had happened twice before since he had taken up his post at the *Questura* in Via Pesaro. Now the pattern was about to be repeated for a third time - that a protracted lull in the crime rate in Pescara was unexpectedly interrupted by events that would demand his full attention and that of his team of police officers. He was in the middle of his mid-morning call to Sonia. He had received the latest update on the number of disposable nappies that had been added to the planet's waste and the attempts by his daughter to enunciate her new words.

"Nothing to report this end, *amore*," Beppe reassured Sonia. "Some old man reported a violent dispute coming from the flat above him - turned out they had the television turned up too loud. The woman upstairs apologised and told us her grandmother was as deaf as a post and hadn't bothered to put her hearing aid in."

"Ah, the problems of an ageing population!" Sonia had commented drily.

That was the moment when officers Oriana Salvati and the redoubtable Lina Rapino entered Beppe's office through the door he kept open at all times unless he was in private discussion.

"*Con permesso, capo,*" said Oriana as they stepped over the threshold. Beppe waved them in as he sent a rapid *bacio* through cyber space.

"We've just had a report in that a lady walking back from the shops with her dog along Viale Kennedy has been shot at – or rather the dog has," explained Oriana.

"Her account is a bit confused, *capo*," continued their latest recruit, *Agente* Rapino, an officer in her forties who had been transferred to Via Pesaro from the young offenders detention centre. "She didn't hear a shot but her dog suddenly yelped and she could see blood oozing out of the animal's shoulder. Could be a pellet from an airgun, we thought."

"You'd both better go and find out what's happened," said Beppe. "Let me know as soon as you get back, Oriana, Lina."

It didn't sound particularly threatening, but one could never be too sure, thought Beppe.

But this seemingly minor incident seemed to act as the trigger for what occurred just a couple of minutes after the two police women had departed on their mission.

His internal desk phone rang. It was his chief, the *Questore*, asking him to come up to his office. "As soon as conveniently possible", the *Questore*, Dante di Pasquale, requested in his habitually genteel tone of voice. Beppe could find no excuse to delay the visit although he had a premonition that something out of the ordinary had provoked his chief's summons.

"I fear you may consider that what I am about to ask you to do comes at a most untimely moment," began the *Questore* –

35

thus confirming Beppe's fears. The *commissario* let out a sigh as he looked at his chief.

"*Mi dica tutto, capo,*" Beppe said in a resigned voice.

"It's not *that* bad – as far as we know, Beppe. I've just had a call from our colleague in L'Aquila – you remember him from our 'Sleeping Beauty' days, I'm sure."

"You mean *Ispettore* Fabrizio De Sanctis, *capo?* Of course, I remember him well – a conscientious officer and a thoroughly nice guy."

"He's asking for our help. Or rather, I should say, he's asked specifically for *your* help."

Beppe let out another involuntary sigh at the prospect of having to tell Sonia that he would have to leave her side at this poignant moment in their lives. Beppe raised an eyebrow in his chief's direction, inviting him to elaborate.

"A lady called Rebecca Zannetti has reported her husband has gone missing," said the *Questore,* pausing deliberately to allow his senior officer to make the obvious comment along the lines: "What's this got to do with us?"

Instead, Beppe looked at his chief and replied:

"You would hardly have invited me up here if the missing person had been some ordinary mortal who has wandered off or abandoned his wife, *vero, capo?*"

"*Appunto,* Beppe. The missing man is called *Professore* Donato Pisano – and he's the chief scientist at the underground physics laboratory just outside L'Aquila."

As far as Beppe could recall, he had never heard of an underground physics laboratory in Abruzzo. He nodded sagely at his chief, not wishing to utter the words 'What underground physics laboratory?' He was mindful of his last major case involving the poisonous mushrooms. Whenever he had expressed ignorance of frescoes in a certain church in Loreto Aprutino, or the existence of waterfalls outside a village called Farindola, he had inevitably been assailed by his team of officers with the chorus: "But, *capo,* EVERYBODY in Abruzzo knows about..." thereby reminding him that he was the outsider from Calabria.   Accordingly, the *commissario* merely raised an astonished eyebrow and waited for his chief to fill in the details. Dante di Pasquale smiled knowingly and added kindly:

"It's one of Abruzzo's lesser known institutions, Beppe. Most *Abruzzesi* go about their daily lives without concerning themselves about what goes on in the Montenero physics laboratory. Apparently, they are spending millions of euros waiting to catch sight of some elusive subatomic particle called a neutrino."

Beppe might have known he could not hoodwink his *capo* who had clearly read the signs of bewilderment on his second-in-command's face.

"That's all *I* know about this laboratory, Beppe," he added. "You have *carta bianca* to do what you think fit as far as I am concerned. But this disappearance risks being a bit too high profile an event to be ignored. However, I absolutely insist that you take two officers with you this time, Beppe. I don't want you disappearing again as you did during the mushroom poisoning case."

"May I explain all this to Sonia tonight, *capo?* I'll pick a couple of officers to go with me and set off tomorrow morning."

"Of course, Beppe - I'm sure our vanishing physicist can wait another few hours - if it's not already too late for him," he added ominously.

* * *

Beppe approached Pippo first and asked if he would be willing to accompany him to L'Aquila.

"I'm going to ask our *Orso Bruno* to do the driving, as you still seem to be limping a bit after your knee operation, Pippo. But I would really appreciate your presence during this journey – and this investigation..."

"What's it all about, *capo?*" Pippo asked, adding that his driving was no longer impeded by the lengthy operation he had undergone in Rome as a result of the rash intervention on his part to save his chief's life.

"I'm happy to hear that, Pippo. But I would like to take my own car too. I might be able to drive back to Pescara some nights. And if we have a second car then you'll be able to take a break to be with your *fidanzata*, Mariangela – just in case this investigation turns out to be more involved than it seems to be."

"What's it all about, *capo* – precisely?" Pippo reiterated.

"It appears that the chief scientist from that physics laboratory under the mountains has vanished under circumstances that may well be suspicious..."

Beppe vainly hoped that Pippo would ask him what physics laboratory he was talking about – just to hear himself saying the words: "But Pippo, *everybody* in Abruzzo knows about..." But his colleague merely nodded.

"That's as much as I know, Pippo," concluded Beppe, who went off to find Luigi Rocco.

The *Brown Bear* – as Luigi Rocco had been nicknamed by the other police officers because of his imposing stature and his tendency to speak with a deep-throated growl – was a man of few words.

"*Agli ordini, commissario,*" was his sole response to Beppe's request to drive Pippo to L'Aquila. He did not even ask whether Beppe himself would be with them.

"I'll take my car and follow you, Luigi. We might well need two cars when we get to L'Aquila. I'll fill you in with the details tomorrow."

Luigi Rocco nodded amiably enough but declined to complicate life with a verbal riposte.

Officers Oriana Salvati and Lina Rapino presented themselves back at the *Questura* well after midday.

"All sorted out?" Beppe asked them.

"No, *capo,* not really," replied Oriana. "As you know, Viale Kennedy is a residential area. The blocks of flats are all between 8 and 12 storeys high."

"We met the lady whose dog was wounded," continued Officer Rapina. "She couldn't tell us anything we had not already gathered..."

"She was so worried about the wound to her dog's leg and the animal was in obvious discomfort. So we decided to take her and the animal to the nearest vet..."

"You did the right thing," Beppe assured them.

"Good thing we did, *capo,*" continued Lina Rapino. "The vet found a 0.22 airgun pellet in the dog's left leg. So we were right about the airgun. But..."

"From the direction the lady and her dog were walking up Viale Kennedy, we know that the gun must have been fired from one of the flats on that side, but we came back to check with you before spending time making enquiries in all the flats," said Oriana.

Any indecision as to whether the police should get further involved was resolved just after lunchtime by a second resident just off Viale Kennedy reporting that he had been working in his greenhouse when three of the plastic windows had been punctured by what sounded like a small bullet.

"One of them felt as if it was aimed at *me!*" he had claimed.

"Take Danilo and Gino with you," Beppe had told Oriana and Lina Rapino. "At least we've narrowed down which *palazzo* the shots must have been fired from. Well done, you two. See what you can find out and we'll all meet here at five o'clock. I need to talk to the whole team. It looks as if I shall be out of the police station for a couple of days..."

By five o'clock, the whole team bar two of its members were waiting in the meeting room.

"Alright, let's get started, *ragazzi.*" said Beppe. "Where are Lina Rapino and Danilo Simone?" he asked casting his eyes round the room.

"Lina is downstairs with our airgun criminal, *capo.*" said Oriana Salvati with a mischievous smile on her face.

"Can't she just lock this person up in a cell?" asked Beppe.

"A bit tricky, *capo* - our 'suspect' is a twelve-year-old girl."

There was a murmur of shocked surprise from the gathered officers.

Something like this was bound to happen, thought Beppe, as he explained to his team that he and Officers Caffarelli and

Rocco were being called away to L'Aquila to track down a vanishing physicist.

"I'm sorry. Our absence seems to have been badly timed. I shall have to leave you in charge, Giacomo," said Beppe to his longest serving officer.

"We'll manage, *commissario,*" Giacomo D'Amico reassured his chief.

"But keep me posted about the twelve-year-old girl," said Beppe, thinking how ably Sonia would have dealt with this unusual miscreant. "Has she got a name, by the way?"

"At first, she claimed her name was Monica Bellucci…"

This revelation provoked subdued laughter from the assembled team of officers.

"She sounds as if she is going to be trouble, *capo.* Her acting skills might well prove to be equal to that of the real life actress," continued Oriana. "She told us she didn't know where her ID card was kept. In the end, I got her to admit her real name is Rosa Orlando – she sounds as if she's from the deep south of Italy – Puglia, I think. I'm not very good at local accents."

"What about her parents?" asked Beppe.

"We're still working on that, *capo.* Rosa was very evasive about the subject of her parents. She keeps on telling us that she has to go home to look after her younger brother. That's why Danilo isn't here. We all decided someone needed to stay in the flat – on the top floor, by the way."

"Let Giacomo know as soon as you've tracked the parents down, Oriana, Gino," said Beppe looking at each of them in turn.

"We'll go back to the flat after the meeting, *capo,*" said Gino.

"The apartment is in a total mess," added Oriana. "The kitchen is filled with unwashed dishes and saucepans and the oven is covered in grease. We might as well do some cleaning while we wait for the parents to turn up. Oh, and by the way, *capo,* we've confiscated the airgun."

There was nothing else Beppe could do but leave the whole problem to be sorted out by his team. He thanked Oriana and Gino, apologised to everyone and left the *Questura.* Unusually, he was heading back home by six o'clock.

* * *

The next morning, the three officers set off in the direction of L'Aquila in two separate cars. Pippo was driving Beppe's own car whilst Beppe himself travelled in the police car with the *Orso Bruno.*

"That way I can tell Luigi what little I know about this disappearing physicist," explained Beppe.

He had managed to reassure Sonia that he was not going to be in danger. She made him reiterate his promise that he would never attempt to act without the presence of his two colleagues. She was fascinated by the story of Rosa Orlando.

"We could have done with your magic touch dealing with that young lady, *amore.*"

"I bet Oriana Salvati will prove to be more than able to deal with this girl Rosa," Sonia predicted with quiet conviction.

Beppe had been surprised and - he was obliged to admit to himself - a little hurt that the love of his life had taken the news of his departure so calmly. He tried to convince himself that this was nothing to do with the fact that he was no longer the sole centre of Sonia's life. He was aware of the shifting currents below the surface of their marital relationship. He experienced a momentary stab of sadness – quickly suppressed.

L'Orso Bruno drove with steadfast purpose – never too fast and never giving his chief even a sidelong glance. Beppe would not have felt uncomfortable had the journey to L'Aquila been accomplished in total silence. But he felt obliged to tell his newest male recruit the little he knew about the reason why they were heading for the mountains.

"The chief physicist from the Montenero laboratory has vanished, Luigi. His wife reported him missing a couple of days ago. So we're going to help our colleagues in L'Aquila track him down..."

Beppe thought he heard a grunt of acknowledgement from his colleague. It was all Beppe had been anticipating by way of response. It was to his total astonishment, therefore, when Luigi Rocco – still without taking his eyes off the road – began talking:

"I believe the chief scientist, Professor Pisano, has been upsetting the scientific community all over Italy and beyond with his assertion that certain neutrinos have been observed to travel at faster than the speed of light, *capo*. His assertions are based on recent experiments where they fired bursts of neutrinos from the CERN laboratory near Geneva to our own physics lab just outside L'Aquila – the Montenero laboratory."

"How on Earth did you know about that, Luigi?" exclaimed Beppe. "I am truly impressed."

"Just a bit of reading of the scientific journals I came across on the web, *capo*. I've always been interested in physics – I attended a *Liceo Scientifico* when I was a teenager."

"But why should such a statement by this professor cause such a global furore?" asked Beppe, stifling his surprise at this series of revelations from a colleague whom he had hitherto regarded simply as a reliable if rather stolid member of the human race.

"That's a bit complex, *capo*. First of all, because it flies in the face of Einstein's mantra that the speed of light is constant - that is already hard enough for most physicists to swallow. Secondly – and this is a more subtle reason – if the professor's assertion turns out to be true, then the Americans would be very upset because it wasn't them that discovered it first..."

"Are you being serious, Luigi?"

"If this professor is right, the whole of theoretical physics is turned on its head. Americans are paranoid about any discovery that does not emanate from them. There have been other examples in the past. So, *capo*, I would say we should keep an open mind about Donato Pisano's disappearance. There could be a less obvious motive behind it all."

The *Orso Bruno* fell silent again and concentrated on the winding road to L'Aquila.

Beppe felt compelled to add some words of recognition, which only went a fraction of the way to expressing his stupefaction.

"Thank goodness I decided to bring *you* along on this investigation, Luigi. I am sure you will be invaluable. Thank you."

"*A disposizione, capo.*"

Beppe had the distinct feeling that he would be exploiting his young colleague's offer *'to be at his disposal'* on many occasions over the next few days.

4:   *Giada's dilemma...*

Giada Costa's feeling of relief on leaving the two Americans to their own devices was to be short-lived. She had hoped to wash her hands of the whole issue and delude herself into believing she had nothing to do with subsequent events. All she desired was to carry on her tranquil existence in this land of never-ending delights whilst cultivating her comfortable and reassuring relationship with Gianni. Even the risk of earthquakes did nothing to detract from her vision of living out her life in this part of the world.

She had already secretly decided – without ever putting the thought into concrete terms – that she would accept Gianni into her life on a permanent basis should he ever make her a romantic offer along those lines. The word 'marriage' never took on a precise shape but lurked happily enough in the outlands of her mind.   She had sighed contentedly as she was driving back towards L'Aquila after dumping the two 'agents' - or whatever they claimed to be - back in Collecorvino.

She decided, on arriving at her apartment, that she would say nothing to Gianni about her official role in life - however guilty she was feeling about the deception. He would quite understandably take it the wrong way and assume he was being exploited because of his position as second-in-command at the laboratory.

Giada was content to maintain her cover activity of giving private maths or guitar lessons to the children of middle-class parents in L'Aquila. She would have been happy not to charge them anything but considered she should maintain the illusion of being an ordinary, single woman struggling to make a living. She deliberately made out to the parents that she had almost reached the limit as to the number of private lessons she could cope with. In fact, it was just a token handful of eight to sixteen-year-olds who turned up mid-afternoon at her modest apartment. She had even turned down a couple of evening lessons with the excuse her books were full. This was the time of day when she could meet Gianni; moments which had become sacrosanct.

Such a meeting was scheduled two days after she had happily abandoned agents Lombardi and Vitale to their own fate. She had tried to expel from her mind all conjecture as to how they would spend their time - on their unspecified 'official business'. Giada simply did not want to know.

It was a Friday evening. Gianni and Giada had established the routine of beginning their weekend together by Giada driving to Gianni's house in Monticchio – where he owned a traditional stone house, lovingly and cosily restored after suffering damage during the 2009 earthquake.

Giada knew something was wrong as soon as she heard Gianni's voice over the phone. She had called him to check that he was home before driving the few kilometres from L'Aquila out to Monticchio in the encroaching twilight.

The only words she coaxed out of him were decisive – almost abrupt:

"I'd rather tell you *di persona*, Giada. Come over as soon as you can."

Giada knew her worst fears were about to be realised.

* * *

Gianni delivered the news solemnly as soon as Giada stepped into his living room through the solid wooden front door which opened directly on to the street. He pulled a heavy blue curtain across the doorway as he told her without preamble:

"*Il professore* Donato Pisano has gone missing, Giada. Even his wife doesn't know what has happened to him."

The shock to Giada's system was instant and the physical change to her features was apparent to her partner as the colour drained from her face.

"Giada, you look as if you've seen a ghost. I know it's puzzling – and very worrying but…. well, you've only met him once…"

Giada stammered some rapidly concocted explanation out of sheer desperation.

"I don't know…you've talked about him so much. It's so unexpected, that's all. And it must have affected you deeply, Gianni."

"Yes, we are all very shocked at the laboratory - especially his secretary, Eva. She is taking it very badly…"

Giada could not help but notice that Gianni himself was displaying some other emotion which did not correspond to the sentiment which his words were intended to express. Was there not a hint of relief in his eyes which Giada could not fully comprehend? And then, it occurred to her that the principal scientist's disappearance solved her partner's dilemma; his fear that Donato Pisano's fanciful revelations would jeopardise their research projects had been laid to rest at a single stroke.

"But there must be some kind of hint as to how the professor…" began Giada managing to reassert some hold over her inner turmoil.

Gianni looked thoughtful for a moment before replying.

"I can't think of anything definite, Giada. It might well be that the *professore* couldn't face up to admitting in public that he had made such a catastrophic error in his calculations. Maybe he has just taken himself off somewhere…"

"But surely he would have told his wife, Gianni," Giada pointed out, playing her part as the rational companion. She must not overdo the act.

"I really don't know, Giada."

Gianni's next casual words, expressed as an afterthought, put her back on her guard in an instant.

"The only unusual occurrence was the arrival of a couple of American-Italians. The secretary, Eva, said they were very persistent ... and not at all friendly. They were not the usual kind of visitors we get at the laboratory. But I can't really see a connection between this couple and Donato's just vanishing into thin air."

Giada could see a link that was blatantly obvious, but suppressed the thought instantly.

"Now, I understand, some *commissario* from Pescara is on his way to L'Aquila to investigate," added Gianni with a trace of exasperation in his voice.

* * *

The natural affinity between Giada and Gianni, added to a determined effort on her part not to think about the disturbing disappearance of Donato Pisano, salvaged what might have become a strained weekend. They spent Saturday morning in bed indulging in the glorious oblivion of love-making. With their sense of intimacy restored, they drove to Pescara and had lunch at a fish restaurant along the sea-front, followed by a hand-in-hand walk along the three-kilometre-long promenade. They crossed the ultra-modern pedestrian suspension bridge which curves round as it straddles the river *Pescara* at its very mouth and sat on a bench in the shade of the pine trees in the *Pineta Dannunziana.* Giada asked many questions about Gianni's family in Modena. She discovered that he had been married for two years before splitting up with his wife four years previously. There had been no children he explained with obvious nostalgia in his voice. He stated simply that he felt far more relaxed with Giada than he ever had during his brief marriage. She felt a warm sensation spreading through her body and squeezed his hand. "Me too," she said omitting to add she was comparing their relationship to one with a man she had been with in the States many years previously. She remained suitably vague about her motives for coming to live in Italy.

"I feel more at home here than in any other place I have ever lived," she stated simply.

In the evening, they went to the cinema and saw a new film just out – a romantic comedy called *Sei mai stata sulla luna?* *(Ever been to the moon?)* Gianni had read up about the film and had decided it would appeal to both of them. Giada was flattered that her partner always went to so much trouble to think about their outings beforehand. She loved not having to make decisions about where to go or what to do. It took away her part of the responsibility on the rare occasions when they were disappointed by a destination or when a restaurant did not live up to their expectations. On this occasion, Gianni's choice of film allowed them to forget the outside world completely for a couple of hours.

The setting of the film was divided between Milan and Nardò - in the deep south of Puglia. A beautiful thirty year old blonde, working for a prestigious fashion magazine, travels down to Nardò where she has inherited a *masseria* in the middle of nowhere. She immediately sets about the task of selling the old farmhouse, despite it being permanently occupied by a cousin of hers called Pino - seemingly a simpleton whose main contributions to life consist of miming the meticulous preparation of cups of imaginary coffee for his visitors and dressing up as a priest with the manifest purpose of persuading everyone to let him hear their confession.

The farm is run by a suitably unshaven Raoul Bova, *(A well-known Italian actor)* who plays a single father in charge of a forthright nine-year old son, whose sole wish is to acquire a new mother. After endless clashes, Raoul Bova and the blond from Milan discover how deeply in love they are as she is steadily captivated by the beauty of the Salento countryside and the rugged charms of the farmer. A host of other characters contribute to the creation of "a delightful comedy of manners according to the critics", Gianni had quoted.

The couple found they both laughed spontaneously at the same scenes in the film – sometimes when few other members of the audience reacted to the humour; at one point, the exasperated farmer turns to his son and scolds him for pointing out to his dad that he wouldn't have had sex with the woman from Milan if he hadn't fancied her. "Couldn't you just talk like a nine-year-old child for once in a while?" pleads his father. Gianni and Giada were under the impression that they were the only people in the cinema who found the line poignantly amusing.

The final scene was a traditional *festa* in the town square where the whole community joined together dancing the *Pizzica* and releasing Chinese lanterns, with a wish attached, into the night sky. Only at this point do the blonde fashion designer and the farmer realise they are truly in love – an outcome which the nine-year-old son has been plotting throughout the course of the film.

Giada and Gianni had in some subtle way been brought closer by their mutual enjoyment of the film. They talked about it - and their own fortuitous relationship - during the drive back to L'Aquila. It was well past midnight before they tumbled exhausted into bed. Gianni had switched his phone off, not wishing to face the dozens of phone calls and text messages that he anticipated he would have received throughout Saturday.

As soon as he turned the device back on again late on Sunday morning, the spell of the last two days was broken as Gianni was assailed by a barrage of text messages and calls about the missing physicist. Giada stayed until after lunch but realised that Gianni would not be able to give her his undivided attention whilst fending off the encroaching outside world. She reluctantly made moves to take her leave. But Gianni held her in a protracted embrace and, almost imperceptibly, spoke the words she had wanted to hear.

Her resolve not to disclose her true status to Gianni weakened to breaking point. She wanted to tell him about the part she had inadvertently played in Donato Pisano's disappearance – loathing herself for her perceived deception. But, in the end, she stopped herself. She simply could not bring herself to say the words which might shatter their dawning relationship in the blink of an eye.

* * *

That night she slept fitfully. Her sleep was full of disturbing images of the two American agents burying a body under a gnarled old olive tree somewhere in Puglia – in an olive grove that looked just like the ones in the film. Both Monica Vitale and Attilio Lombardi wore grim smiles of self-satisfaction at a job well done.

The final *coup-de-grâce* came on Wednesday morning in the shape of a peremptory phone call from Agent Monica Vitale, demanding that she should pick them up immediately from the taxi driver's place in Collecorvino and take them back to Fiumicino airport.

Her token protests that she had commitments to her students that afternoon fell on deaf ears.

"Tell them you'll catch up with them some other time," replied the female agent.

"But they are my cover, *Agente* Vitale. You should at least have given me twenty-four hours' notice that you intended to..."

Agent Vitale obviously did not want to argue. The next words Giada heard were spoken by Attila-the-Hun.

"Agent Costa, you are in no position to argue with us. We can even take you back to the States with us if we so choose. Your sinecure post in this part of the world can be revoked in an instant. We have that authority. Now... have you any other objections?"

Giada cut off the call. She stifled the desire to tell Agent Lombardi that he could stuff his job, or rather, *her* job. She still did not feel sure enough about her future with Gianni to make such a bold gesture.

The heavy silence during the journey back to Rome was almost absolute. Giada's anger was sufficient for her to break protocol as she drove across the mountains – travelling as fast as she dared to bring the journey to an end as soon as possible.

"Would you mind telling me what you have done with the professor? I think I have a right to be put in the picture."

Attila-the-Hun sneered at her from the front passenger seat.

"You are mistaken, Agent Costa – you have *no* rights. And you have no need to know anything."

From the rear seat, Agent Monica Vitale said in a more conciliatory tone:

"He is in a safe place, Giada. We shall make arrangements for him to be transferred to the States in due course."

"Should you breathe a word of this to *anyone*, Agent Costa, you will most certainly be heading in the same direction. Your usefulness in this part of the world is under severe scrutiny," snarled Attila-the-Hun.

The remainder of the journey was completed in a tense and stony silence. Giada dropped them off on the airport concourse. Agent Attilio Lombardi rescued his suitcase from the boot and walked away without a word or a backward glance. Monica Vitale managed a smile and a brief handshake.

"Tread carefully, Agent Costa," was all she said before following her surly companion into the terminal.

Giada drove back slowly towards her familiar territory, consoling herself with the minimal assurance that the chief physicist was still alive. The chilling words of Agent Attilio Lombardi still rang in her ears. Her days of financial security in this land were in jeopardy. She would have to play her cards astutely from now on. Her one hope for survival lay in her continued relationship with Gianni Marconi. And he *had* implied with those few intense words whispered the previous day that he would be happy for them to live together.

5: *Inizia l'indagine del Commissario Stancato*

(Commissario Stancato's investigation gets under way)

"First stop – the police station, Luigi. We need to make contact with our two colleagues here."

To Beppe's mild surprise, it was Officer Giovanni Palena, Oriana Salvati's partner, who greeted them.

"*Ispettore* De Sanctis has gone round to talk to the chief scientist's wife. I'm under orders to get you a coffee and fix you up with accommodation, *capo*. Then I'll take you round to meet Rebecca Zannetti – the missing man's wife, that is."

They stopped off at a bar before driving to a hotel on the outskirts of L'Aquila. Pippo remarked sadly that the modest hotel, *La Bella Vista,* was overlooking a deserted building site, barely more than a heap of rubble. Pippo sighed. There were still so many reminders of L'Aquila's tragic night of terror two years previously.

"Rebuilding our wonderful city is a slow and painful process, Pippo," said Giovanni to his friend and colleague. "I've chosen this hotel for you because the couple who own it are good people. They're having a hard time keeping afloat these days."

"It seems more than adequate for our needs, Giovanni," stated Beppe simply.

The middle aged couple who owned the *Bella Vista* ushered them to their rooms as if they had been visiting royalty.

Beppe caught the wife looking askance at Luigi Rocco as she opened the door to his room. She must be wondering if the bed is long enough or whether it will collapse beneath his bulk, thought Beppe.

"We can deal with the paperwork later on, *commissario,*" said the wife when the three officers had come back downstairs to the reception area. "Unless, of course, you would prefer to..." she added, remembering she was dealing with policemen. She had formed the impression that the *commissario* with the kindly brown eyes was not the type to be a stickler for formalities. He already seemed to be working out in his mind what his next step should be.

"Later will be fine, *signora,*" he reassured her with a wave of his hand.

Whether out of sheer habit or curiosity, Pippo was idly glancing at the visitors' book. He wore a concerned frown. It had been almost a week ago since a couple of guests had signed in – and at least one week had elapsed since any visitors had booked into the hotel prior to this couple. It was no wonder the hotel was struggling, thought Pippo.

"Come on, Pippo," said Beppe. "Let's get going."

The impatience in his tone of voice was born of a niggling feeling that he had next to nothing to go on in this case. He had no way of telling whether a crime had even been committed.

* * *

Donato Pisano's wife, Rebecca Zannetti, was the first surprise element in the tentative opening moves of Beppe's enquiry. As so often on previous occasions, Beppe had been dreading the prospect of being faced with a tearful spouse, looking to him for reassurance that all would be well. It was not that the *commissario* felt unsympathetic, merely that he dreaded letting people down. But Sonia had, on occasions, chided him for underestimating a woman's power to resist pointless emotional displays in the face of potential tragedy.

Indeed, Beppe's fears proved to be groundless. Not only did the physicist's wife fail to show anxiety, but she was positively ebullient in her refusal to accept that her husband could possibly have come to any harm.

"I'll leave you in *Commissario* Stancato's capable hands, *Signora* Zannetti," stated *Ispettore* Fabrizio De Sanctis as he took his leave, with handshakes all round.

Rebecca Zannetti had greeted the three new arrivals with a smile and got them to sit round the kitchen table. Officer Luigi Rocco had declined to sit down. He had remained standing stiffly in front of the capacious double fridge-freezer, which appeared dwarfed by his solid physique.

The physicist's wife turned to him and said simply:

"*Agente* Rocco, please sit down with us. My kitchen chairs are as sturdy as the *Gran Sasso* itself – and if they're not, it is time I changed them."

Officer Rocco gave one of his rare smiles and sat down cautiously on a chair.

"Please don't take this the wrong way, *Agente* Rocco, but you remind me of one of those brown bears that roam the mountain tops near here."

Beppe and Pippo chuckled as they explained to her that *l'Orso Bruno* was the nickname he had been given by his fellow officers. Luigi was looking uncomfortable – a reaction which the sensitive lady noticed immediately.

"I just love those creatures to bits – up there on their own, defying the whole of the Italian nation. If I had a choice as to how I should meet my end, it would be to be hugged into oblivion by a mountain bear," she added with a rippling laugh.

Beppe smiled to himself at her skilful choice of words – with just a hint of intimacy to soften her original comment. She was a 'natural' when it came to making people feel at ease, decided the *commissario.*

Luigi Rocco and Rebecca Zannetti exchanged a brief glance which told Beppe instantly how the lady felt about the young officer. The physicist's wife had simply found her comfort zone cached beneath the surface of Luigi's reassuring bulk. Luigi too had read the message clearly. He wore an expression of glowing serenity. Beppe was learning more about his most recent male recruit by the minute. Pippo looked on with mild astonishment at the fleeting and wordless exchange which had taken place.

"Now down to business, officers!" stated the scientist's wife without preamble. "I do not believe my husband is dead. Even less do I believe he would have gone off somewhere without telling me first. So I have to conclude he has been abducted."

It was as if Beppe's investigation had jumped over an invisible hurdle, passing in a single second from abstract conjecture to accepted reality. Beppe noticed Luigi Rocco giving him a conspiratorial look before returning his attention to Rebecca Zannetti's expressive face.

The *commissario* felt he should keep some hold on the situation by not letting the present company jump to unfounded conclusions. It might be that Rebecca was wishing to clutch at this straw of hope to ward off the onset of fear.

"That's quite a big leap of faith, *signora.* I imagine you have more than pure intuition to go on," he stated without a hint of accusation in his voice.

Her reply was unequivocal.

"If you knew my husband, *commissario* – as you undoubtedly will do someday soon - you would know that the only possible conclusion must be that he has disappeared against his will. I knew he was deeply worried about something before he left that morning. He told me the night before that he would be 'put to the test' over the next few days. That's all he would say – apart from promising to explain everything when he got back home that evening; except he never returned."

"Have you been in touch with anyone from the laboratory since his disappearance?" Beppe asked.

"Yes, my husband's secretary phoned me that evening. She's called Eva – I can't remember her surname, if I ever knew it. She was very attached to Donato. He sometimes joked he would have a woman to fall back on if he ever grew tired of me..."

"I'm quite sure nobody could ever tire of you, *signora*," said Beppe with a glint of humour in his eyes.

"Thank you, *commissario*. That is most gracious of you – and I am conceited enough to believe that to be true. Now, where was I? Eva, yes... It was odd that she should phone me out of the blue like that. She obviously had an inkling that something was amiss. She told me Donato had been visited by a man and a woman earlier that day. She had felt uncomfortable in their presence. They had practically ignored all the usual courtesies and just turned up demanding to see my husband."

"Did she notice anything unusual about this couple?" It was Pippo who had asked the question after Rebecca Zannetti seemed to have fallen into a pensive silence.

"Yes, as a matter of fact, she did. Apart from feeling very ill at ease in their presence, she had the distinct impression that they spoke Italian with an American accent. They claimed to represent some advanced scientific research unit near Boston USA."

For the first time since he had sat down round the table, Luigi Rocco stirred on his chair – on which he had been perched as delicately as his frame would allow. He coughed politely and looked pointedly in the *commissario's* direction. His chair creaked noisily as he turned to face Beppe.

"Yes, Luigi, your American connection," he said quietly.

Pippo's brow was furrowed in perplexity. He was evidently not privy to some vital piece of information.

Luigi Rocco growled a few unexpected words in the brief pause after Beppe's seemingly enigmatic comment. Rebecca Zannetti was looking intently at *Agente* Rocco. It was the first time he had uttered a whole sentence since his arrival.

"We understand that your husband has been upsetting a few apple carts over the past few weeks, *signora,*" Luigi ventured before falling silent again.

Rebecca looked surprised that this junior officer seemed to be abreast of events which she assumed had been confined to the Montenero laboratory. She looked quizzically at the *commissario* with the intense brown eyes and disarming manner.

"It's alright, *Signora* Rebecca. I was as surprised as you are now when I learnt that my colleague has been following developments at your husband's laboratory. *Agente* Rocco seems to know exactly what neutrinos are – *and* the trouble they've been causing in recent days."

"So I see, *commissario*," said Rebecca Zannetti. But she was looking admiringly at Luigi rather than addressing the words in Beppe's direction.

"Do *you* go along with your husband's claim that the neutrinos travelled faster than the speed of light, *signora?*" Beppe asked Rebecca pointedly.

She gave a rueful smile before answering his question.

"*Commissario*, the smallest particles I have to deal with are grains of rice or lentils – and when they're cooked and served up on my husband's dinner plate, they seem to disappear at something approaching the speed of light. He's an avid vegetarian."

Pippo's laugh was spontaneous and brought a smile to the face of the other two officers.

"But if you're asking me seriously about Donato's explanation of neutrinos, I can assure you I am totally out of my depth," continued Rebecca. "Now, my husband, on the other hand, is in a class of his own."

"*In quale senso?*" asked Pippo.

"Let me try to put it into words for you. Then you'll understand exactly in what sense I think he is different to us - and even different to his colleagues at the Montenero laboratory."

She paused briefly to collect her thoughts.

"All those scientists up there in the mountains are brainy. They all have first class degrees in maths and physics from the best universities around the world. They understand the way in which particles interact with each other at a level of minuteness that we ordinary mortals simply cannot imagine. You are bound to meet Donato's second-in-command – a physicist called Gianni Marconi. He's a lovely, charming man who has been to this house as a dinner guest on a number of occasions. He and the rest of the team talk about sub-atomic particles in the same way as we would talk about the ingredients for a new pasta dish. It's a privilege just listening to them. But... how can I put it? They are super-technicians."

"But your husband is more than just a super-technician, *signora* Rebecca. Is that what you are trying to tell us?" prompted Beppe gently.

Rebecca Zannetti nodded.

"Yes, in a nutshell. Donato has another layer to him. He is possessed of an imagination and a sense of mystery about creation which the others do not share. He often tells me that his whole team seem to be missing the point of what they are supposed to be doing. He believes that we humans have been set an immense and complex puzzle by..."

"By God you mean, *signora?*"

It was the voice of Luigi Rocco which had filled the *lacuna* left by the unfinished sentence.

"Thank you *Agente* Rocco. I couldn't quite bring myself to say the word. But do you all see what I'm driving at? All the scientists up there, arrogantly – that's the word my husband used - believe they know all there is to know about the cosmos. Whereas my husband believes firmly that our journey of discovery to unveil the secrets of the mystery of creation has barely begun."

"I agree with your husband entirely, *signora,*" stated Luigi Rocco in his deep bass voice.

Beppe was moved by what was being said in this house perched half way up a mountain range in a country which he thought he understood. He was deeply affected by the fact that an apparently ordinary police officer in his charge shared a sense of the hidden mystery behind the veil of everyday normality.

"Thank you – both – very much," Beppe said simply. Pippo was looking somewhat nonplussed. He was feeling redundant.

"Coffee?" asked the physicist's wife, breaking the spell.

"Do you have children?" asked Pippo, wishing to bring the conversation back to earth.

"Yes, we do - a son and a daughter. My son is studying particle physics at Pavia University and my daughter is in her first year at the University of Salento – Lecce – studying nanotechnology. They have their father's brains, you see," said the lady, sipping her coffee and nibbling a sweet biscuit.

"Do they know their father has disappeared?" asked Beppe cautiously.

"Yes, I had to tell them. I didn't want them finding out when the story hits the media – as it inevitably will. But I told them to stay where they are – that they shouldn't worry."

"I suppose you had better let me have a photo of your husband," Beppe said, regretting the necessity to be practical. "I shall need to recognise him when we find out where he is," he added with a grin.

Rebecca Zannetti sent a head-and-shoulders photo of her husband to all three officers via her iPad. It was a professionally taken photograph and the missing physicist's initials DDP, followed by the date when the photo was taken were printed in the bottom left-hand corner.

"He's a good-looking man, *signora* Rebecca," stated Beppe simply.

"You didn't think I'd marry an ugly man just because he has brains, do you, *commissario?*"

The complicit smile was back on her face again as she stood up to lead them to the front door.

"I'm happy you three are looking out for Donato, *agenti*. I like you all and I feel reassured."

She held out her right hand to Beppe and then Pippo, but she had hooked her left arm under the *Orso Bruno's* right arm in a natural gesture of fondness.

"That's quite some woman," Beppe said quietly to Pippo as they got into the police car and headed back towards the police station, where *Ispettore* De Sanctis was waiting to take them to lunch. *Commissario* Beppe Stancato wore an expression that clearly suggested that food was the last thing on his mind. Pippo pointed out to his chief that the scientists at the Montenero physics lab would also be at lunch anyway. Beppe sighed and accepted the inevitable delay.

* * *

Luigi Rocco looked impassive as he negotiated the winding road out of L'Aquila which would join the *autostrada* which, in its turn, led up to the laboratory. He showed no hint of what was going through his mind. But a perceptive *commissario* read a softened expression in his brown eyes.

An appointment had been made with the physicist who was now technically in charge of the research projects following the disappearance of Donato Pisano. The second-in-command bore the name Gianni Marconi, just as Rebecca Zannetti had indicated.

Professore Marconi's patent reluctance to meet the three police officers responsible for investigating Donato Pisano's disappearance had been audibly apparent when the young officer from the police station in L'Aquila, Giovanni Palena, had telephoned him to notify him of the visit by the *commissario* from Pescara.

"Does it have to be today, *agente?* It would be far more convenient if the interview could wait for a couple of days. After all, there is very little that *I* can tell this *Commissario* Stancato..."

Beppe made a covert sign to Giovanni to hand over the phone to him.

"*Buongiorno, professore,*" Beppe began sweetly, "*Commissario* Stancato speaking. You gave the impression when talking to my young colleague just now that we would be intruding on your precious time. I apologise if I have gleaned the wrong impression. I would suggest that your cooperation is essential to our enquiry."

There was something about the timbre of this senior officer's voice which unnerved the physicist. There was an indefinable hint of a threat which could not be ignored.

"No, no, *commissario,* forgive me. It's just that I am inundated by enquiries from colleagues, which I am not yet used to dealing with."

Professor Gianni Marconi agreed to see the *commissario* at four o'clock. There was no way of delaying this interview with the investigating team from Pescara, he realised.

Pippo was looking at his chief in admiration.

"How do you do it, *capo?*" he asked. "Every time, too!"

"Practice, Pippo – nothing else. What I am wondering before we have even met this gentleman is why he should be so reticent about meeting us..."

6: In the hall of the Mountain King...

The police car driven by Luigi Rocco had plunged into a tunnel on the A24 *autostrada* which passes beneath the Gran Sasso mountain range on its way to Rome. They seemed to drive for an eternity through the ten kilometre long tunnel.

"I presume you have visited these laboratories before, Luigi?" asked Beppe who had not managed to conceal a hint of anxiety in his voice. He hated tunnels and his latent fear of enclosed spaces was beginning to surface.

"*Sì, capo.* We have to travel five kilometres along the tunnel before we reach the entrance to the Montenero laboratory. We're nearly there," he added reassuringly.

Beppe closed his eyes and forced himself to take deep, even breaths. Finally, Luigi Rocco turned right into another tunnel which led off the A24. Almost immediately, the police vehicle was brought to a halt in front of a solid-looking metal grill.

"Now what?" snapped the *commissario.* "Do we have to ring on the doorbell or something?"

Unperturbed, Luigi Rocco got out of the driver's seat and stepped onto the shiny stone floor.

"I hope this is going to work, *capo.* I was a passenger on a minibus tour when I first came here some months ago."

To Beppe and Pippo's astonishment, Luigi Rocco walked unhesitatingly up to the gate and placed his powerful hands on the vertical metal bars.

"Is he going to wrench it open by force?" whispered an awed Pippo, not sure whether his words had been spoken in jest.

To the couple's further amazement, the *Orso Bruno* clearly uttered the words *"Tau neutrinos"* into a panel on the gate. With well-oiled grace and a slight humming noise, the metal gate slid into the mountain-side. Luigi Rocco drove them through the gate into the entrance of the laboratory. They immediately came to a vast car park as the tunnel widened out on both sides. Luigi Rocco drove slowly towards the far end until he found a free space as near to the end of the cavernous parking area as possible. Pippo's sharp eyes scanned a bank of CCTV cameras set high up on the rocky walls. Beppe glanced at the screen of his mobile phone - the time was twenty to four.

A woman of about forty-five was waiting expectantly for them at the entrance to the car park. She looked flustered, as if meeting police officers was a new experience for her.

"Good afternoon, *agenti,*" she said, holding out a hand to Beppe and then to Pippo. "I'm Eva Petrarca."

"Ah yes, *signora,*" said Beppe. "You must be Professor Donato Pisano's secretary."

The lady looked surprised and relieved all in one go.

"Thank you so much for coming, *commissario,*" said Eva effusively. "I'm so glad someone is taking the professor's disappearance seriously at last."

Pippo exchanged a rapid glance with his chief on hearing the secretary's unexpected words. Beppe's face, however, gave nothing away.

"And this is *Agente* Rocco, *Signora* Eva," said Beppe assuming it must be Luigi's imposing physique which had unnerved the secretary. But the shock on Eva's face, he was convinced, was genuine. Eva Petrarca started involuntarily as she turned to where Luigi was standing rugged and statue-like on the fringe of the little group.

"I'm so sorry, *Agente* Rocco," she said. "I didn't see you standing there."

Beppe and Pippo laughed spontaneously at the notion of an invisible *Orso Bruno.*

"I know it sounds stupid, officers. I didn't mean to ignore you, *Agente* Rocco. I think I must be overwhelmed by all of you arriving like this at our laboratory."

She held out a delicate hand to Luigi Rocco, who took the tips of her fingers gently in his massive paw and bowed his head in greeting, saying *"Piacere, signora,"* as softly as he could.

"Maybe you should take us to the *professore, Signora* Eva. We don't want to keep him waiting."

Eva smiled knowingly. "Follow me, officers. We have to take the lift up to the administrative area."

She led them through the massive vault that housed endless banks of tubes, cables and cylinders which rose from floor level up to the roof of the cavern twenty metres above their heads.

"It's more like a modern day cathedral – but devoted to Physics rather than God," said Pippo reverentially.

"*Il Professore* Pisano would probably have told you that the two things are closely linked," Eva Petrarca added nostalgically.

"There are two more caverns just as big as this one," explained Luigi Rocco.

"It's ironic, isn't it," added Beppe, addressing no one in particular. "Here you are chasing particles that are almost massless, from what I have understood, and yet..."

"The more minute the particle, the more massive the equipment needed to detect it," observed Luigi Rocco.

In his mind, Beppe made an analogy between this officer's massive frame and the amount of hitherto undisclosed sparks of knowledge that appeared to be stored within it.

The lift carried them soundlessly upwards for what seemed to be an eternity to the *commissario*. When they stepped out of the lift, Pippo and Beppe gasped in surprise. They were out in the open again and could even see L'Aquila in the distance.

"The admin block, staff quarters and the canteen are all above ground," explained Eva. "Didn't you realise that?"

Beppe shook his head. He wanted to get on with his investigation and cover as much ground as possible in one visit to this place. Only Luigi appeared to be in his element.

Eva led them to the modest office where Professor Gianni Marconi was expecting them. The door bore the title *Prof. D. Pisano.*

"At least this office still seems to be expecting its occupant to return," thought Beppe who, despite himself, felt overwhelmed by the scale of the whole place and the strangeness of the circumstances that surrounded the investigation he had been landed with.

"Pippo, would you like to go with Eva – if I may call you that, *signora* – and have a chat to her about matters from her perspective?"

Pippo was obviously taken aback. He was used to backing up his *capo* but this witness's account of events was likely to be vital. He looked quizzically at Beppe. But Pippo was faced with one of his chief's meaningful stares. He understood that he was being entrusted with what could turn out to be a crucial interview.

Pippo nodded and said: "Let's go to your office, *Signora* Eva."

He assumed an air of self-importance which he was not feeling.

"*Le faccio strada, agente,*" said Eva, walking slightly ahead of Pippo. She was relieved that she could finally unburden her fears to just one other person in authority. It would feel less like an interrogation. She found this young officer quite unintimidating. Glancing behind her, she noticed he was walking with a slight limp.

"How did you get your injury, *Agente* Pippo?" she asked kindly.

"Playing football, *Signora Eva,*" Pippo lied.

* * *

Gianni Marconi took a seat behind his absent colleague's desk and invited Beppe and Luigi Rocco to sit on the chairs facing him on the other side of the desk – despite there being a separate round conference table in an adjoining room to one side of the office. Beppe held a well-established belief that people who put a desk between themselves and their interlocutors felt a subconscious need to put up barriers. There were two photograph frames standing on the desk with their backs to the police officers. Beppe wondered if the substitute physicist had already placed photos of his own family on the desk.

"Well, *commissario*," began Gianni Marconi, "what would you like to know?"

There appeared to be nothing to dislike about this man, Beppe decided. What puzzled him was that the scientist seemed to have already made up his mind as to the fate of Donato Pisano.

"I was hoping, *professore*, that *you* would be willing to share with *us* what you know about the professor's disappearance."

Unexpectedly, Gianni Marconi opened a folder and retrieved a sheet of paper which he handed over to Beppe.

"This e-mail arrived this morning via my own PC, *commissario*. If you would like to read it...?"

The *commissario* took the sheet of paper and read it quickly.

Esteemed colleagues and followers of our project around the world,

I have thought long and hard about my position at the Montenero physics laboratory in the light of my recent and most public claim that neutrinos covered the distance between CERN in Geneva and our own laboratory here in Abruzzo at significantly more than the speed of light. I now realise that my claim defies the accepted laws of physics as laid down by Einstein and Paul Dirac.

I attribute my misinterpretation of the facts simply to an unchecked fault in our atomic clocks. In a subsequent experiment, in which the beam of neutrinos was shot to us in a less concentrated pattern, the particles appeared to obey the accepted laws of physics.

In light of my arrogant assumption that I could single-handedly overturn the laws of the cosmos, I have no choice but to resign from my position at the Montenero Laboratory. I prefer to allow my highly competent colleagues to continue their research into the transformation of neutrinos from muon into electron neutrinos on their journey through the rocks – without my quantum interference, so to speak.

I am writing this letter from an undisclosed location. Copies will be sent to all the appropriate scientific journals and authorities – as well as to the RAI.

I wish my team of colleagues the best of scientific luck and a special thanks and farewell to my long-suffering second-in-command, Professor Giovanni Marconi.

(signed) Donato Carlo Pisano

Beppe scanned the e-mail rapidly before handing it over to his colleague. Luigi Rocco read the text slowly. The frown on Luigi's face grew increasingly pronounced as he proceeded with his reading. Beppe turned to Gianni Marconi and put a question to him in the most innocent tone of voice he could muster.

"Did you know your colleague's middle name was Carlo?"

"I...I don't see what that has to do with anything, *commissario*," stuttered the scientist, who seemed inexplicably unnerved by the simplicity of the question. The *commissario* continued to stare at Gianni Marconi, one eyebrow raised. He was evidently expecting a reply to his trivial question. It was a disconcerting experience. Over the span of his career, Beppe had developed this technique until it had become a fine art. By maintaining his silent stare, the other person inevitably felt obliged to fill the hiatus with words – any words.

"No, *commissario*, I am quite sure I never knew what Donato's middle name was. But I still don't see that his middle name makes any difference to the content of this email," finished Gianni Marconi petulantly.

"I take it, *professore*, that you do not believe your colleague's claim that the neutrinos travelled faster than light?" continued Beppe.

"No, *commissario*, I don't. The scientific community has believed for more than a century that nothing measurable can travel faster than the speed of light. Donato's interpretation of our experiments is quite impossible in the light of this accepted scientific precept..."

It was a shock to Beppe – but even more so to the physicist - when Luigi Rocco broke into the interrogation with a deep growl.

"So, how do you account for quantum entanglement, *professore?*" he asked.

The expression on the scientist's face was so comical that Beppe laughed out loud.

"I make no apologies for my young colleague's contribution to our interview, *professore.* You might well wish to satisfy Officer Rocco's curiosity on another occasion – if you can. Meanwhile, I think that will be all for now," said the *commissario* standing up, still smiling at Luigi's incursion into the interrogation.

A look of relief passed quickly across Gianni Marconi's face. But it was short lived. "We shall need to talk to you again very soon," said Beppe. "And of course, we shall need to take your computer away for our technical team to see if they can trace back where the e-mail was sent from. And I'd like to keep the paper copy of the e-mail too."

Luigi Rocco had stood up at the same time as his *capo* and had made as if to walk round the other side of the desk. It was enough to stem the tide of protest that was about to erupt from the physicist's lips.

"I promise to return it as soon as possible, *professore,* maybe even by tomorrow. And I do sincerely apologise for the inconvenience. Whatever you may think, I am becoming increasingly convinced that *Professore* Donato Pisano was abducted against his will. Therefore, he might well be in danger."

"But surely, you have no sound logical reason to believe your theory of foul play, do you, *commissario?*"

"Yes, I do. In the first place, he vanished at the same time as that couple of unidentified American visitors arrived last week – a matter that you have not seen fit to mention. And secondly, he disappeared without contacting his wife, Rebecca Zannetti. She stated categorically that her husband would never have gone away anywhere without telling her first. I am sure you must be acquainted with the lady in question, *professore?*"

Gianni Marconi merely nodded in acquiescence. He had the grace to admit to himself that he had been wrong-footed right from the outset by this disconcerting police inspector from Pescara - not to mention his terrifyingly well-informed colleague, who reminded him more of a Sumo wrestler.

"I'm sorry, *commissario.* But, you know, I never saw this couple. I was only told about them by Eva Petrarca – Donato's secretary."

"That's alright, *professore.* I quite understand your reluctance to think the worst about your colleague's disappearance. It's a natural reaction in your position."

Gianni Marconi was unsure whether he was being censured - but every sentence uttered by this police officer seemed to carry some concealed implication that he could not quite put his finger on.

Luigi Rocco had taken the laptop from Gianni Marconi's hands and had returned to his chief's side of the desk.

"Now we must go and rescue our colleague – who has been talking to Eva. Perhaps you could show us the way, *professore?*"

Gianni Marconi left the *commissario* and his junior officer with a shake of the hand and a promise of close cooperation whenever it was needed. Gianni was left with the uncomfortable sensation that he had been unmasked.

As soon as the scientist had gone back to his 'adopted' office, *Agente* Rocco turned to his chief and began talking.

"That letter was as phoney as a thousand euro banknote *capo.* It makes me certain that *Professore* Pisano left clues in the text to show he was being forced into writing it."

"*Bravo* Luigi - and I am equally as sure that Gianni Marconi *knows* it's a phoney letter. By the way, did you get a look at the photos on his desk when you relieved him of his laptop?"

"Yes, *capo,* they were both photos of the same woman – a pretty-looking thirty-five year old I'd say. Nothing like Donato Pisano's wife – and too old to be his own daughter."

"Luigi, thank you for your support - you're proving to be indispensable in this investigation."

"*Grazie, capo,*" said Luigi, beaming with pleasure.

"And when we are on our way back to L'Aquila, perhaps you would be so kind as to explain – in layman's terms – what on earth *quantum entanglement* is supposed to mean. At the same time, you can explain to me why you thought the e-mail made you so suspicious. But right now, we had better go and see how Pippo has fared with Eva Petrarca."

7:   *Pippo's non-quantum entanglement...*

All that could be seen of *Agente* Pippo Cafarelli as Beppe and Luigi stepped into Eva Petrarca's office was his tousled mop of curly black hair. The rest of him was obscured by the presence of at least five other women - apart from Eva – crowded around a desktop computer. They were all peering at the screen and giving a voluble running commentary on what they were seeing.

"Look... there! That's them getting out of that silver-grey Punto."

"Notice the way they are keeping their heads down..."

"As if they don't want us to see their faces..."

"Now watch this bit, *Agente* Pippo," said a voice that could have been Eva's.

"Look carefully," continued the same voice. "The man takes something that looks like a golf ball out of his pocket. He appears to drop it but it rolls across the floor just in front of them..."

The CCTV recording was partially obliterated by what appeared to be patterns of electronic interference which disappeared only when the couple had passed out of view.

"Those two are professional agents. That was some sophisticated device to fool the CCTV cameras. Eva, it certainly looks as if your suspicions about this couple are justified." It was Pippo's voice speaking for the first time.

One of the 'girls' in the entourage had stuck Pippo's police kepi on her head at a jaunty angle. Her auburn-coloured curls were sticking out beneath the rim of the hat as she peered intently at the screen.

"I didn't like the look of that pair at all when I caught a glimpse of them in the corridor the other day," she added informatively.

The *commissario* coughed politely from where he and Luigi Rocco had been observing the scene from just inside the doorway.

The effect was instantaneous. The young woman who had donned Pippo's hat whipped it off her head and replaced it on the desk next to its owner. The whole group - except Eva – scattered in a scented cloud of perfume like naughty schoolgirls at the unexpected arrival of their teacher.

Beppe smiled and said in a reassuring voice:

"*Signorine* – your contribution to our investigation is most welcome. Please feel entirely free to talk to us about any trivial memory you might have of those visitors. Anything you say could prove vital to us in our search for Donato Pisano."

There was a consentient murmur of approval from the five secretaries now back at their own desks.

"I *did* notice the man was wearing a pretty revolting body deodorant, *commissario*," piped up the auburn-haired girl who had been wearing Pippo's hat.

There were suppressed giggles from her companions.

"You may be surprised to learn, *signorina*, that criminals have given themselves away with far more trivial slip-ups than that," Beppe reassured her. He knew he had won the trust of this group of women but half wished that Sonia had been present. Oriana would have coped well too. He must remember to call up the *Questura* in Pescara to see how Oriana was getting on with the twelve-year-old girl who took pot-shots at passing dogs and gardeners.

The *commissario* mentally shook his head to clear it of all extraneous thoughts. With the exception of Luigi Rocco, standing behind him, everybody in the spacious office was looking at him in expectation of his next move.

"*Che bell'uomo!*" muttered one of the young women as if to herself. Beppe was not clear which man in the room was being referred to as handsome. Probably Luigi Rocco, he thought abstractedly.

It was Pippo's voice that called his chief back to the immediacy of the investigation in hand.

"Come and have a look at this CCTV footage, *capo*. It shows that American couple arriving on the day when the professor vanished."

Beppe walked over to Eva's desk followed closely by *Agente* Rocco, who stood behind the group looking intensely at the screen. Pippo replayed the CCTV footage showing the suspicious couple getting out of their car and walking towards the entrance to the laboratories. The same zig-zag lines appeared on the screen, obscuring the visitors' faces as they drew nearer.

"We were about to watch a later recording as the couple left about half an hour afterwards with the *Professore*," explained Pippo as he slipped another DVD into the tower of Eva's computer.

"You should watch this bit, *commissario*," added Eva unnecessarily, since the three police officers' eyes were riveted to the screen. The image clearly showed the two American 'agents' – as Beppe had already taken to calling them - walking back to their car with their backs to the camera. The female agent had an arm tucked under that of the professor and the male agent was walking on the professor's right flank. Beppe was on the point of opening his mouth to ask Eva: "Are you sure the one in the middle is really our Professor?"

Before he could get the words out of his mouth, the three policemen were taken by surprise on seeing the head of the man being escorted out of the laboratory briefly swivelling round to catch the CCTV cameras. Beppe and company instantly recognised the face of Donato Pisano from the photo supplied by his wife, Rebecca. They experienced a physical shock when the figure of the professor mouthed a silent word in the direction of the cameras. Pippo, whose eyesight was perfect, looked at his chief in horror. In an instant, the male agent had moved behind Professor Pisano, blocking the view from would-be observers. They didn't need to be expert lip-readers to decipher what he was saying.

"He just said *'Aiutatemi', capo* - as plainly as could be!" *(= Help me)*

"We're going back to talk to *Professore* Gianni Marconi now," stated Beppe angrily.

"I think he's just left the laboratory while we were talking, *commissario*," said Eva nervously. "He told me this morning he might be leaving early – he had to help a friend of his move house, or something..."

Yet there was a hint of triumph in her eyes that did not escape Beppe's notice. "Shall I book *Il Professore* Marconi in to see you first thing tomorrow morning, *commissario?*"

Beppe smiled and nodded at Eva. He realised that he had found an ally in the camp.

"We shall be taking the CCTV recordings with us, Eva. Could you and *Agente* Pippo print off some pictures from the DVDs? *Agente* Pippo will know what we're after. Come on, Luigi. We're going back to Professor Marconi's office. I just have this feeling..."

The *commissario* left the sentence unfinished. He spotted the difference in Donato Pisano's office as soon as they stepped through the doorway. There was only one photo on the desk. Without a word he picked it up and showed it to *Agente* Rocco.

Luigi merely nodded curtly. The photo showed Donato Pisano with his wife and his two children. Professor Gianni Marconi had removed the two photos of the young woman which had been on his desk a mere twenty minutes beforehand.

* * *

"Can you talk to me while you're driving, *Agente* Rocco?" asked Beppe.

Luigi's enigmatic question, which had appeared to unnerve Professor Gianni Marconi, was niggling away in Beppe's mind. He had an aversion to his colleagues and those closest to him knowing more than he did on any subject about which he remained in ignorance. It was not, he claimed, that he held it against other people for being better informed than he was, but rather that he blamed himself for being one step behind. Thus, whilst investigating the mushroom poisoning case, he had felt compelled to make a solo detour to visit the *Vitello d'Oro* waterfall near Farindola – with well-nigh catastrophic consequences to himself. He had persuaded himself – only half-successfully – that he was motivated by curiosity rather than envy.

"You mean what I said about quantum entanglement back there to that substitute chief physicist, *capo?*"

"*Appunto,* Luigi!" replied Beppe brusquely.

"Well, it's all totally counter-intuitive, *capo...*" warned Luigi, "but all the more fascinating just because it flies in the face of reality as we perceive it."

Pippo's ears pricked up. He stopped reading the e-mail, purportedly from the missing physicist, which he had been studying with an intense frown on his face. The *Orso Bruno* was about to surprise them all over again, it seemed.

By the time Luigi had finished talking, they had arrived back at the hotel. It was the longest Beppe and Pippo had ever heard their colleague talk – uninterrupted - during the fifteen months since he had joined the team. Pippo jokingly said afterwards that he wished they had thought of recording his speech for posterity – before he had begun talking.

"It all started in Paris, in the nineteen-nineties," Luigi Rocco had begun in his deep bass voice whilst he steered the police van unerringly down the winding roads towards L'Aquila. *"This French physicist called Alain Aspect had succeeded in isolating a discrete photon – that's a light particle by the way – and fired it out of a kind of gun. Then he got round to firing a second photon out of a parallel gun simultaneously with the first photon. I'm sorry, capo, I can't tell you about the mechanics of it all – only what he observed from his own experiments. He was just tinkering around a bit to observe if anything odd happened if he deflected one of the photons as it came out of the gun. He simply could not believe what he saw and he had to redo the experiment*

hundreds of times to make sure he wasn't imagining the impossible. He noticed that as soon as he deflected one photon, the other photon simultaneously followed the first one – as if they were in some way linked by an invisible force. But the point is, capo, that since the deflection of the second particle happened simultaneously to the deflection of the first particle, the communication between the two particles must have travelled faster than the speed of light. Scientists have carried out similar experiments repeatedly – the communication between particles seems to work even across vast distances. This impossible-seeming affinity between particles got called 'quantum entanglement'. And it made the scientific world squirm with embarrassment. Nobody has been able to explain the phenomenon in a satisfactory manner since then. Professor Marconi was obviously very unhappy when I mentioned it to him – that's why I believe he's treading on very thin ice when he denied the results of Donato Pisano's neutrino experiment...

"We've arrived at the hotel, *capo*," stated Luigi Rocco to his bewildered colleagues. "Would you like me to tell you both why I think that e-mail which Professor Marconi showed us was as full of holes as a colander?"

"I think I need a shower first, Luigi. I need to digest what you've just told us before we discuss the e-mail. Let's all meet in the lounge in thirty minutes time. Pippo...?"

"I agree, *capo.* I've been looking at that e-mail too. It just doesn't add up…"

As Pippo inserted the key into the lock of his bedroom door, he was distracted by the sound of the couple who owned the hotel in the bedroom opposite his. The door was as wide open as the window. The couple were spraying an aerosol can into every corner of the room and muttering inaudible comments to each other. To his amusement, Pippo heard them say the word 'fumigation' before he let himself into his own room and headed for the shower and a change of clothes for the evening.

Beppe's shower must have lasted all of fifteen minutes and drained the hotel's hot water tank down to the last centimetre. His mind was turning over and over again the words of his colleague, Luigi Rocco. If this 'quantum entanglement' was true, then didn't it imply that the whole of creation must be invisibly linked together? He got to thinking about Sonia and concluded that in some way he and she were intimately 'entangled' by invisible particles that bound them inextricably together even when they were apart. The phenomenon might even go some way to explaining their frequent instances of telepathy, he thought. He idly wondered if Sonia was having a shower at the same moment as he was – just before *his* shower water turned icy cold as the hotel's ancient boiler system failed to keep up with demand.

*　*　*

It was still too early to think about dinner – being only seven o'clock – when the three officers, dressed in civvies, met downstairs to discuss the e-mail purportedly sent by Professor Donato Pisano to his second-in-command.

"So, *ragazzi*. What made you think the e-mail was not as it was supposed to appear?" asked Beppe, wondering if they had spotted the same inaccuracies as he had.

Pippo had just felt uneasy about the whole tone of the letter, with very little else to go on.

"Why did *Professore* Donato Pisano call his second-in-command Giovanni and not Gianni?" said Pippo.

Beppe nodded and waited to see if either of his colleagues had noticed anything odd about the signature.

"I guess you also spotted that he had signed himself *Donato Carlo Pisano, capo,*"
continued Pippo. "That's why you asked Gianni Marconi if he knew his colleague's middle name was Carlo. On the photograph Donato Pisano's wife uploaded for us, it bore the initials DDP, as I remember."

"Well spotted, Pippo," Beppe complimented him. "It's not a lot to go on but…"

The *commissario* did not finish his sentence because Luigi Rocco had coughed politely.

Beppe smiled.

"I hoped you would have something to add, Luigi," he said. "Pray, enlighten us further."

In the next few minutes, Luigi did exactly the opposite. By the time he had finished speaking Pippo and Beppe's minds were reeling.

"The science was all wrong, *capo,*" began Luigi. "In the first place, when he apologised about ignoring *'the accepted laws of science laid down by Einstein and Dirac'*... Well, quite simply, Dirac never agreed with Einstein about the fixed speed of light. He had already understood that quantum physics had upset Einstein's interpretation of the cosmos."

Beppe and Pippo were just staring open-mouthed at their colleague.

"Secondly," continued Luigi almost shyly, "he went on about *neutrinos arriving at the laboratory in a less concentrated pattern seeming to travel below the speed of light.* It was the opposite way round. The neutrinos only seemed to obey the accepted laws of physics when the beam of neutrinos was more concentrated. When they were scattered, they appeared to arrive faster than the speed of light. In reality, the professor made his team carry out the experiment hundreds of times since the first experiment took place months ago. He got the same contradictory result on most occasions... That's what I understood when I read that article."

"Anything else, Luigi?" asked Beppe, hoping not to end up even more confused than he felt already.

"Oh yes, *capo*. He talked about *the transformation of neutrinos from muon to electron neutrinos.* It wasn't like that at all. They were studying the transformation of Muon neutrinos to Tau neutrinos. Something completely different! The whole e-mail was full of mistakes that a physicist like Donato Pisano would never have made. And I'm sure Professor Marconi knew that too," concluded Luigi Rocco.

"Well done, Luigi!" Beppe complimented his junior colleague in admiration.

"Interestingly enough, *capo*," Pippo added. "Eva Petrarca, the professor's secretary, you know, gave us a DVD of an interview he gave some weeks ago in which he explained why he thought his interpretation might be right. She told me that Donato Pisano was a very modest man. He always wanted to persuade people by scientific arguments. He was never dogmatic. Maybe we could watch that DVD too?"

Beppe appeared not to be listening to Pippo. He turned to Luigi instead. His words took Pippo by surprise. Luigi merely nodded while only his eyes gave away his inner pleasure.

"Luigi, would you mind going back to see Rebecca Zannetti this evening? I want you to ask her two things. First of all, confirm that her husband's middle name is not Carlo. And secondly, ask her if last time Gianni Marconi came to their house he came alone – or whether he had anybody else with him."

Luigi gave his usual curt nod. He had understood the implication perfectly.

"When you get back, Luigi, we'll go and get something to eat," suggested Beppe. "I know just the place," he added smugly, hoping to be one step ahead of his colleagues.

"You mean Remo Mastrodicasa's *agriturismo,* don't you, *capo?*" said Pippo, thereby ruining the effect.

Since their colleague, Remo, had decided to exchange his police pistol for a cook's wooden spoon, only Giacomo D'Amico, to Beppe's knowledge, had taken his wife to eat in the beautiful setting of the country villa confiscated by the State from the Mafioso boss, Gianluca Alfieri. Remo and his partner, Marta, had taken over the running of this farm-restaurant which specialised in the cuisine of Abruzzo. Giacomo had returned full of praise for the food which they had eaten. The country restaurant had been renamed *La Bella Addormentata* in honour of Beppe's first major case on Abruzzo soil.

Luigi phoned Donato Pisano's wife, Rebecca Zannetti, to ask her if he could come round and clarify a couple of minor points. "If it isn't an inconvenient moment," said Luigi. The *Orso Bruno* smiled at her reply.

"Don't wait about for me, *capo*. I've just been invited to dinner."

The *commissario* acknowledged Luigi's words with a mock gesture of silent admonishment involving the thumb and first two fingers of his right hand pressed together and wiggled loosely from the wrist. However, Beppe's eyes expressed what his colleague, Pippo, put into words:

"In bocca al lupo, Luigi!"

Beppe felt that the *Orso Bruno* deserved some reward for his contributions to day one of their investigation.

* * *

Abandoned to their own devices, Beppe and Pippo were engrossed in watching the DVD of Donato Pisano's TV interview with the journalist. The recording had been supplied by Pescara's local television company, TV-Tavo, following one of the professor's rare public appearances a month or so previously.

Everything that had been said about the Vanishing Physicist – by his wife and by his secretary – was wholly vindicated by the video recording. The chief scientist was relaxed, unassuming and the least confrontational person one could imagine. He had opened the session by smiling at the journalist interviewing him, saying:

"It's funny, but I trust you completely, Gabriele. I've often been criticised for being too gullible about people who interview me. My wife tells me I assume that everyone is as transparent as I am. But there you are! I can't help it, I'm afraid..."

Il Professore Donato Pisano covered just about every point which the three officers had discussed – even about muon neutrinos mutating to tau neutrinos on their journey through the mountains. Beppe doubted that many viewers had understood what he was saying. But they would have appreciated his candour and his modest demeanour. He rounded his talk off on a theological note – having been asked by the journalist whether he believed in God or not.

"Most days, yes, I do. Absolutely!" had been his gentle reply.

Just as Beppe and Pippo had decided to replay the DVD interview, for its sheer entertainment value, the couple who owned the hotel walked into the lounge.

"Have you solved your problem with the bedroom upstairs?" asked Pippo kindly, since the couple still looked mildly frustrated by whatever problem they had encountered.

"It will resolve itself in time," answered the husband resignedly.

"It was that American-Italian who stayed with us for a couple of days, *agente* Cafarelli," explained the wife. "He must have had a personal hygiene problem – because he wore this overpowering deodorant all the time. We simply cannot get rid of the smell."

The hotel owners looked alarmed. The two police officers had frozen in their chairs. They were staring at them with alert, wide-open eyes.

"Show them the photo we got from the CCTV cameras, Pippo," said Beppe tersely.

"It's not a very clear picture, *agenti*. But yes, I reckon that's the couple who stayed here a week ago..."

8:   *Food for thought...*

"Couple?" asked Beppe rather more abruptly than he had meant to. "I apologise, *signori.* We're not accusing you of anything – far from it. You could be instrumental in helping us solve a very difficult case. Until you told us about the man with the strong deodorant, we didn't really know where we were going. When you say 'couple', do you mean they were... married, for want of a better word?"

"Oh, no, *commissario,*" replied the wife. "They had separate rooms. But she was *più simpatica* than the man – at least she smiled occasionally."

"They were more like business partners. They both spoke perfect Italian, but they had a strong American accent," clarified the husband.

Pippo stood up and helped himself to the visitors' book. He pointed out the two people whose names he had spotted earlier on that day.

"Do you mean these two, *signori?* M. Vitale and A. Lombardi – from Boston?"

"Yes, they're the ones. They arrived on May the eleventh – as you see."

"So, you must have registered their documents in the usual way?" asked Beppe.

The hotel owners were looking shifty. It was the wife who spoke up first.

"I'm sorry, *commissario*. I asked to see their documents – which they showed us immediately. But when I said I needed to hang on to the documents while we registered their names on the official site, they became very... diffident."

"The woman asked us – all very politely – if we could complete the formalities the following morning. They had just arrived from the States that afternoon, they explained. They said they were exhausted," added the husband.

"They paid us – in cash – for four nights. We couldn't believe our luck, *commissario*. We are really struggling to keep this business going at the moment. So we didn't want to appear to be too pushy," continued the wife. "But they only stayed two more nights and then we never saw them again."

"They must have sneaked out with their suitcases early in the morning while we were sleeping. We never lock the main entrance door. I would guess they must have rented a car at some point. I'm so sorry, *commissario*. I know we should have insisted, but that guy was... difficult to deal with. He looked threatening whenever we tried to explain we needed their documents because Italian law demands that..."

"You won't get into any trouble, *signori*," Beppe reassured them. "What happened on the first morning – just after they arrived?"

"Oh, that nice-looking young woman who had brought them to the hotel the previous evening came and picked them up again sometime after eight o'clock..." began *la signora*.

"What young woman?" asked Beppe, who had been about to ask how the two Americans had known about their hotel - which certainly wouldn't have been the obvious first choice for American visitors who were unfamiliar with L'Aquila.

"I don't know who she was, *commissario*. But she must have been a local girl."

"What makes you say she was a local girl?" asked Beppe, whose mind had begun to make connections which nobody else would have thought of on such slender evidence.

"She wasn't dressed as if she came from far away," replied *la signora*, looking embarrassed at the vagueness of her peculiarly feminine deduction. "But she said something like she reckoned we would probably welcome new guests as we were a bit off the beaten track... She was very pleasant and friendly. Not like that couple."

"Did she give you her name?" asked Pippo.

The couple shook their heads apologetically.

"Are you certain the American couple didn't mention her name when they said goodnight to her?" asked Beppe, hoping to jog a memory.

The couple both shook their heads again.

"No, *commissario* - the man was very curt and dismissive towards her."

"Would you recognise her if you saw her again, *signori?*" asked Pippo.

"Oh yes, *agente*. She was a very pretty woman," said the husband, with the first smile they had detected on his face since their arrival. The scowl from his wife was barely perceptible.

"She didn't like the American couple at all," added the wife. "They had been waiting outside the hotel for a good fifteen minutes before she drew up that first morning, *agenti*. The man was very abrupt with her. I could tell by her face she didn't really want to give them a lift."

There was nothing else to be gained from asking further questions. Neither of the hotel owners had registered what car this 'pretty woman' had been driving. The two police officers had made a vital connection. Beppe was all too aware that identifying this young woman could be crucial.

"We've got to find her, Pippo," said Beppe.

"Why do you say that, *capo?*" asked Pippo – more to satisfy his curiosity than because he doubted the truth behind his chief's words.

"If she arrived with their suitcases in her boot, where do you think she must have picked them up from, *Agente* Caferelli?"

"Of course, *capo!* From a railway station or an airport – maybe she went to Fiumicino to fetch them."

"Appunto!" stated Beppe.

* * *

Before the *Orso Bruno* abandoned himself to the task of fulfilling Rebecca Zannetti's fantasies about being hugged into a state of oblivion by a mountain bear, he managed to send Beppe a text message, which was as brief as most of his communications with the outside world had been up to that particular day.

'Middle name Davide – GM's companion, Giada' Beppe read out to Pippo.

"We might as well go and get something to eat," said Pippo hopefully. Luigi's brief message had determined the next phase of their investigation. There was little else they could do that night – and Pippo was hungry. The *commissario* gave in with a good grace and they drove in Beppe's own car to Remo's *agriturismo* just outside the village of Monticchio.

Beppe felt a strange sense of nostalgia as the two of them stepped inside the massive hallway of the vast house where the rescue of the twenty-two-year-old Serena Vacri had taken place. What a transformation! The space where the Mafioso's seventieth birthday party had been filled with his family members from Naples was now a bright, cheerful dining room half full of diners who were already eating. A subdued buzz of conversation filled the spacious dining area.

When Beppe's favourite ex-officer recognised his former *capo* as he and Pippo stepped over the familiar threshold, Remo's face was suffused with blushing pleasure. It was all Beppe could do to stop Remo standing to attention and saluting him.

"I think an *abbraccio* is more appropriate on this occasion, Remo," suggested Beppe, who proceeded to hug his former colleague warmly.

Remo shook Beppe enthusiastically by the hand as he turned to Pippo:

"Nice to see you back here again so soon, Pippo. How is Mariangela?"

Beppe felt the familiar pangs of something akin to envy as soon as he realised that his junior colleague and his *fidanzata* had beaten him to it – and, above all, had done so without telling *him.* He managed to master his own baser reactions on this occasion.

"Well, at least, I suppose you wouldn't have suggested coming back here if the food had been bad, Pippo," said Beppe with only a touch of severity.

"I told Marianagela about our Sleeping Beauty, Serena Vacri, *capo.* She wanted to know why this *agriturismo* was known as *'La bella addormentata'* – so I told her. Then she simply had to come and see the place for herself. As for the food, *capo,* you'll be able to judge for yourself."

Pippo was all too familiar with his chief's foibles and had become a past-master at dealing with him diplomatically.

Beppe had the grace to smile at his younger colleague, secretly admitting defeat.

"I guess you two must be in this part of the world to look into the disappearance of that physicist, Donato Pisano," stated Remo Mastrodicasa out of the blue.

Beppe's eyebrows shot up in surprise. As far as he was aware, there had been no public announcement in the media about Donato Pisano's plight.

"I always said you should have remained in the police force, Remo," said Beppe. "How on earth did you...?"

"Just rumours, *capo.* Lots of the scientists from the Montenero Laboratory come here and eat – when they grow tired of their own canteen food. Donato Pisano has been here a number of times – with his wife and once with his son and daughter too," added Remo nonchalantly. Now let me get you a menu. I can see Pippo is hungry."

The *commissario* had a thoughtful expression on his face – which had nothing to do with the prospect of food, Pippo reckoned.

Although the need to eat took second place when Beppe was involved in an investigation, he became a true *gourmet* as soon as the food arrived at the table. In the end, he and Pippo, bewildered by the choice on the menu, had instructed Remo to serve up whatever he thought fit. They even allowed him to choose the wine on their behalf. For only the second time on Abruzzo soil, Beppe ate a generous helping of *cacio e uova,* and complimented Remo on its excellence, appreciating the distinctive combination of tender pieces of lamb, scrambled egg and rosemary.

But when the meal was over, Beppe reverted to investigative mode. Remo had been reluctant to give them the final *conto,* insisting that the honour of serving his ex-colleagues was reward in itself. Both Beppe and Pippo had equally insisted that they had to pay for what they had eaten. In the end, a *prezzo d'amico* had been agreed between both parties.

"Do you by any chance have surveillance cameras here, Remo?" asked Beppe.

"Yes, we do, *capo,*" replied Remo, unable to find an alternative way of addressing his former chief. "There's one in the car park and a second one just inside the hallway. The place is so big, that we need to see when clients arrive. The screens are in the kitchen. You want me to check up on who comes here from the Montenero laboratory, I assume."

"Well, we're looking out for a gentleman called Gianni Marconi – he's standing in for *Il Professore* Pisano. But we're more interested in seeing who accompanies him," said Beppe.

"I don't recall seeing that name on any credit card receipts...eh... *capo.* But we'll certainly keep an eye out for the name. You're welcome to look at our DVD video footage - although we tend to reuse the DVDs after a week or so has elapsed. We're not really geared up for intensive surveillance here."

"Thank you, Remo," concluded Beppe, once again giving his embarrassed ex-colleague a warm hug. "I shall come back here and bring Sonia with me next time," he promised. *"E congratulazioni,* Remo. *La cucina è eccezionale!"*

Remo gave his two clients a bow and a radiant smile at the compliment he had received about the standard of his cooking.

"Where's your *fidanzata,* Marta?" asked Pippo as there had been no sign of Remo's girlfriend.

"She's still busy in the kitchen. Why don't you both come back one Monday? We're officially closed on Mondays to give the staff time off, but we would be delighted to rustle something up – and eat it with you," Remo suggested.

As the *commissario* headed back towards the main entrance door, he took a few steps down to the cellars – where Remo had shot the Latin American doctor in the heart, thereby saving the life of their colleague, Oriana Salvati. It had been the overwhelming shock of that single act of violence which had ultimately determined Remo Mastrodicasa to abandon police work in favour of devoting his life to catering.

When he re-emerged from the cellar, Beppe noticed Pippo was in urgent conversation with Remo. The latter had another even broader smile on his face.

"Now what's Pippo up to?" Beppe wondered.

In the car, going back to the hotel in L'Aquila, Beppe made a valiant effort not to ask what Pippo and Remo had been discussing. Sensing his chief's suppressed curiosity, Pippo relented.

"Mariangela and I are getting married this year, *capo*. She has already made up her mind that the reception will be held at Remo's *agriturismo* - if only because of its name. She was engrossed for hours on end when I was telling her about our 'Sleeping Beauty' case."

"How will Mariangela's father react to that, I wonder? Won't he be hurt that she doesn't want to have the reception at *La Vestina?*"

"We're getting married in Penne – at the *comune*. But she says there's no way the reception will be held at her father's *trattoria, capo*. She said she would probably start waiting on her own guests out of sheer habit."

Beppe laughed at the image conjured up of the ex-waitress, Mariangela, wearing a waitress's short black skirt, black tights and a white pinafore at her own wedding reception.

The words 'best man' came to mind but were suppressed. Pippo had been best man at Beppe's marriage to Sonia. He wondered – not very casually - whether he would be asked to return the compliment.

The mention of Sonia had reminded Beppe how remiss he had been about phoning her. He would do so as soon as they got back to the hotel and he had retired to his bedroom.

Luigi Rocco had not returned from his 'mission of mercy'. Beppe suspected they would not see the *Orso Bruno* again before dawn.

Beppe was dialling Sonia's number when his phone began ringing of its own accord. A glance at the screen confirmed what he knew already. It was his beloved Sonia calling *him* at the same instant in time. They certainly both had quantum entanglement, Beppe decided, enjoying his conscious use of this newly acquired concept – which seemed to encapsulate the spirit of this long first day of their mission. He gave Sonia a potted version of events.

"Luigi Rocco has been worth his weight in gold – so to speak," Beppe concluded, not sure whether his metaphor was apt when applied to their *Orso Bruno.*

"Please come back soon, *amore,*" said Sonia with quiet passion. "*Mi manchi un sacco.* Veronica is missing you too."

"Can you tell that in a fifteen month old baby girl?" asked Beppe, wanting it to be true.

"Of course I can, Beppe!" replied Sonia crossly. "I'm her mother!"

They talked for another ten minutes about nothing in particular – just so as not to leave each other too soon.

As soon as they had stopped talking and Beppe was lying on his bed planning what had to be done the following day, his phone rang again. He hoped it was Sonia. But it was his senior colleague, Giacomo D'Amico, calling him from the *Questura* in Pescara.

Giacomo would never call him just to ask how he was getting on, Beppe knew. It would have to be something serious.

"What's wrong, Giacomo?" asked Beppe without preamble.

"Nothing that we can't handle, *capo*. But I thought you ought to know. Forgive me if you were about to fall asleep."

"I'm all ears, Giacomo."

It was obvious that, despite the gravity in his voice, Giacomo was taking a certain perverse delight in relating what was happening back at the police headquarters in Pescara.

"It's just that war has broken out here in Via Pesaro, *capo*. Officers Lina Rapino and Oriana Salvati had practically to be pulled apart. They were having a massive and very public row by the reception desk. It looked as if they would come to blows. We seriously considered putting one of them in the cells below – just to cool off."

"What on earth was it all about?" asked Beppe quite astounded at what he was hearing.

"It was a fierce disagreement about how they should deal with the twelve-year-old girl, Rosa Orlando. You know, the air rifle girl..."

"How is the situation right now, Giacomo?"

"Oh, the *Questore* himself had to come back to the police station – from an official dinner he was attending. He's just about to grill the two ladies – separately, I am told. I believe I heard him mutter under his breath *'I wish Beppe were here'* chief..."

At that moment in time, so did Beppe – wish he was there.

"Kindly keep me posted, Giacomo..." concluded Beppe. He could not think of anything more constructive to add.

9: *Oriana Salvati's new approach to policing...*

"Amore mio," began Oriana, speaking with her customary *élan* to her *fidanzato*, Officer Giovanni Palena in L'Aquila. "I simply cannot walk away from this problem. This girl is only twelve. We haven't managed to get hold of her parents because Rosa – that's the girl's name – just isn't cooperating. I'm not sure even she knows exactly where her parents are. She keeps on reassuring me they will be back next weekend. She says they have to travel up to Bologna to work. On top of all that, she has a little brother who is only seven. She's the only one who this kid brother has got in the world..."

"But surely one of the other officers can help you," pleaded Giovanni. "You can't carry the whole weight of this on your own."

"Oh, Danilo and Gino are helping me whenever they can – even if it's just to keep me company. They're good colleagues – as you know. And then there's this older female officer called Lina Rapino – I've told you about her, haven't I, Giovi? But she's got this fixation in her mind that only discipline will have any effect on the girl. She keeps telling me that I'm too kind and that my kindness will merely be taken as weakness..."

Giovanni Palena sighed.

"Well, you must follow your instincts, *amore*. I'm quite sure you know what you're doing. *Allora...* I guess I shall see you when I see you. *In bocca al lupo*, Oriana."

"Mille grazie, Giovi. I knew you would understand."

"Just be careful. This girl sounds a bit crazy and unpredictable to me. It isn't normal for a kid of that age to start taking pot shots at people – or dogs – with an airgun."

"Don't worry, Giovi. I know how to deal with her," stated Oriana with her usual bravado. *"Un bacione,"* she concluded, sending a noisy kiss into cyberspace.

"I must be slightly crazy myself," thought Oriana as she plodded up the stairs to the top floor where Rosa Orlando and her little brother were no doubt waiting for her arrival. The lift, residents had informed her, tended to be unreliable.

She always dreaded returning to the flat after a day's normal police work. She had personally escorted Rosa and Stefano – Steffi – to school that morning. She had previously gone to the trouble of cornering the headmistress of Rosa's school, filling her in on the details of everything that had transpired. The *direttrice* of the local *scuola media* which Rosa attended fitfully was as helpful and understanding as she could be. To the youthful and dedicated Oriana, this middle-aged head teacher seemed worn down by the stresses of her profession.

"Rosa spends more time in my office than she does in the classroom, *Agente* Salvati. There are only two or three teachers who can cope with her. Now you've told me that she is bearing the responsibility of her little brother and that her parents are hardly ever there, I can quite understand why she is a very disturbed girl. I'll try and keep an eye on them after school hours. If Rosa fetches her brother from the *scuola elementare*, she can bring him back here until I have to go home."

"You are very kind, *Signora Direttrice*," said Oriana. "We'll get the matter sorted out as soon as we get hold of the parents."

"*In bocca al lupo, Agente* Salvati. You are going well beyond the remit of your duties as a police officer. *Grazie di cuore.*"

But despite the head teacher's valiant efforts, the two children were usually home by six o'clock – plenty of time to mess up all Oriana's attempts of the previous night to put some order back into the chaos in which they lived. Oriana shared one 'defect' with Rosa – she never made her bed. There seemed little point in tidying up something that would be rumpled beyond recognition only five or ten minutes after the occupants returned to it. Whenever *Agente* Rapino was on duty at the children's apartment, she made Rosa make her bed and tuck in all the sheets in hospital fashion. Her insistence produced momentary tidiness but created a state of almost permanent hostility between herself and her charges. Like the children they were beneath the skin, Rosa and Steffi slept in the same double bed. Oriana tumbled into the vacant parents' bed – never before half past ten – and slept until dawn. She had found some clean but un-ironed sheets and a duvet to go on the bed.

During her frequent altercations with her older colleague, Oriana argued against involving the city's social services until the parents returned.

"They'll separate the kids," argued Oriana. "Can you begin to imagine what that will do to them both, Lina?" she would state angrily. "They'll become more of a problem than ever."

So far, Oriana's fiery conviction had won the day. But the tension between the two female officers would inevitably explode sooner rather than later.

The rapid decline towards open warfare began with a Pescara football team shirt – with its vertical marine blue and white stripes representing the sea and the surf of the Adriatic, with the embroidered image of a dolphin rising out of the water sewn onto the right breast of the garment.

Oriana Salvati found the shirt attached to the outside surface of the entrance door of the apartment. It had been stretched out and held in place by strips of adhesive tape. The sleeves were spread out horizontally and flattened against the wooden door panels as if it was on display. Oriana's curiosity was increased by the fact that the shirt looked clean and ironed – unlike all the other clothes she had found scattered about inside the apartment.

She rang the doorbell. She could hear Rosa whispering furiously to her brother. She could even make out his voice protesting feebly at whatever his sister was ordering him to do.

Rosa's voice turned aggressive and Steffi evidently caved in under the onslaught of his sister's verbal attack.

"Poor kid!" thought Oriana as Rosa opened the door a few centimetres, peering suspiciously to see who was there. She was clutching a white envelope in one hand. For the first time in their brief acquaintance, Rosa smiled as soon as she realised who it was. Oriana had changed into ordinary clothes instead of wearing her uniform. Rosa opened the door wide but the smile had vanished as soon as it had appeared – to be replaced by the look of sullen defiance which Oriana had grown accustomed to over the last couple of days. Nevertheless, thought Oriana, Rosa's initial reaction had been spontaneous. It could be an indication that her strategy stood a chance of success. She would go out of her way to inform her elder colleague about this small sign of progress, which, Oriana felt, vindicated her unconventional approach to their problem child.

"I have to win her trust before we can do anything with her," she had repeatedly told her colleague, Lina Rapino.

With a deft movement, Rosa opened a drawer in the sideboard with a key hung round her neck attached to a blue cord. She replaced the white envelope which she had been clutching and locked the drawer again with a practised casualness which did not escape Oriana Salvati's attention.

"What's she up to?" thought Oriana, deciding to bide her time rather than challenge her *protégée* immediately.

"I've made us something to eat," said Rosa with a display of smugness, which Oriana interpreted as a feint to cover up her furtive act of opening and relocking the drawer.

"Steffi," she called out. "Come and have something to eat with us." Her voice had a hint of affection and pleading behind the simple command, in contrast to the dismissive tone of voice which Oriana had overheard through the closed door.

Oriana had a flash of insight as when one unexpectedly sees a familiar figure transformed into a person one doesn't recognise. A veil had been removed to reveal a glimpse of the real Rosa - her lithe figure, her olive complexion and searching brown eyes set in a sharp face struck Oriana forcibly. Rosa was even developing breasts, she noticed with a slight shock. The girl was on the verge of becoming an adolescent. Oriana had also noted with curiosity that Steffi had emerged from his bedroom wearing a boy-sized version of the Pescara football shirt. It would give her an opening conversational gambit when she next tried to strike up a dialogue with this subdued and diffident seven-year-old boy.

"Aren't you going to try my pasta *all'Amatriciana*, Oriana?" asked Rosa, bringing Oriana's mind back to the present.

Oriana's smile was genuine. This ruffian of a girl had never called her by her first name until this moment. Oriana felt the first twinge of affection towards her.

"It tastes delicious, Rosa. Just like the real thing..."

"It *is* the real thing!" Rosa pointed out, her sharp features pinching slightly as the look of defiance threatened to return. "My mum taught me how to make it. She's a brilliant cook."

Oriana looked at Rosa. She recognised that the girl's retort had been delivered in precisely the same tone of voice that she adopted with her colleagues whenever she felt challenged. Rosa was a kindred spirit.

"It's really tasty, Rosa," she conceded graciously.

Oriana looked at Steffi, his tousled head of black hair bent low over his plate, steadily spooning the pasta into his mouth. She could clearly see a teardrop forming which fell softly into his plate of pasta. It must have been the mention of his mother that had provoked this secret emotional response.

Oriana felt an overwhelming desire to protect these two vulnerable human souls. An image of Giovanni, her *fidanzato,* sprang unbidden to her mind. But she did not have time to assimilate or analyse her thoughts - because somebody was knocking on the entrance door of the apartment. The knock sounded like a pre-arranged signal – otherwise, why hadn't the visitor just rung on the doorbell as Oriana herself had done?

Rosa looked at Oriana and shrugged her shoulders by way of apology at the interruption to their meal. But the observant police officer read the look of guilt in the girl's eyes before she stood up and walked away from the table with her back to the two diners. She went through the same ritual as before – deftly unlocking the drawer and taking out the white envelope. As Oriana suspected she would, Rosa re-locked the drawer before going to the main door. The girl was clearly concealing something which she did not want Oriana to know about. But it was the expression of alarm on Steffi's face that was far more telling than Rosa's reaction. He had stopped eating and was staring after his sister, his eyes wide with apprehension.

"Who is it, Steffi?" whispered Oriana.

The boy merely shook his head wordlessly.

But the expression of fear on Steffi's face gave way to one of mute relief when his sister returned seconds later, surreptitiously stuffing what appeared to be a wad of folded twenty euro notes into the back pocket of her jeans. Oriana had only caught a fleeting glimpse of the blue-coloured banknotes before they vanished with a conjuror's sleight of hand.

Rosa coolly resumed her place at table and picked up a forkful of pasta.

"Who was that, Rosa?"

"Oh, just the landlord," she replied smoothly without looking directly at Oriana. "He comes by once a week to collect the rent. That's why I keep it locked up in that drawer."

It was a masterful performance on Rosa's part. Oriana knew she was lying because of the quantity of cash she had pocketed. But accusing her outright would serve no purpose.

"I didn't have the correct money. He gave me the change in twenty euro notes," added Rosa to cover her tracks when she suspected Oriana might not have been convinced by her explanation.

Rosa even managed an ingenuous smile in Oriana's direction, but the wariness showed in the expression behind her eyes.

Oriana smiled brightly and asked her young charge in all innocence:

"Why have you stuck a Pescara football shirt to the door, Rosa?"

It was obvious that Rosa had been expecting the question and had concocted a plausible reply.

"Oh, that was Steffi's idea. He's just mad about football and he's a big Pescara supporter – *vero Steffi?* He wants to be in the *Calcio Pescara* junior team as soon as he's old enough."

Rosa's performance would have been totally convincing had it not been for Steffi's reaction. He had turned a bright red and was looking wildly at Oriana – obviously appealing to her not to challenge his sister's words.

"That's great, Steffi," replied Oriana. "You must tell me all about the junior Dolphin Team sometime very soon. I love football."

The look of relief on the seven-year-old's face was short-lived. There was a prolonged ring on the door bell. Somebody was obviously very anxious for the door to be opened without delay. Rosa was frowning in puzzlement. Steffi, too, seemed to be more perplexed than alarmed. Oriana worked out quickly that the usual signal must have been that a caller would knock on the door.

"It's probably one of our nosy neighbours," stated Rosa. She got up to answer the door, not stopping to open the drawer this time. In the brief few seconds that Rosa was out of sight in the hallway, Steffi looked at Oriana with an expression on his face that clearly said he did not want to be a part of this charade. But he could not manage to find the words to express his confusion in the brief time during which his sister was out of sight. His expression was transformed into comic surprise at what happened next. Even Oriana's face registered momentary bewilderment. The two of them witnessed the spectacle of Rosa walking backwards into the room whilst staring angrily in front of her.

It was like a scene from a spaghetti western. A split second later, the uniformed figure of *Agente* Lina Rapino appeared – walking forwards in perfect step with the retreating Rosa. She was holding up the Pescara football shirt by the sleeves as she advanced into the living room.

"*I* know what you are up to, young lady," the police officer was saying in accusing tones.

To Oriana's surprise, Steffi looked at her with his hand covering his mouth. There was no doubt about it – he was concealing an uncontrollable giggle. Oriana grinned back at him with a shrug of her shoulders whilst trying to bite her lower lip as if to suppress a burst of laughter.

"Good evening, Officer Rapino," said Oriana, who had regained her self-control. "Would you like to explain what is going on?"

Oriana knew she needed to get a grip on the situation – mainly because she had more than an inkling of what was going on, but also because Rosa was looking cowed, guilty and defiant, all rolled into one. Rosa could erupt into anger at any moment, unravelling in an instant the fragile bond of friendship which she, Oriana, had been at pains to create.

"Displaying a T-shirt on a door is a ruse invented by that club, The Night Owl, to show their 'clients' that their choice of illegal substances can be collected from the particular location where it's displayed. Your favourite *protégée* is a *spacciatrice*, *Agente* Salvati – a drug-dealer," concluded Lina Rapino triumphantly. "Now, will you stop protecting these two children?"

"No, I won't, *Agente* Rapino. They need our help and protection even more than ever."

Oriana had stood up from where she had been sitting - an unfinished bowl of *Fusilli all'Amatriciana* growing cold in the centre of the table.

"Is this true, Rosa?" asked Oriana gently – knowing full well that it was.

Tears of anger had appeared in the corner of Rosa's eyes.

"Yes, it's true, Oriana. But there's this bastard at the night club who comes round and threatens us both. He says he'll lock me up in a dark cellar out in the countryside and nobody will ever see me again if I don't do as he says..."

Now Rosa was crying like a child. Her little brother had moved to her side and was holding her hand whilst looking desperately at Oriana – his only friend in the world as far as he could make out.

"It's true, Oriana," said Steffi. It was the first words he had ever spoken to her.

"I believe you, Steffi," said Oriana walking over to where the two children were standing. She stood behind them and placed an arm round both their shoulders.

"This situation cannot be allowed to continue, *Agente* Salvati," stated the older police officer. "We have to notify the official authorities immediately."

Oriana gently told the two children to go to their bedroom while she talked to her colleague. When the two police officers were on their own, Oriana said:

"Don't do anything precipitous, *Agente* Rapino, *la prego!* I will deal with the drugs. I know where they are hidden. You must allow me to handle these children in my own way. Your presence makes a difficult situation even more fraught. Please go back to Via Pesaro now – and trust me."

Agente Rapino made as if to leave but could not relinquish her deep-rooted disciplinary principles.

"You can beg me all you like, Officer Salvati. I can't stand by and let you carry on mothering these two kids. I shall have to inform the *Carabinieri* as to what is going on. *They* will know how to deal with these two...children."

Oriana suspected her colleague had been about to say 'criminals' rather than children, but had thought better of it.

"Trust me, Lina – please!" repeated Oriana. "They *are* only children – even if they have gone seriously astray. Where is your humanity?"

Agente Rapino had paused. Oriana's words might have struck a chord in a kinder part of her being. But Oriana felt sure she would return to the police station and carry out her threat of informing their colleagues in the *Carabinieri.* She would firmly believe she was doing the right thing.

As soon as the door had closed behind Lina Rapino's departing figure, Oriana walked over to the locked drawer. She knew what she had to do and she knew equally that it would provoke a violent reaction from Rosa. She would instinctively feel her life was at stake. The threats from the man from the Night Owl were, Oriana suspected, very real in Rosa's mind.

Pippo Cafarelli had taught Oriana how to open simple locked drawers with a piece of wire. It took her all of five seconds to achieve her first step. She carried the drawer to the table and tipped its contents out. She was amazed at the quantity of little white packets there were.

She called the children back into the kitchen. As she had expected, the look of anger on Rosa's face was alarming to behold. She looked like a volcano which was on the point of erupting.

"I understand somebody is making you do this, Rosa," began Oriana calmly. "But my colleague is almost certainly calling the *Carabinieri* as I am speaking to you. In about thirty minutes, they will arrive outside this apartment. They will take you both away and Steffi and you will end up in social care – separated from each other..."

Rosa was breathing rapidly as she fought with all the conflicting consequences in her mind.

Oriana split open a packet and poured the white powder into the palm of her hand. She walked to the toilet near the kitchen and poured the contents into the toilet bowl and flushed the substance away. When she walked back into the kitchen, the scene had changed dramatically. Steffi was standing in mute horror as his sister was charging at his only ally and friend,

Oriana, screaming abuse and holding a lethally sharp kitchen knife in her hand. Rosa had completely lost control of herself.

Oriana felt sorry for Rosa even as she prepared to defend herself. "Poor child," she thought. Rosa just could not grasp what was happening to her body as she reached her intended victim. An arm appeared from nowhere and held her wrist in a grip of steel. In the same instant, her intended victim's torso had twisted round and a leg had somehow managed to find its way under her charging body. She felt herself rising into the air and somersaulting over her own head. She hit the kitchen floor surprisingly softly but her wrist had twisted round at such an angle that she had let go of the knife, which scuttered harmlessly across the floor.

Oriana was preparing for her next defensive judo move. But she stopped in total astonishment as she saw the expression on the twelve-year-old girl's face. It could only be described as a look full of loving admiration.

"How did you do that, Oriana? PLEASE will you teach me how to do those things?"

Steffi was clapping his hands gleefully. A broad grin lit up his features - no doubt for the first time in ages.

"Teach me too," he cried.

Oriana knew in that instant she had achieved her wished-for breakthrough.

10: *In which Professor Marconi becomes entangled...*

"Should I go and knock on Luigi's bedroom door, *capo?*" asked Pippo.

"Did you hear him coming back to the hotel last night, Pippo? I didn't."

Pippo shook his head. But on a gesture from his chief, Pippo headed for the *Orso Bruno's* bedroom, his knuckles poised to rap on the door.

Pippo was startled when the door was opened from within and the massive frame of Luigi Rocco appeared already clad in his uniform."

"Buongiorno, Agente Cafarelli," he growled pleasantly.

Pippo swallowed the temptation to make any ribald comments he had formulated in his mind as to his colleague's evening spent in the company of the missing scientist's wife, Rebecca Zanetti.

A brief glance on Beppe's part took in the serene look on Luigi's face and he concluded that, on a personal level, the *Orso Bruno* had not wasted his time.

"Did you learn anything new last night, Luigi?" he asked – his tone of voice modulated to imply a hint of a *double entendre.* Pippo concluded that his chief was better versed than he was in the art of innuendo.

If the *commissario* had hoped to embarrass his young colleague, any irony was wasted.

"Apart from the fact that she uploaded a photo of Gianni Marconi's *fidanzata* – the girl called Giada - taken during a recent dinner party, I didn't learn anything new, no *capo.*"

"And was it the same girl as we saw on the two photos on Professor Marconi's desk yesterday?" asked Beppe.

"Yes, *capo* – there's no doubt about that. I also learnt that the professor's wife is desperately anxious about her husband – despite her putting on a brave face for our benefit yesterday," added Luigi.

"That is quite understandable. Well done, Luigi!" said Beppe without ambiguity.

They rapidly swallowed their morning cups of hotel coffee and brioches before standing up to leave the dining room. Beppe was clutching Professor Gianni Marconi's confiscated laptop under his arm. It would have to be taken back to the *Questura* in Pescara to be passed on to the technicians at some point during the day.

As the hotel owner's wife came up to the table to clear away their plates and cups, Beppe laid a hand on her arm.

"Just a minute, *signora.* I would like you to look at another photo for me," said Beppe, nodding meaningfully at Luigi, who fished out his phone and found the photo of Giada – in the company of two other unknown guests.

"Do you recognise this young woman, *signora?*" asked Beppe.

"I'm not sure, *commissario,*" replied the lady. "It could be..."

Beppe noted her reluctance to commit herself. He remembered their exchange of the previous evening and the salacious smile on the face of her husband at the memory of the young woman who had come to pick up the two Americans.

"Could you fetch your husband, please *signora?* It might jog a memory with him."

The wife was gone several minutes before she returned with an unshaven husband still in his dressing gown and pyjamas.

"It's my husband's morning off," said his wife feebly. Beppe thought that this pattern of behaviour might be the norm in light of the sparse numbers of guests they seemed to attract.

"Buongiorno, signore," said Beppe. "Could you please take a look at this photo and see if you recognise anyone?"

With bleary eyes, the hotel owner searched for a pair of battered reading glasses from his dressing-gown pocket and peered at the photo on Luigi's *cellulare.*

His face lit up for a brief moment before he replied:

"Why yes, *commissario* - that's the girl who came and picked up those two Americans. How did you manage to...?" he began.

"We're pretty good at our job, *signore,*" was Pippo's immodest contribution to the exchange. But inside, he silently acknowledged that it was his chief's intuitive ability to make connections that nobody else would have dreamt of which had led them to this crucial point in their investigation.

"How does he do it?" Pippo asked himself with a touch of secret envy.

But the *commissario* was thanking the couple as he stood up purposefully.

"Come on, *ragazzi.* We've got a lot of ground to cover today."

* * *

The appointment made by the secretary, Eva Petrarca, to grill Professor Gianni Marconi was not until 10 o'clock.

"To the police station here in L'Aquila first please, Luigi – we need to get Inspector De Sanctis and *Agente* Giovanni Palena involved in a covert search for this Giada woman. I don't want to alert *Professore* Marconi that we are aware of her existence just yet. He might warn her that we are on to her. It might well be the case that *he* does not realise his girlfriend is involved with this couple of Americans."

"*Bravo, capo,*" said Pippo, realising that Beppe had spotted a potential link between the 'substitute' professor, his *fidanzata* Giada and the two Americans. His chief had also understood immediately that it would be wrong to jump to hasty conclusions about any firm connection between these four individuals.

"This woman, Giada, might have met the Americans by pure chance in L'Aquila and shown them to our hotel," added Pippo quietly.

"*Appunto,* Pippo!" said Beppe. "But my instinct tells me that there is far more to all this than mere coincidence."

"*Sono d'accordo, capo,*" concluded Pippo.

The *commissario* went into precise details with Inspector Fabrizio De Sanctis and his junior colleague, Officer Giovanni Palena. They would find out discreetly who this young woman called Giada was – and where she lived.

"There shouldn't be too many women called Giada in L'Aquila," said Giovanni as he accompanied Beppe and his team to their police van.

"I understand your *fidanzata,* Oriana, has been making waves in Via Pesaro during my absence, *Agente* Palena," said Beppe with wry humour.

Giovanni sighed audibly.

"So she tells me, *commissario.* She seems to have taken two parentless children under her wing. I understand from Oriana that she is going to give them lessons in self-defence. She's managed to convince your *Questore* that what she is doing counts as essential police work – he's taken her off routine police duties until the kids' parents turn up..."

"She is a remarkably persuasive young woman," said Beppe.

Giovanni Palena sighed again.

"Don't I know it, *commissario!* Apparently, she has uncovered a drug distribution racket out of some night club in Pescara which has sunk to the level of involving this twelve year old girl in its criminal activities. Your *Questore* has assigned the drug dealing aspect to another lady officer – the one whom Oriana nearly came to physical blows with."

Beppe felt relieved. He had been convinced his chief would settle the dispute with his usual gift for diplomacy. But it was good to have confirmation of this. He need not be distracted during this crucial morning. He left the laptop computer belonging to Professor Marconi at the police station to be picked up later. The trio were heading up towards the mountain laboratory by twenty past nine.

* * *

Il Professore Gianni Marconi was ensconced behind his desk, smiling his welcome while his arms were spread out on the desktop – a subconscious gesture which was intended to convey his readiness to be cooperative in any way he could to the three police officers sitting on the other side of his desk. Beppe Stancato had witnessed similar body-language a thousand times before during his career. The false bonhomie was, thought the *commissario,* a tell-tale sign that the scientist was concealing something. Nevertheless, Beppe was sure that he was not dealing with a bad man. Beppe was growing increasingly conscious of the urgent need to locate Professor Donato Pisano before his fate was sealed – whatever that fate might be. The image of the chief physicist turning his head to the CCTV cameras and mouthing the words *"help me"* was vivid in his mind. There was a sinister aspect to this abduction which should not be underestimated.

During the drive up to the mountain laboratory, Beppe had briefed his two colleagues as to how he wanted them to contribute to the interrogation.

"Subtlety is the keyword," he had concluded. "And above all, don't forget – I want no hint that we have already identified his *fidanzata.*"

According to the *commissario's* instructions, the three police officers sat immobile, looking fixedly at Gianni Marconi. Just as Beppe had intended, the scientist was looking at each of his inquisitors in turn, wondering who was going to speak first. Pippo waited until the scientist was looking at one of the others before he addressed the unsuspecting scientist:

"Why did you swap over those photos on your desk as soon as we had left you yesterday, *professore?*"

Beppe was secretly delighted that the unexpected attack had unnerved the scientist so easily. His shoulders hunched forward, his attempt at a spritely welcome collapsed in the blink of an eye. He felt himself blushing. Gianni Marconi had the impression that his interrogators must be endowed with X-ray vision. What added to his bewilderment was the fact that the young officer who had fired this question at him had not even been present in his office during yesterday's conversation.

"I don't know, officers," he stammered. "I suppose I felt a bit guilty about replacing Donato's photograph with my own so soon after his..."

Before Gianni Marconi had a chance to recover his composure, Beppe whipped out the letter purportedly written by Donato Pisano and threw it on to the desk under the professor's nose.

"You know better than we do, *Professor* Marconi, that this letter you received is more full of holes than a colander. It could not possibly have been written by your colleague unless he was under extreme duress. It is obviously an attempt to alert you that he is in danger."

Gianni hesitated, trying to formulate some protest.

"Would you like my colleague here to point out the series of deliberate scientific errors which Professor Pisano inserted into the text, *professore?* Quite apart from the fact that you must be aware he supplied you with a false middle name. Luigi, tell Professor Marconi about muon neutrinos and tau neutrinos..." added Beppe piling on the agony.

Luigi took the stricken scientist through the sequence of false statements one at a time until Gianni held up his hands in surrender.

"How do you know all this, *Agente* Rocco?" asked Gianni Marconi despite himself.

"I'm interested in your work in this laboratory," Luigi growled at him, leaving a lot of unanswered questions about ordinary policemen being well versed in advanced physics.

Beppe nodded at Pippo. It was time to change tack.

"Have you seen the CCTV footage of Professor Pisano leaving with those two Americans, *professore?*" Pippo shot at him.

Gianni shook his head guiltily.

"My secretary told me I should take a look. But I haven't had time since..." replied Gianni Marconi, aware how feeble his excuse sounded as soon as he had uttered the words.

"Show him, *Agente* Caferelli," said Beppe, producing the CD. "Put this in to your desktop computer, *professore.* You will find it very telling."

The substitute professor turned as white as alabaster when he clearly lip-read the words "Help me" in the brief second that Donato Pisano's face was turned towards the video camera.

"Now, *professore,* perhaps you would like to explain why you have been so reluctant to be open with us," suggested the *commissario* in gentler tones.

Gianni Marconi's whole body language was transformed. His countenance relaxed as he let out a sigh of relief.

"I'm sorry, *commissario.* You are quite right, of course. But you need to understand the stresses of the last few months – ever since the moment when Donato Pisano made the discovery of our neutrinos seeming to arrive at faster than the speed of light. He was like a dog with a bone. We had to waste hour upon hour redoing the experiments. And, yes, your colleague was quite right..." Gianni Marconi was looking at Luigi Rocco, who sat impassively in his chair. "... I immediately spotted the anomalies in that e-mail which supposedly came from Donato. It really threw me when I realised your colleague understood the difference between Tau, Muon and Electron neutrinos! Congratulations, *Agente* Rocco."

Luigi was obviously sticking rigidly to his chief's injunction that they should not display any reaction to Professor Marconi's words. He continued to stare impassively over the scientist's shoulder.

"Yes, congratulations, Luigi," said Beppe with a grin. "You are allowed to acknowledge the professor's compliment."

A brief nod from the *Orso Bruno* and a deep-throated utterance which might have contained the words *"grazie professore".*

"You were saying, *professore,"* said Beppe.

"Yes, *commissario.* I was trying to put into words the stress which Donato Pisano's discovery caused us all. If he had gone public with his theory about faster-than-light neutrinos – which he did in the end – the whole future of our laboratory would be threatened. We wake up every morning with the fear that a cash-strapped central government will simply axe the whole project. I know this smacks of self-interest, but the lives of tens of top-class physicists are on the line – and we *were* slowly making ground-breaking discoveries."

"So, *professore,"* said the *commissario* in his most conciliatory tone of voice, "it would be true to say that you were relieved when Donato Pisano disappeared?"

Gianni Marconi had the grace to blush.

"Yes, *commissario,* I felt relieved. But it never occurred to me that his life was in danger. I wasn't even convinced that the two Americans had taken Professor Pisano away with them. But when you showed me that CCTV footage just now, I realised just how wrong I must have been. But I still don't see what possible interest the Americans might have in our experiments that they cannot find out freely for themselves..."

It was Luigi Rocco whose gruff voice supplied a possible explanation.

"Americans hate it when they feel their dominance in *any* field is under threat – scientifically or financially. There have been a number of discoveries they have managed to stifle at birth, *professore*. There was a man who produced copious amounts of methane gas from chicken shit – enough to guarantee the death of the oil industry if it were ever allowed to be developed on an industrial scale. Then there was the scientist who claimed he had produced nuclear fusion from the hydrogen molecules in water..."

There was a nod of acquiescence from Gianni Marconi as Luigi ceased talking.

The scientist had fallen silent again - obviously debating with himself whether he should be open about his personal life too. He had had a pang of guilt when he had considered the possibility that this group of police officers might have seen the photographs of his *fidanzata* on Donato Pisano's desk the previous day. Should he be straightforward about her too – to be on the safe side? He could not be caught out hiding anything else from them – however innocent.

Beppe signalled to his two colleagues with an imperceptible hand gesture that they should not interrupt the professor's thought processes. The *commissario* could sense that Pippo Cafarelli was actively wondering how to nudge the professor into divulging something else about his private life. The *commissario's* spider-like patience paid off in a most unexpected manner.

"And then, officers," continued Gianni Marconi with a look of embarrassment on his face, "I have just embarked on a new relationship within the last month or so. I realise how pathetic this sounds, but I have had nobody in my life since I got divorced four years ago. It was another totally selfish reason for not upsetting the *status quo* here at the Montenero laboratory – our job security..."

His voice tailed off.

Pippo, the *commissario* knew, had become adept at the art of asking seemingly innocent questions with an almost boyish curiosity. Another subtle hand gesture to encourage his closest male colleague to go ahead.

"I'm guessing that she must be someone who works here in the laboratory, *professore.* It's so difficult these days, isn't it, to meet new people outside working hours? I know this from my own experience."

The substitute professor's response was spontaneous.

"No, *Agente* Cafarelli. As it happens, I met her quite by chance – here at the laboratory. She turned up one day with one of the regular coach loads of visitors who come here on an organised trip to find out what we do here. You'd be amazed at the number of people who are curious about our scientific research projects," Gianni Marconi added, looking meaningfully in Luigi Rocco's direction.

Beppe's team knew the routine well by now – keep looking expectantly at the person concerned until they feel obliged to continue talking under their own steam.

"When I had completed the usual guided tour, this engagingly pretty woman in her thirties came up to me and asked if she could put a few more questions to me – to satisfy her own personal curiosity. By the time we had finished, her coach party had left, so I offered to take her back to L'Aquila. It all started from there really."

"Ah, so she lives in L'Aquila, does she? That's fortunate for you both, *professore.* It's so difficult to hold down a relationship with a girl who lives in Milan, isn't it?" said Pippo encouragingly.

"Yes, we got on like a house on fire from the outset. Now, she is in the process of moving in with me. We took a few of her personal things – like clothes – from her apartment to my house yesterday. That's why I left so early," added Gianni Marconi apologetically. His secretary, Eva Petrarca, had made great play the day before of the fact that the *commissario* had wanted to talk to him again but had discovered he had already left.

The *commissario* waved a dismissive hand at the scientist.

"So I guess you two have been seeing each other on a daily basis, *professore?*" asked Beppe in his most ingenuous tone of voice. He had understood perfectly that this decent man was trying to assuage his own sense of guilt about his missing colleague. If he and his team were to get closer to the truth, then it would have to be now while Gianni Marconi was in a state of mind to talk freely.

"Yes, we have, *commissario* – every day. Apart from a couple of days about a week ago when she had to go and pick up some cousins who had flown into Fiumicino airport. But I was so involved with trying to stop Donato going public about his faster-than-light neutrinos, that I didn't even have time to miss her."

"Did you meet her cousins?" asked Pippo, who was holding his breath. He had understood precisely the direction in which his chief was heading.

"No, I didn't. She told me she had taken them to somewhere in Molise – Venafro, I think she said. I believe she took them back to Fiumicino a few days later. Apart from that..."

"So, your new *fidanzata* isn't Italian then?" asked Pippo.

"Well done Pippo!" thought Beppe. "You're a budding *commissario!*"

"Oh no, she's Italian alright! Believe me – she has all the characteristics of a full-bloodied southern Italian woman," replied Gianni smiling proudly at the thought. "Her parents are

Sicilian although they are third generation American Italians. But she's got Italian nationality and has made Abruzzo her home, she assures me."

The sudden change in atmosphere was tangible. The look on Gianni Marconi's face had become thoughtful. The simple and accidental mention of the word *'American'* had triggered a connection in the scientist's mind.

Beppe Stancato stood up abruptly. Pippo and Luigi followed suit a split second later.

Beppe held out a friendly hand to the scientist.

"Thank you so much for your time and your cooperation, *professore.* We won't need to trouble you again. I'll get your computer back to you by the day after tomorrow at the latest."

Gianni Marconi nodded distractedly as he shook hands with Pippo and Luigi. He was obviously still deep in thought, his brow furrowed with the mental effort involved.

Beppe Stancato was feeling smug. The merest hint of a conjecture which had been in the back of his mind had just been promoted to a guarded probability.

"Are you thinking what I'm thinking, *capo*?" asked Pippo.

"It's quite possible, *Agente* Cafarelli."

"The American connection again," said Luigi Rocco.

11:   *In which time is of the essence...*

"We think we've tracked down the girl called Giada, *commissario,*" said Giovanni Palena as soon as they arrived back at the police station. "It was easy enough. We went through the list of rented properties in the *comune* as soon as we discovered that nobody with the first name of Giada owned a property in the city. There are only three girls with that name in the whole of L'Aquila – and two of them are in their teens."

"Obviously, you discovered her surname too?" snapped Beppe in his anxiety to push matters forward.

"Of course, *commissario.* Her surname is Costa. We didn't do anything else until you got back, naturally. Here's her address – it's not far from the city centre – or what's left of it," concluded Giovanni Palena with a touch of bitterness.

Beppe was handed a piece of paper with an address on it. He noticed with mild curiosity that Giada Costa lived next door to the house where the seismologist whom they had arrested during the 'Sleeping Beauty' case had lived.

"We know where *that* street is," Beppe commented, handing the piece of paper to Pippo, who reacted with a quizzical glance at his chief.

"By the way, an interesting point, *commissario - la Signorina Costa* seems to have rented the apartment above too," added Giovanni Palena.

"No shortage of money, you mean," suggested Beppe.

"*Appunto, commissario!*"

"Thank you for being so efficient, Giovanni. Now, we're going back to the hotel, *ragazzi*. I'm going to leave you until tomorrow and take this computer to our technicians. There's another matter I need to attend to in Pescara, too," added Beppe without enlightening them.

Pippo understood he was being put in charge of the crucial next step in their investigation. He looked reprovingly at his chief, who remained quite unperturbed.

"All I want you two to do is park some distance away from the apartment and check up on this Giada Costa. We need to look inside her apartment to see if we can find anything concrete to link her to that American couple. You have a free hand, *Agente* Cafarelli - I trust you understand what I am saying. I cannot escape the feeling that the time we have left to catch up with *Professore* Donato Pisano is running out. Use my car of course. I'll drive the van back to Pescara - it's too conspicuous. And Luigi – I hope you brought some civilian outfit with you – apart from your pyjamas, that is. You two are going undercover. Just see how far you can get before I come back tomorrow – probably not before lunchtime."

* * *

"The *commissario* is an outstanding boss," stated Luigi Rocco following a protracted silence which had lasted almost twenty minutes. Not that one felt a great need for conversation when in the *Orso Bruno's* presence, Pippo considered.

They had been sitting in the car about fifty metres down the street from Giada's apartment for nearly an hour. Luigi Rocco's idea of civilian clothing did not differ all that much from the pyjamas which Beppe had jokingly referred to, thought Pippo. The loose-fitting silk shirt and beige trousers were rounded off with a pair of dusky pink trainers. The whole outfit was topped off by a huge pair of black-framed sun-glasses. Nobody could call Luigi Rocco inconspicuous – even at the best of times.

Pippo was beginning to exhibit symptoms of restlessness – or maybe hunger.

"Yes, Luigi, you are right. No other *commissario* I know would trust his junior officers enough to just hand over an investigation as he just did. But," Pippo added meaningfully, "he does have one fault which you might not be aware of..."

"What's that, *Agente* Cafarelli?"

"He doesn't need food when he's in the middle of an investigation. The problem is he forgets that ordinary policemen like us *do* need to eat."

Luigi Rocco smiled.

"I was beginning to notice," he said. "Why don't you walk back to that bar in the *piazza* back there and get us a sandwich? I'll stay here and keep watch."

"Thanks, Luigi. I could do with stretching my legs for ten minutes."

Pippo was out of the car like a shot. He hadn't even thought to ask his colleague what filling he wanted in his *panino.*

As he couldn't resist the idea of eating a *porchetta* sandwich himself, he avoided making a decision on behalf of his colleague by ordering the same filling for him. With a frame like Luigi's it was unlikely that he was fastidious over his food. He became aware how little he knew about the *Orso Bruno* – somehow one did not do small-talk with him. It was only in the last couple of days that he had begun to appreciate that there were many hidden facets to his character. He bought two bottles of *San Benedetto* mineral water and wandered back to the car at as slow a pace as he could justify. He must have been gone longer than he had intended. He had wasted some time eating his own sandwich outside the window of a tobacconist, curious to read the small ads that people selling old cars, bicycles and pasta-making machines had left in the window, casually scribbled in poor handwriting. One neatly printed card stood out announcing that a 'local teacher' was offering maths and guitar lessons at €25 an hour. There was a tiny photo in one corner of the card which seemed vaguely familiar to Pippo.

More than a quarter of an hour later, he reluctantly climbed back into Beppe's car and handed the sandwich and water to his colleague.

Luigi took one massive bite out of the sandwich without bothering to lift up a corner of the bread to see what was inside. He must have been hungrier than he had let on. A beatific grin spread across his face.

"*Grazie, Pippo,*" he said. Pippo was momentarily shocked at being called by his first name – for the very first time by this colleague. "My favourite filling of all time! How did you know?"

"You look like a *porchetta* man, Luigi," he replied cheerfully.

There was a pause while Luigi finished his first mouthful.

"Looks like we shall be stuck here for a bit," said Pippo bitterly.

"Not necessarily, *Agente* Cafarelli," replied the *Orso Bruno,* reverting to the strict observance of protocol. "As soon as you left, a teenage boy of about fifteen turned up clutching a guitar case. His mother drove off and left him on the pavement. He rang on the doorbell of Giada Costa's apartment but nobody answered. He looked at his watch and seemed to be debating whether to call his mum to come back and pick him up when our good lady turned up in that light blue *Cinquecento X.* I guess he must be having a lesson of some sort..."

Pippo was out of the car in an instant.

"Still hungry?" asked Luigi maintaining the deadpan face he always wore when he was being humorous.

"No, Luigi – but I just saw an advert in a shop window for a young woman who gives guitar and maths lessons. There's a tiny photo of Giada Costa in one corner of the card – I didn't recognise her at first. But more importantly, there's a phone number on the card."

The two police officers had to sit outside for a further hour, before the teenager and his guitar re-emerged from the apartment to be picked up by the mother some ten minutes later. Giada Costa did not appear until a further thirty minutes had elapsed. She was trailing a small trolley suitcase behind her. She drove off at a sporty pace and disappeared out of sight.

Pippo looked at Luigi meaningfully.

"Are you ready for a bit of undercover work, Luigi?" asked Pippo. His heartbeat had increased considerably at the thought of the risk they were taking.

"You remember what the *commissario* told us," he replied simply. "I would guess *Signorina* Costa won't be back for some time."

"Right, come on, Luigi. Keep thinking about our vanishing physicist!"

Pippo was convinced that his *capo* had deliberately returned to Pescara to give his lock-picking junior colleague free rein to carry out a bit of unofficial poking about to see what he could unearth.

"We're just taking a short cut, *Agente* Cafarelli," Beppe would have said.

After all, the worst thing that could happen would be that they were arrested by the local police for breaking and entering.

* * *

Il Professore Donato Pisano was experiencing the wildest range of thoughts and emotions in rapid succession since his adolescent years. His predominant feeling was anger, followed close on its heels by a sense of nostalgia for his wife, Rebecca. It was a constant torment to him to know how anxious she must be - having been left in the dark as to his fate. Those wretched Americans had been alarmingly efficient. He had begun to experience boredom for the first time in years. Enforced inactivity played on his nerves far more than a fear for his own safety – which was strangely absent, he noted.

It was the anger which had first driven Donato Pisano to berate his 'prison warders' – as he referred to them to their faces – for serving him the wrong sort of food.

"I'm a vegetarian," he proclaimed when he was first served up with a lamb casserole by the couple in whose extensive disused wine cellar he was being held captive. He simply refused to touch the plate which had been placed in front of him.

"I can't help it," he stated when he saw the look of discomfort on their faces. "If that couple of American crooks who brought me here had done their research properly, then you would have known that I don't touch meat – in any form."

The celebrated physicist relented when the wife apologised. There was no point, he reasoned, in antagonising this couple who had been assigned the task of keeping him alive – for how long he had no way of telling. The couple must be approaching the age of retirement. The husband was obviously of farming stock – he was short and stockily built. His wife was not all that much less substantial in physique than her husband.

"But I'm not a vegan," he added in a more conciliatory tone of voice. "I'm happy to eat fish, cheese, pulses and as many vegetables as you care to serve up."

"We'll see what we can do, *professore,*" promised the wife.

His 'prison' was not that uncomfortable in as much as there was a rudimentary shower and toilet. The absence of daylight was the source of his greatest unease. He had been supplied with a clean tracksuit and pyjamas, both of which were several sizes too big – more likely cast-offs belonging to the farmer.

Donato understood that the couple must be under orders to make sure he was looked after as far as his captivity allowed.

The following day, he was given some pecorino cheese, a plate of pasta in tomato sauce and a half litre carafe of red wine.

"At least I know that I'm still in Italy, *signora*. Your cooking is very good."

The compliment had brought a brief blush of pleasure to the wife's face – quickly banished as her husband muttered something coarse under his breath from his position by the heavy steel door. The professor could hear farm animals and a tractor – but no traffic at all during the daylight hours.

"Where am I, exactly?" he dared to ask.

"We cannot tell you that, *professore*," said the farmer gruffly. He spoke in a very pronounced *Abruzzese* accent – which at least went part of the way to answer Donato's query.

The following day, it was his boredom which prompted him to demand pens and a proper A4 sized *quaderno*. This Italian word for an exercise book was not covered by their local dialect. He had to mime the meaning with his hands followed by a scribbling gesture of someone holding a pen.

"I'm bored during the daytime – and at night," he said. "I'm going to use the time down here to begin a book I've been meaning to write for ages."

"We'll get you what you want later on today when we're in town," said the wife, almost kindly. Her husband looked on, begrudging the extra effort involved in satisfying the whims of their captive. Nevertheless, Donato reckoned, they were almost certainly being remunerated generously for their illegal task with copious amounts of American money.

That evening, he was given a generous helping of *Fusilli alla Norma* – his favourite dish – a bottle of *Montepulciano d'Abruzzo,* a packet of cheap pens and a hundred page blue spiral-bound exercise book.

"Delicious, *signora!* Thank you! The *fusilli* you use are much better than the usual dried pasta," he commented.

"It's Giuseppe Cocco's pasta, *professore* - our local pasta maker."

The farmer, standing guard by the steel door, growled at his wife:

"You talk too much, woman!" he said rudely.

Donato Pisano kept an impassive face as the wife removed his empty plates, and wished him goodnight.

Inside, Donato Pisano was feeling jubilant. He felt he had won a small victory. He now knew where he was being held prisoner. One of the most famous pasta makers in Italy had his factory in a small town called Fara San Martino, in the province of Chieti. Not that it helped him at all in practical terms, he realised, as he settled down to begin writing the opening words of his book about the mysteries of mankind's erroneous perception of Time.

"*Noi esseri umani diciamo spesso che facciamo una determinata cosa solo per ingannare il tempo. Ma in realtà è*

il tempo stesso che inganna noi." These were the opening words he had been mulling over for months. Now, finally, they were on paper. It was a small triumph which counteracted the feeling of total powerlessness to control his own destiny.

(The Italian expression meaning to 'kill time', ingannare il tempo, translates literally into English as 'to trick time' or 'to cheat time'. Thus the professor's opening sentence is a play on words: 'We human beings often say that we are doing such and such a thing to trick time. In reality, it is time itself which is tricking us.')

It was midnight by the time he had finished two pages to his own satisfaction. He said 'good night' to himself and *'Buona notte, amore'* to his wife and headed for his single iron-framed bed.

* * *

Opening the main entrance door which led on to the street had been, in Pippo's words, *un gioco da ragazzi* – child's play. The street level floor led to the cellars and a flight of stairs took them to the main entrance door to the apartment itself. There was a simple Yale lock and a heavy-duty security lock which Pippo did not like the look of.

"We might not get any further than this first lock, Luigi," confessed Pippo as he inserted a thin blade into the Yale lock and released the pins with a click. To Pippo's surprise, the door opened with a gentle push.

"This doesn't look good, does it *Agente* Pippo?" growled his colleague.

Pippo liked the sound of the compromise title by which he had been addressed but was puzzled by Luigi's comment.

"What do you mean, Luigi? We're in, aren't we?"

"I mean, if there is something in here that Giada Costa needs to conceal, she would surely have used the security lock as well," concluded Luigi Rocco.

Pippo looked at his colleague with ever growing respect.

"Let's hope she just had a momentary lapse of concentration, Luigi."

They put on a pair of forensic gloves and stole into the apartment like a couple of furtive schoolboys trespassing in some local farmer's orchard.

They both made a bee-line for Giada Costa's computer desk in her study room. It housed an array of equipment which seemed more extensive and sophisticated than what one would normally find in an average person's home.

There followed a silent mime between the two police officers in which the one was goading the other to switch the equipment on.

"I don't suppose she's got the apartment bugged," whispered Pippo furiously.

"So why are we whispering?" asked Luigi logically.

"What's that black box contraption on the desk next to her computer?" asked Pippo, still talking in a stage whisper.

Luigi Rocco was incapable of maintaining a whispered voice.

"I've only seen one of those gadgets once before, *Agente* Pippo. It's a decoding machine that is usually plugged in when you are making phone calls and Skype calls when you want them to be encrypted. That is a *very* advanced piece of equipment for a normal user to possess. Plus, it's made in America!" added Luigi on examining the device more closely.

Giada Costa's computer was switched on and was asking for a password.

"This is as far as we are going to get, Luigi," muttered Pippo. "Have a look through all this paperwork on her desk. I'll try my luck with a password or two."

Luigi Rocco discovered a day-by-day desk diary with an increasing number of blank pages in it as it reached the present day. He went back a week or so and found something interesting. It was an entry which said simply – in English:

Skyped Agent Moretto DASR Boston – see CD transcript.

The note had been written on the page dedicated to May 10th. The *Orso Bruno* gave a grunt when he turned to May 11th. Anyone else would have let out a cheer. The note, once again in English, said:

Holy shit! Fiumicino – Flight AZA 1209 out of Boston. Arr: 11.35. Pick up M.Vitali plus A. Lombardi. Giada had written what could have said '*CIA bastards!*' next to the message. She had apparently thought better of it and scribbled over the offending words.

Luigi Rocco was about to impart the news to his colleague that they had already found what they had come to look for. They both froze at what they heard next – a key turning in the lock of the entrance door to the apartment.

"*Merda puttana!*" said Pippo in a savage whisper. "She's home already. We'll have to pretend to be burglars, Luigi, and get out of the flat as quickly as possible – pretend to push her out of the way as we run for the door..." suggested the ever resourceful Pippo.

After a few agonising seconds of tension, when nobody came into the apartment, Pippo realised what had happened. Giada Costa had returned because she had remembered about the security lock and had simply come back to correct the omission.

"We're locked in, Luigi!" he said unnecessarily to his passive colleague.

After his heart rate had steadied again, Pippo faced the inevitable task of phoning his chief to inform him of their plight.

"We did find out quite unequivocally that she is involved with the two Americans who turned up," explained Pippo apologetically.

To Pippo's astonishment, the *commissario* apparently found the whole episode hilariously funny.

"My priority, it seems, *Agente* Cafarelli, is not to rescue you guys but to arrest Giada Costa – so she can't get back into her own flat and incriminate you two."

After his outburst of mirth, Beppe apologised. He explained that his reaction was probably born of sheer relief that they were finally heading in the right direction.

"Just hang on there, *ragazzi*. I'll get you out as soon as I possibly can."

It was not to be until much later that night that the two police officers heard the apartment door being unlocked and the cheery voice of their *commissario* reassuring them that it was him on the other side of the door. They had raided Giada Costa's fridge – with their forensic gloves on – and made use of her bathroom and shower just to pass the time.

Pippo had finally given up attempting to discover Giada's password. If she was really part of some American covert organisation, she would have avoided any of the more obvious tricks people use to disguise a memorable combination of letters and numbers. The two men had had a competition to try and assign words to the letters DASR. Without having his guess confirmed until many hours later, it was Luigi who had hit the nail on the head. Pippo had suggested the letters stood for the *Directorate of American Secret Research.* He had rashly bet Luigi €20.

The pair of officers had also managed to unearth the CD recording of the Skype conversations Giada had had with someone called Agent Moretto – quite enough to allay any doubts as to her direct involvement with the two Americans who had abducted Donato Pisano. All in all, their covert – and illegal - investigation had paid off, Pippo argued as they whiled away the time before their release. They had found a chess set in a cupboard and played two games together. Pippo was glad he had not bet on the outcome of the chess contest. He had had his fill of Giada's goat's milk cheese and biscuits. Images of his meal at the *Agriturismo della Bella Addormentata* came back to taunt him.

* * *

Beppe was in the company of the Archbishop of Pescara when he received Pippo's call. He had hesitated to admit to his two colleagues that he felt the need for some practical spiritual guidance in this particularly sensitive investigation. It appeared so far that nobody had been murdered. Yet he found it repugnant that another nation, rather too prone to using subversive bullying tactics to maintain its position of world dominance, should feel free to abduct an entirely innocent Italian citizen for its own political ends.

He had paid a brief visit to Via Pesaro where he had dutifully left Gianni Marconi's laptop computer with his two technicians. He had reassured himself that peace had been restored between his two lady officers before taking himself off to the *Cattedrale di San Cetteo* to see the Archbishop, Don Emanuele – by appointment. After his visit, he had intended to spend the night with Sonia and his little family before returning to L'Aquila the following morning. Pippo's phone call, informing him that he and Luigi had managed to get themselves locked into Giada Costa's apartment put paid to his intended family visit.

"At least it means we are getting somewhere, *amore*," he told Sonia apologetically.

"I'm sure we shall still be here for you when you get back," Sonia had reassured him. "Besides which, Mariangela is here with me. She appears to love babies. You had better warn Pippo about that when you return to L'Aquila," she had added. Sonia had been highly amused by Beppe's account of Pippo and Luigi's imprisonment in Giada Costa's flat.

The Archbishop had been enthralled by the whole sequence of events leading up to Professor Donato Pisano's abduction by the two American agents.

"I'm surprised that his disappearance hasn't been reported by the media," he had said to Beppe.

"We've managed to keep a lid on it so far. Most of the scientists believe he's on leave. Not even a team of loquacious secretaries have broken the silence. They have been told that any word to the outside world would put the professor's life in jeopardy. But I fear every minute of the day that the truth will leak out. That's why I came to see you, Don Emanuele," concluded Beppe feebly.

Never one to shirk a spiritual challenge, Don Emanuele led his friend to the cathedral and, kneeling on the steps leading up to the altar, he held his shaven head between two hands and seemed to fall instantly into a deep trance.

He didn't move for ten minutes. When he stood up again, he looked thoughtfully at Beppe with a puzzled smile on his face.

"The Good Lord is not being very forthcoming today, Beppe, but I get the impression that the professor is alive and well. But the strange thing is, I had a vivid image of him writing in a blue exercise book – with a blue pen."

Don Emanuele led Beppe back into the presbytery and offered him a cup of coffee. It was at that point that Beppe received the phone call from Pippo Cafarelli – who at least was able to reassure his *capo* that they had found a firm link between Giada Costa and the two American agents.

"You see, Beppe? The Holy Spirit works in mysterious ways!" proclaimed Don Emanuele with an angelic grin on his face.

12:   *Una svolta per l'Agente Giada Costa...*

(A turning point for Agent Giada Costa)

Beppe had purloined the best car he could find in the police car compound. It was an unmarked dark blue FIAT Punto with a turbo-charged engine, hands free telephone and, of course, equipped with a sophisticated Satnav guidance system.

As soon as he was heading out of Pescara on the main route to L'Aquila, he called Fabrizio De Sanctis. This usually serious police inspector reacted with an amused chuckle when Beppe explained that Officers Cafarelli and Rocco were imprisoned in an apartment where they had no legal right to be.

"Don't be concerned, *commissario,* we'll send a couple of uniformed officers to wait outside Giada Costa's apartment. If she turns up, we'll say a neighbour has reported something suspicious going on. We'll borrow her key and let your lads out without *la Signorina* Costa seeing them. Leave it to us."

"*Grazie mille, ispettore,*" said Beppe.

"What do you want us to do with Giada Costa?" asked Fabrizio De Sanctis.

"I'm working on that. I shall be back with you in a couple of hours' time," Beppe reassured him.

Beppe was mulling over in his mind the parting words of Don Emanuele. He was thinking – not for the first time since he had known the Archbishop – how extraordinary it was to find a human being who was so patently certain in his own mind that an invisible power was at work somewhere in a dimension beyond human comprehension. It was disturbing and yet reassuring at the same time.

It was getting on for seven o'clock and darkness was falling as he drove without haste towards his destination. His mobile phone rang.

It was difficult for Beppe to escape the belief that some hand other than his was guiding this investigation as soon as he heard the familiar voice of Remo Mastrodicasa ringing in his ears:

"*Capo…*Beppe, you'll never guess who's sitting at one of our tables right now - Professor Gianni Marconi and his *fidanzata*. They arrived for an early supper. They are engaged in a strange conversation. She looks as if she's pleading with him and he's just listening to her talking. I'm not sure whether he's angry or hurt at what she's saying. Every time Marta goes over to the table to ask them if they're ready to order, he just waves his hand and says: *Ci dia ancora un' attimino per cortesia, signorina.*"

Beppe thought quickly.

"*Senti Remo.* Keep them there as long as you can. Offer them something on the house if you need to. *E grazie mille! Arrivo subito!*"

Beppe called Fabrizio De Sanctis as soon as he had finished talking to Remo. In a few urgent words, he told the inspector what he wanted him to do. Then he pushed the accelerator pedal down almost to the floor and ignored the impassive female voice emanating from his Satnav system warning him of a series of sharp bends on the road ahead.

* * *

Giada was picking nervously at the various *antipasti,* which they had finally ordered simply because neither of them felt in the mood to indulge in the pleasurable task of pouring over a menu before making the final decision about what to eat. Giada did not appear to be appreciating how good the food tasted. Gianni Marconi was already half way down a bottle of *Montepulciano d'Abruzzo.*

"*Io ti amo, Gianni,*" Giada was saying pleadingly, with tears welling in the corner of her eyes as she earnestly tried to convince him that she had never meant to deceive him. "I knew that something good was happening between us after we had been out together that first time, Gianni. Please believe me," she said, letting the tears run down her cheeks.

"So, why didn't you tell me who you really are as soon as we began going out together?" he asked. Gianni was clearly torn between the desire to believe her expression of love whilst combatting the feeling that she had duped him for so many weeks.

The plate of *antipasti* remained half eaten but the level of wine in the bottle had sunk even lower.

When Marta came over and asked them if they had finished eating the *antipasti,* Gianni Marconi asked for the bill.

"I'll put the food in some tinfoil for you, *professore,* then you can take it home with you for when you're feeling a bit more hungry," offered Marta kindly.

Gianni had the presence of mind to reassure her that the *antipasti* were delicious. Giada nodded in agreement - her head still lowered over her plate, not wishing to show her tears.

"Please let us offer you a coffee and a *digestivo* on the house, *signori,*" said Marta, mindful of Remo's injunction to keep the couple sitting at the table for as long as possible.

To Remo's relief, he spotted a uniformed Fabrizio De Sanctis and Giovanni Palena walking casually down the hallway leading to the dining room as he was placing the cups of coffee and the little glasses of *genziana* on the couple's table.

The two police officers headed with quiet purpose towards the couple.

"We are sorry to disturb you both," said the *ispettore,*" but we urgently need your assistance in our enquiry regarding your missing colleague, *Il Professore* Donato Pisano. We believe, *Signorina* Costa, that you might have some vital information concerning his disappearance."

The tears on Giada's face had vanished, leaving her eyes slightly red. The look on her face was one of sheer incredulity. There was no way her role in Donato Pisano's abduction could have come to light...was there? Her disbelief that she had been unmasked turned into a deep suspicion that it must have been her *fidanzato* who had betrayed her. She looked accusingly at him.

Gianni knew her intimately and read the signs instantly. He managed to maintain his calm.

"No, Giada... This has nothing to do with me," he stated firmly.

"Now, *Signorina* Costa...Giada. If you would be good enough to come with us..." said *Agente* Palena kindly.

"May I come too?" asked Gianni Marconi.

"Of course you may, *professore*. Your companion is not under arrest. We urgently need her help – that's all," *Ispettore* De Sanctis reassured them. Giada whispered hurriedly to Gianni saying she would feel embarrassed and guilty if he came with her to the police station. He did not need too much persuading to go home, promising to pick her up later.

"Don't worry, *professore*," the inspector reassured Gianni. "We'll take care of getting her back home when we've finished talking."

Gianni Marconi's offer to pay the bill was declined.

"Please come back again whenever you feel up to it," said Remo Mastrodicasa, shaking Gianni Marconi's proffered hand.

* * *

When Giada was ushered into an interview room, she was surprised to find another plain-clothed detective sitting at the table. He stood up courteously as she entered the room. She knew instantly who he was from the accurate and detailed description that her *fidanzato* had given. It was that *commissario* from Pescara. She would not give in as easily as her scientist boyfriend had, she decided. How she wished she had had time to convince Gianni of her unwilling participation in this sordid affair. Maybe now *was* the time to come clean about everything. But she feared that she would lose everything she held dear, everything good that had happened to her in the last couple of months. She dreaded above all that she would be deported back to the USA.

The *commissario* was smiling at her with a disarming kindness in his brown eyes. She secretly knew which way she would have to go. Just a token resistance maybe!

"I'm *Commissario* Stancato, *Signorina* Costa," he began. "I wonder if you would be so kind as to lend me the keys to your apartment - Giada."

"Commissario!" she said in a voice which expressed shock, surprise and a touch of moral indignation to absolute perfection.

Beppe had guessed correctly that breaking Giada would not be quite so straightforward. He had anticipated his next move and had interrupted the magistrate while the latter was enjoying his dinner only minutes before returning to the police station. The magistrate had grumbled but Beppe had informed him that it was to do with the abduction of the chief scientist at the Montenero laboratory. The sixty-year-old legal representative had expressed horror and ignorance of the event. A phone call to *Ispettore* Fabrizio de Sanctis, whom the magistrate knew well, confirmed the *commissario's* claim.

Staring at Giada, Beppe assumed an apologetic air - two could play at this game - and casually laid the *mandato di perquisizione* obtained from the magistrate on the table in front of Giada.

She shrugged her shoulders and handed over the keys to her apartment. One did not attempt to argue with an official search warrant.

"Anything to help, *commissario*," she said seemingly at ease with herself and the situation. A young woman police officer stepped into the room and sat down smiling at Giada.

"I'll be back in fifteen minutes, *Signorina* Giada. *Mi scusi...*" said the *commissario*.

Giada barely had time to consider whether she should call her lawyer – an idea which she rejected on the grounds that it would look like an admission of guilt. She considered the idea of simply leaving the police station and rejoining Gianni. After all, she argued, she was not under arrest and, therefore, under no legal obligation to remain.

The reluctance to take to her heels, she analysed, was due to some instinct which told her that *Commissario* Stancato was not a man to be trifled with. Gianni had already told her how the three police officers who had turned up the day before had worked as a team to put him at a psychological disadvantage. It had been a very effective ploy, he grudgingly admitted.

"That *commissario* from Pescara is deceptively easy-going," Gianni had told her. Now it would be her turn to be subjected to his steady and unnerving gaze. She knew that in the end she would have to surrender. Some instinct of self-preservation – or simply the habit of leading a double life in this country – came into play. But Giada Costa also knew her own nature all too well. She was a Sagittarian by birth and by inclination; she loved the cat-and-mouse verbal games that could be played to establish who was the master – or often the mistress. It was no accident that she enjoyed the game of chess –

the only game ever invented, she would often claim, in which there was no element of chance whatsoever.

She was astonished how soon the *Commissario* was back in the room, clutching her diary and a CD.

"So you went to Fiumicino and picked up the two American agents from the DASR. What were their names? Monica Vitale and Attilio Lombardi? You brought them back to L'Aquila and deposited them at the Hotel *Bella Vista* on 11th May... Am I right so far, Giada?"

Giada did not react. Her mind was working very fast. Surely, even this police inspector could not possibly have had time to digest the contents of the diary – and the CD? Then it occurred to her what must have transpired.

"*Commissario!* I can't believe you would sink so low!" she said in tones of mock moral indignation. "I do believe you sent your henchmen into my apartment when I went out this afternoon. I noticed a couple of individuals in a car just down the road from my home as I left. One of them was about the size of a mountain. I must have shut them inside when I came back to lock the main door properly. I would find the situation highly entertaining – if it were not for the fact that my privacy has been violated. You have some very careful explaining to do before I call my lawyer."

For the first time in many years, Beppe knew he had been wrong-footed. Giada Costa was a highly intelligent woman. He would have to think very rapidly to extricate himself from this dilemma and regain the upper hand. The lady police officer sitting in the room with them held her breath – and said a mental prayer for this nice *commissario* who spoke with such an engaging Calabrian accent.

To Giada's astonishment, her adversary let out a deep and regretful sigh. He was shaking his head from side to side as if he had some very bad news to impart. In the quietest voice he could muster whilst still being audible, he said:

"I hoped I would not have to resort to this, *Signorina* Costa – Giada. But it looks as if I have no alternative. I shall have to phone Cosimo Moretti in the Boston branch of the DASR – and explain to him that your cover has been blown."

It was undoubtedly Beppe's most spectacular shot in the dark of his whole career. But he could tell that his words had hit the mark. He had struck at the core of Giada's worst fears. Her face drained of all colour.

Then, seconds later, to Beppe's total disbelief, Giada's face broke into a radiant smile.

"Sorry, *commissario.* I shall stop playing games with you from now on. May I just ask you one single question?"

Beppe nodded in assent.

"It wasn't my *fidanzato* who put you on the right track, was it?"

"No, Giada. Rest assured. We worked it out for ourselves. But I think your partner had a suspicion about your involvement yesterday afternoon for the first time. He made a probably false connection between your family being in America and your possible link to that couple whom you picked up at Fiumicino."

Giada nodded.

"Yes, Gianni is a very intuitive kind of person," she said as if to herself.

"May I suggest, Giada, we meet up with you tomorrow morning at your apartment? We've all had enough for one day. Shall we say at nine o'clock?"

Beppe looked at the lady policewoman, who had been riveted to her chair, listening avidly to this dramatic exchange of words. Just as good as an episode from *Commissario Montalbano* on Rai Uno, she reckoned.

"Would you be so kind as to take *la Signorina* Costa to wherever she wants to go, *agente?*"

"And what if I should want to go back to my own apartment, *commissario?*" asked Giada teasingly. "Would you give me my keys back?"

Still playing games, thought Beppe. He leant back in his chair and fixed Giada with an unblinking stare. He could hold this disconcerting gaze for up to twenty seconds – unbeknown to Beppe, Pippo had once timed him during an interview. Without taking his eyes off Giada's face for an instant, he reached into his pocket and placed the keys to her apartment on the table exactly half way between them.

In the end, Giada smiled, stood up and said in mock resignation:

"Maybe I'll just go back to Professor Marconi's place after all, *commissario.*"

* * *

The young police woman was back at the police station in less than twenty-five minutes.

"I'm sorry *agente,*" Beppe said to her. "I should have asked your name earlier on."

"*Agente* Valentina Ianni, *commissario.* Ianni is the most common surname from L'Aquila," she added pertly.

"I'm sorry to take advantage of your willingness to help yet again, *Agente* Ianni. "I'm going to ask you one more favour – it could be very important."

Officer Valentina Ianni was secretly delighted to be able to help this engaging *commissario* from Pescara.

"I want you to drive back to where you left Giada Costa – the house of *Professore* Marconi, presumably?"

Officer Ianni nodded.

"I'm going to follow you in my car. Then you can go home and relax. Is that alright with you?"

"Agli ordini, commissario," replied Valentina, sorry that she was not going to be in the same car with him.

* * *

Beppe was acting out of pure instinct. He parked himself where he could keep an eye on Professor Gianni Marconi's house and Giada's sky-blue *Cinquecento X* – both so tantalisingly near Remo's *agriturismo,* his empty stomach reminded him. He could always call either Pippo or Luigi – now back at the hotel *Bella Vista,* he assumed. One of them could come and relieve him while he went to get something to eat. It was a new experience for him to be hungry during an investigation. He had expended a lot of nervous energy dealing with Giada Costa, he reckoned. And he was certain in that intuitive part of his mind, which rarely let him down, that the young woman who was the key to this investigation had not quite finished for the day. There was a wild feminine element to her nature which had not quite been tamed.

It was Pippo who came to support him, feed him and keep him company until midnight – at which point Beppe sent his friend and colleague back to the hotel.

"I'm going to be here through to the early hours, Pippo," he predicted.

Beppe's analysis of Giada Costa's mental and emotional state was accurate to a fault. He quite simply needed Giada to know that he knew.

Behind the snug walls of Professor Marconi's house, Giada was striving to convince her *fidanzata* that, when they first met, it was admittedly true she had had an ulterior motive for visiting the Montenero laboratory, but that afterwards she had been driven only by the desire to be with him again.

"I could not possibly know that I was going to fall for you, Gianni. After the visit of those American agents who abducted Donato, I just wanted to cut myself off from the whole sordid business. But it's not that straightforward, don't you see? If you are acting as a covert agent for the USA, they can send you anywhere in the world. You don't just resign without putting your own personal life in jeopardy. You *must* understand, Gianni. They can threaten you with all kinds of things – my parents and their farm, for example. They put pressure on you and use any threat they can conjure up to keep you in line. That bastard Attilio Lombardi – the one who stank of deodorant – threatened to take me back to the States with them. He inferred I was doing nothing useful in Italy and that my life had become a sinecure, paid for by the American tax-payer.

When you offered me a way out – living with you – I was overjoyed. I felt hope that I could really live my life out in a place I love – with the man I had fallen for. *Please* Gianni! Don't reject me now. I *know* you feel about me the same way I do about you..."

But Giada's pleas had snagged on her partner's male pride. He was still feeling that undercurrent of resentment that she had taken him for a ride so easily. And, deep inside himself, he detected the ignoble feeling that, if she confessed her part of the abduction fully to that *commissario,* it might lead to Donato Pisano's release and his subsequent reinstatement. Didn't *anyone* understand just how much chaos and stress his crazy fantasies about faster-than-light neutrinos had created?

"We'll sleep on it Giada. OK?" Gianni said with little warmth. *"La notte porta consiglio,* as they say."

He had not hugged her, kissed her on the forehead, nor had he held her tight for an instant before falling asleep as he usually did when they were too weary to make love. She lay awake for hours by his side, panic and fear about her future going round and round in an endless loop - until she could stand it no longer. It was half past three in the morning when she crept out of bed, leaving her partner's insensitive, sleeping form where it was. She slipped on some clothes, grabbed her car keys and stepped out into the sombre pre-dawn darkness.

Beppe had predicted exactly that this would happen. He did not have time to feel smug - he was caught unawares by the speed with which the blue *Cinquecento X* shot off into the night.

Giada did not head for L'Aquila. As soon as she got out of Monticchio, she took a relatively minor road and headed south east towards a town called Barisciano, which Beppe had never heard of. He assumed that Giada was just driving for the sake of driving – with no particular destination in mind. As there was nothing else on the road at that time of the morning, it was not difficult for him to keep her red tail lights in view, even if he had to travel at more than eighty kilometres an hour to keep up with her. He slowly closed the gap between them. It was time to let her know she was being followed.

The next town to be signposted was called Capestrano. Beppe was none the wiser.

Giada became aware she was being followed after she had been driving for some fifteen minutes. She smiled to herself.

"At least *somebody* is anxious not to lose me," she thought, "even if it is only that *commissario.*"

She found Beppe's nearness reassuring. She could not explain why.

Beppe was only a couple of hundred metres behind her when her car suddenly pulled into the side of the road with the emergency lights flashing. He slowed down and pulled in behind her. She had remained seated in her car. Beppe walked towards her – not wishing to scare her with the sight of a strange man approaching her at four in the morning. He need not have been concerned. As he drew level with the *Cinquecento X,* Giada lowered the window.

"*Buongiorno, commissario.* I've just run out of petrol," she said contritely.

Beppe laughed quietly. He knew that she would not give him any more trouble from then on. Her rebellious streak had run its course.

"I suppose I shall have to give you a lift home, Giada," he said kindly.

Between them, they manoeuvred Giada's car off the roadway completely.

"We'll come and pick it up later - and bring a spare can of petrol," he said.

Some twenty-five minutes later, they arrived outside Gianni's house. It was not even five in the morning. Giada showed no immediate signs of wanting to get out of the car.

"I'm dying for a cup of coffee, *commissario,*" said Giada. "But I don't suppose..."

Beppe started up the motor and drove to Remo's *agriturismo.*

"How can you be so sure that the owner will open his doors to you at this time of day?" asked Giada mystified by his assuredness.

"Oh, Remo used to be a policeman in Pescara. He's the most obliging person I know – and I helped him out one or two times," said Beppe.

Ten minutes later, they were sitting round a table in the kitchen. A pyjama-clad Remo served them coffee and biscuits.

"We shall have to have a longer talk later on today, Giada. But I have to ask you the obvious question immediately..."

"No, *commissario*," replied Giada without waiting for the question. "I'm truly sorry. I haven't a clue where that couple of Americans took the professor. They would most certainly have destroyed the professor's mobile phone so its whereabouts could not be traced. And they would have turned off their own devices for the same reason. They might even have whisked him off to the States for all I know."

"No, Giada, we believe he is still on Italian soil. We checked with the airport police in Rome. Besides which, it would have been too risky to abduct him in full view of all those travellers, not to mention the airport security systems. No, they're keeping him somewhere in Italy and they'll come back to get him when they've made suitable arrangements to smuggle him out..."

Giada was impressed by the *commissario's* thoroughness and his logic.

"Well, *commissario,* all I can tell you is that I drove them to some taxi-driver called Gregorio Mazzaferri in a village called

Collecorvino. This man keeps a couple of cars to rent out. After that, they wouldn't have anything to do with me until they needed a lift back to Fiumicino airport."

"Do you happen to know whether their hire car had a GPS device fitted to it?" asked Beppe.

"Oh, I do hope so, *commissario!* But he was just a small-time operator. That's why that Attilio character picked him. I don't know the answer to your question."

"We shall have to go and see this taxi-driver as soon as you have had a bit of a rest, Giada. I'll send my officers to pick up your car this morning."

"You mean the pair who raided my apartment, *commissario* - the nice-looking young one and the officer who looks like a Sumo wrestler?"

"I apologise, Giada."

"Maybe I'll forgive you if they go and fetch my car for me," said Giada mischievously. But the fight had gone out of her, Beppe noted with relief.

Giada's phone rang. She stood and walked away from the table when she saw who was calling her.

"Giada, amore... Where are you? I've been so worried about you. It was awful waking up and finding you gone. And then I saw your car was missing too..."

"I'll be home in a couple of minutes, Gianni," she told him.

Gianni Marconi was waiting for her by the front door. He was smiling with relief.

"Ten o'clock, *Giada.* I'll pick you up from here. I'm sorry but this visit simply cannot wait."

"I'll be ready, *commissario,* I promise."

Without a word, Beppe handed over the key to her apartment.

"*Grazie, commissario,*" she said with a complicit smile lighting up her face. "*Lei è super simpatico! Grazie di essere stato con me stanotte.*"

("Thank you, commissario. You are really nice. Thank you for being with me last night.")

13:   *Rosa Orlando defends her rights...*

To Rosa's surprise and discomfort, a uniformed Oriana Salvati came into the school building as her classmates were leaving, having been dismissed after the final lesson of the day by their teacher. Rosa bridled at the sight of her new 'parent'. The angry pout on the twelve-year-old girl's face would have disconcerted anyone but Oriana.

"Nice to see you too, Rosa!" smiled Oriana sweetly.

"What are *you* doing here, Oriana?" Rosa asked sullenly.

"There is something the three of us have to do before we go home for our next lesson in self-defence, young lady. Now let's go and pick up Steffi."

Oriana nodded amicably at the school's head teacher and led Rosa off the premises. Inexplicably, Rosa slipped her hand into Oriana's as they left the building.

"That lady policeman was my auntie," Rosa would inform her classmates the following Monday morning. She would kill anyone who dared to utter a word in contradiction.

Steffi's reaction was very different; he ran towards Oriana and put his arms round her waist in an affectionate hug. His sister let out a scornful rebuke, stifling her envy that she could not allow herself the same overt expression of affection as her younger sibling. It was down to Oriana herself to put an arm round each of their shoulders as she drew them closer to her. Rosa barely resisted now she was out of sight of her peers.

"Now, Rosa and Steffi, listen to me and promise me you won't be afraid. We need your help to put that nasty man from the Night Owl behind bars..."

Steffi turned as white as a sheet and his eyes grew big with fear. As Oriana had expected, Rosa dug her heels in.

"You've been good to us, Oriana, and we both...like you a lot."

Just for an instant, Oriana was certain Rosa had been about to say the words *'Ti vogliamo bene,'* probably for the first time in her young life. But she had stopped herself and downgraded her verbal assessment of their relationship.

"But there's no way I'm going to go up and point a finger at *him.* He'll hunt us down and lock us up in a dark cellar just as he threatened. You've no idea just how nasty he can be."

Oriana crouched down to be on the same level as the children.

"I know it's a lot to ask of you, *ragazzi,* and if you refuse, then we'll just go home like on a normal day."

After less than a week, Oriana realised, they had already established a pattern which had become part of their lives. Oriana stifled the little voice inside her which tried to tell her how rash she had been in becoming involved with these two children. "What's done is done," she told herself. She could hardly abandon them now.

"I promise you this man will never know you are there, Rosa. We will be upstairs in my boss's office and we will be watching the man on a television screen. Trust me, please!" pleaded Oriana. "I promise you that he will never be able to get to you again. He'll be *al fresco* until you are both grown up. In any case," Oriana smiled, "you'll soon be able to defend yourselves like a pair of black belt champions!"

Rosa and Steffi looked at each other. Oriana sensed she had won them over. They just nodded and the three of them walked over to where Oriana had parked her car. Both children remained tensed up all the way to the *Questura* in Via Pesaro.

"What about that other police woman who made us make the bed every time we began watching *L'eredità* on Rai Uno?" asked Steffi. "Will she be there too?"

"I'm certain we can manage to avoid her as well, Steffi," Oriana reassured him.

* * *

Sitting perched on stools high up in *Questore's* spacious office, they could look out of the window and see the River Pescara running past the window on its short remaining journey to the Adriatic. Even the presence of the uniformed *Questore,* Dante Di Pasquale had put them at their ease. He had shaken them by the hand as if they had been adults and quietly thanked them for their courage in coming to the police headquarters.

The children's eyes were riveted on the large TV screen as they watched the man who had provoked so many nightmare images of terror in their minds, sitting handcuffed yet defiant at a table. He was being interrogated by Giacomo D'Amico and Officer Lina Rapino.

"Is that the man, Rosa? Steffi?" asked Oriana quietly.

"*Sì, è lui!*" replied the two children in unison.

Steffi had a crooked little smile on his face as he listened to Officer Lina Rapino questioning the man, whose Eastern European name they learnt for the first time.

"That's how she spoke to us when she wanted us to make our bed," muttered Steffi.

The *Questore* turned the sound down and sat the little group round a table.

"Just a few questions, Rosa and Steffi," the senior policeman said quietly. "Would you mind if we recorded what you say? That way, we will be able to prosecute that man without your having to appear in court."

To Oriana's secret joy, their two faces turned to her as they sought her approval for the request. She smiled and nodded.

"How did you first meet this man, Goran Bosovic?" asked the *Questore?*

The two children inexplicably froze at the suddenness of the question. Oriana looked at her chief and signalled her puzzlement with an unobtrusive shake of her head. She looked encouragingly at them both but they were reluctant to divulge the answer.

"*Dai, ragazzi!* You're not going to be in trouble. I'm here to make sure nothing happens to you," said Oriana.

It was Rosa who finally broke the silence. Was that a quick look of disappointment from her brother that she was betraying a dark family secret?

"It was our *papà* who invited him round one evening," she admitted against her will. "He told us this man was here to keep an eye on us while he and *mamma* were away."

Even Oriana looked shocked at this unexpected answer.

"He came round a couple more times on his own," blurted out Steffi, "with those little white packets. That's when he told us he would lock us in some cellar and throw the key away if we ever told anyone about what was going on."

Steffi's eyes were full of tears. The *Questore* nodded his head at the technician who turned off the equipment.

"That will be all, *ragazzi.* You have been truly courageous. *Grazie mille!* Now, Oriana can take you home if you want."

Dante Di Pasquale shook their hands solemnly and smiled a paternal smile at them both. "You, young lady, remind me of my own daughter when she was your age. The likeness is striking."

"What does she do now?" asked Rosa, emboldened by the implied compliment.

"She's a doctor at a big children's hospital in Rome, Rosa."

Rosa had a dreamy look in her eyes. It was as if she was looking into the possibility of enjoying a future in her own right. Oriana once again felt a stab of joy mixed with fear in her heart.

Oriana left the kids by the reception desk while she went to change into her civilian clothes again. When she returned she found officers Danilo Simone and Gino Martelli talking animatedly to 'her' two children, who were enthusiastically demonstrating the judo and karate moves they had learnt, delivering imaginary blows to Serbian drug dealers and other enemies who might come their way.

"Remind us never to cross *your* paths, *ragazzi!*" Danilo was saying as Oriana approached the little group.

* * *

Back in the flat in *Viale Kennedy,* the snacks had been quickly made and eaten. Oriana had promised them a pizza after their energy-consuming self-defence session. The mattress had been dragged off Oriana's bed – the absent parents' mattress, she reminded herself. Steffi had shown real talent. He was able to kick an imaginary foe much higher than himself and the speed with which the action was delivered was breath-taking for a seven-year old, thought Oriana. What Rosa lacked in strength she more than made up for with her boundless energy and the look of warlike concentration on her face, as she confronted her invisible opponents.

Both the children were engaged in their warm-up exercises whilst Oriana – the black belt in nearly every form of martial art known to man – was issuing orders and encouragement from the edge of the king-size mattress. None of them had heard the door opening. When the three of them paused, ready to learn their next Karate move – the *hasami-zuki* Oriana had explained – the group became aware that a man and a woman were watching them from the hallway. The children froze. The looks on their breathless faces – pink from their exertions – had reverted to the expression which Oriana remembered on their first acquaintance.

In those first two seconds, Oriana learnt things which made sense of the situation she had landed herself in. The mother was in her mid-thirties at most, dark-skinned and sexually charged, and she was dressed in a provocative manner which made her main occupation in life instantly apparent. The father was older, shorter in stature than the mother and squat in build - a bully who had exploited his partner's sexual attraction ruthlessly.

"Mamma," muttered Steffi under his breath. His lips wanted to form a smile but the expression on the father's face froze the smile before it could form.

"Che cazzo fai qui? Chi sei tu?" snarled the man in Oriana's direction - his vulgarity instantly plain for all to hear.

"She's our friend," shouted Rosa in anger and despair all in one go. Life appeared to Rosa to have regressed in a split second of time. Her father took two steps towards her, his hand raised ready to strike his daughter round the head. Oriana was too far away to intervene. The man's hand was already close to its vulnerable target. The force of the threatened blow would knock Rosa over.

Then it happened. Rosa's arm was raised rigidly with fist clenched to intercept and deflect the blow just as Oriana had taught them. The man looked astounded as the blow failed to reach its target. His surprise turned to excruciating agony as Rosa delivered a vicious kick to her father's crotch.

"Mio Dio," thought Oriana, delighted despite herself, "I don't recall teaching her *that* one!"

The father remained doubled-up in pain but he managed a look of hatred in Oriana's direction as she began to make a phone call for back-up. The children's mother continued to look nonplussed at nobody in particular, unable to know how to react without explicit permission from the children's father.

"You needn't bother phoning the police, *signorina*," the man managed to sneer, still clutching his midriff. "I'll deal with you before they ever get here!"

"*Papà* – she IS the police," called out Steffi, half in anger, half in warning.

"And she's our friend!" shouted Rosa a second time.

The father made his fatal mistake at this point, charging across the room towards Oriana his head lowered, the pain in his genitals apparently forgotten. Oriana had uttered a few precisely chosen words into her phone - explaining the situation she was faced with to whoever had picked up her call in Via Pesaro.

"NO, Luigi!" screamed the kids' mother finally finding her voice. But it was too late - Oriana simply side-stepped nimbly at the last moment. With a swiftly aimed kick to his backside, she propelled the father headlong into the wall under his own impetus. He collapsed on the floor almost unconscious.

Rosa was grinning again. Steffi did not know whether to applaud or cry, so he began to do both. The mother seemed quite indifferent and sidled off towards the bathroom and locked the door behind her.

"*Disfunctional,*" thought Oriana.

"Come on kids," she said. "Let's get this mattress back on the bed again."

The father was recovering, although he made no attempt to get up.

"We haven't done nothing wrong," he said, attempting to defend himself even from his defeated position on the floor.

"How about neglecting your children, for starters, *signore?*"

"She's twelve years old. She can be left in charge and it's not breaking any laws..." began Luigi petulantly.

The scorn on the young police officer's face was absolute as she launched into a tirade of words as sharp as a slashing razor.

"That is what *you* think, *stronzo!* You are simply managing to display your total ignorance of the law – in addition to your crass stupidity about almost everything else in your life. You will be charged with gross negligence in respect of your son and daughter. You are obviously unaware that the law on neglect extends well beyond twelve years old. You have been absent for nearly a week during which time we have saved Rosa from a charge of shooting her neighbours with an airgun and stopped her dealing in narcotics – an activity initiated by *you.* You'll serve a jail sentence of at least five years by the time we've finished with you."

Oriana paused for breath.

"Come on Rosa, Steffi. Help me with this mattress, please."

In the bedroom, Rosa spoke anxiously – fearful that they were about to lose even the shred of happiness they had shared with Oriana during the week.

"When will we see you again, Oriana?"

Oriana did not know the answer to Rosa's question. So she spoke the only words of comfort she could think off – fully aware that they were written in stone.

"Don't worry, Rosa. I promise I shan't desert either of you," she said. Gino Martelli and Danilo Simone found the three figures huddled together with their arms round each other. Nobody had thought to shut the entrance door to the apartment, so they had walked in unannounced.

"Ciao Oriana - are these the two miscreants we should be taking away?" asked Danilo cheerfully indicating Rosa and Steffi.

Danilo's comment brought the hint of a smile back to Rosa's face.

Luigi Orlando was led away without protest by the two officers. The mother had emerged from the bathroom and regarded the scene as if it was an everyday occurrence.

"Come on kids. Let's go and get that pizza I promised you."

The mother did not protest but declined to accompany them, following an invitation from Oriana. When they got home again an hour later, the mother was fast asleep on the unmade bed.

"I'll be back soon, *ragazzi,*" promised Oriana, planting a big wet *bacio* on each of their cheeks before walking out into the night. At least she could now spend the weekend with her *fidanzato,* she told herself in consolation for her act of dereliction.

Her car headed at a steady pace in the direction of Loreto Aprutino – for the first time in days.

14: *La bisbetica domata...*

(The shrew is tamed)

Giada was, as she had promised, already waiting outside Gianni's house when Beppe arrived at eleven minutes past ten later on that morning. She jokingly berated him for his lateness.

"I was explaining to my officers exactly where they should pick your car up, Giada," explained Beppe sharply. He was not about to allow this lady to revert to her capricious mood of the previous day.

She took one look at his face and decided she should apologise for her frivolity. Beppe, ever the gentleman, accepted her apology with a slight inclination of his head.

It was she who brought up the subject of Shakespeare, likening herself to Kate, the wildly rebellious woman in that play. She explained to Beppe that she had watched a production of *The Taming of the Shrew* on RAI 5 a few weeks previously and found that the character of Kate reminded her of herself – in her less rational moments.

"Not that I would *ever* portray myself in those terms under normal circumstances, *commissario,*" declared Giada Costa gaily as they headed down the mountain road in the direction of the hilltop village of Collecorvino – some fifty kilometres or so from Monticchio.

"As indeed I would never have thought of comparing you to Kate had you yourself not brought up the subject. Although I

197

concede there might be some superficial similarities between you two," he added. "But don't forget, Giada, in your favour as it were, I believe Shakespeare was under the illusion he was portraying a universal image of the fairer sex when he wrote that play."

Beppe received a round of ironic applause – for his analysis and for his diplomacy, according to Giada.

"But what you did last night was inspired, *commissario*. How did you know in advance that I would do something as irrational as driving myself along a totally unfamiliar road in the early hours of the morning?"

"I just read the warning signs, I suppose," he answered. "Had you any idea where you were heading?"

"Absolutely none at all. If I hadn't run out of petrol, heaven knows where I might have ended up."

"Well, at least we *both* know where we are heading this morning, Giada."

"Yes, *commissario*, we do. As you suggested, I tried to phone the taxi-driver, Gregorio Mazzaferri this morning. He was picking up a fare from Pescara airport. But his wife assured me he would be back by eleven o'clock and that she would make sure he didn't go out again before we arrived. I told her that a well-known *commissario* from Pescara needed his help with an important enquiry."

"*Brava*, Giada," said Beppe.

Silence reigned between the two travellers for several minutes. It was Beppe who broke the lull in conversation.

"I don't imagine you've had much time to talk to your *fidanzato,* Gianni, about your 'other role' in life?" he asked, more out of concern for the survival of their relationship than because it was relevant to the present circumstances.

"No, we shall have to broach that subject later on today. He wants me to give it up so he can make an honest woman of me, *commissario.* At least, he believes me now that it wasn't my intention to deceive him – at least, not after we started going out together seriously."

"Do you mean, Giada, you would like to go on spying on our poor old country? Forgive me being so blunt."

"Absolutely not, *commissario,*" Giada replied emphatically. "Your 'poor old country' as you put it, is *my* poor old country too, don't forget."

"So why can you not simply hand in your notice to this Cosimo Moretto character at the DASR – what *do* the letters stand for, by the way?"

"The Directorate of Advanced Scientific Research, *commissario.* It's an offshoot of the CIA as far as I can gather. I can't keep on calling you '*commissario*'.

"Yes, you can, Giada Costa," replied Beppe, giving her a stern look, "at least while this investigation is on-going. You were about to tell me why you couldn't just hand in your cards."

"Sorry, *commissario.* I'm always too forward in my manners. It must be the American in me. No, the truth is, organisations like the CIA are obsessively secretive. We have to swear life-long allegiance to the USA, to the President – in whatever shape or form he ends up in the White House – and even to God Almighty himself. You don't just 'resign'. You take your allegiance and your often trivial secrets to the grave…"

Giada paused for breath.

"But what role does the DASR play?"

"They are supposed to monitor *any* scientific advance made by *any* other country in the world. Just so the good old US of A can keep one step ahead. I am told that the only place where we have no agent *in situ* is North Korea. But that might just be a joke."

"I see," said Beppe – although he was having some difficulty coming to terms with the concept of America's planet-wide nosiness. "Good job we haven't got men on Mars just yet," he added grimly.

"Appunto, commissario! So you see, if I express a wish to free myself from these comfortable shackles, I shall be 'recalled' to America and 'debriefed' – which in security terms implies isolation, a new identity and being spied on by other off-shoots of the CIA to ensure that I *don't* have any freedom of choice. They even discourage you from forming permanent relations with the

opposite sex – or even the same sex if that happens to be the case."

Beppe remained thoughtful for nearly ten minutes. Giada wisely decided to let him digest what she had just said. She was startled by his words when, only a short distance from Collecorvino, he half turned towards her, never for an instant taking his eyes off the road, and said:

"Let's try to find Professor Donato Pisano first, Giada, and then we'll set about the task of making *you* vanish – on Italian soil, of course."

Giada was too nonplussed to react to his words. She also needed to give him precise directions to the house of the taxi-driver-cum-car-hire-man who may or may not be able to help them. The next few minutes would decide whether the Professor could be located or whether – a more likely scenario thought Beppe with his usual sense of foreboding at this stage of an investigation - he would be faced with the prospect of drawing a complete blank. The thought made him nervous. He sighed as he pulled up in front of a modest detached house below the picturesque historic centre of this unassuming little town.

"I know how you must be feeling, *commissario.* That agent, Attilio Lombardi, deliberately chose to rent a car from this guy – simply because he assumed there would be no tracking system fitted to the car. He didn't want anybody to know where he was going."

"Thank you for your candour, Giada. I do truly appreciate the fact that you didn't come out with some pointless platitude at this stage. You are a good woman."

Giada felt herself blushing despite herself.

Minutes later, the two of them were sitting round the kitchen table sipping the inevitable cup of coffee and trying in vain to turn down politely the offer of homemade cakes and biscuits from the taxi-driver's wife.

"He'll be back in five minutes, *commissario,*" she assured them.

The sound of a chugging diesel engine drawing up outside the house was heard less than a minute later.

"*Eccolo, commissario,*" said the wife.

Beppe's heart was beating faster.

The unkempt figure of Gregorio Mazzaferri appeared nervously in the doorway. His appearance suggested to Beppe that it would have been more in accordance with his image if he had just been collecting eggs from his hen house rather than ferrying passengers around the countryside in a taxi. Beppe had seen the same expression of guilt many times before on the face of ordinary men who instinctively feared that their undeclared cash receipts had been exposed to the police by an ill-wisher. Gregorio's face broke into a shy smile as soon as he recognised Giada.

"This is *Commissario* Stancato from Pescara," said Giada. "Don't look so worried, *Signor* Mazzaferri. You remember those two Americans I brought here about ten days ago?"

The taxi-driver nodded.

"We just need to know, *signore,* whether you had a tracking device fitted to that FIAT Punto they hired – nothing else."

Beppe inwardly thanked this woman for being the one to pose the vital question which he had not wanted to ask.

Gregorio Mazzaferri continued to look nervously at Beppe, who was staring at him intensely.

"I hope I haven't done anything wrong, *commissario,*" said the taxi-driver. "But I just don't trust the punters these days. So, yes, I have a GPS tracking device fitted to both my cars. I never mention it to clients. I haven't rented the FIAT out since that couple used it. I still haven't managed to get rid of the smell of the deodorant that man was wearing..."

Beppe was smiling broadly for the first time since he had begun the quest for the vanishing physicist. He wanted to plant a kiss on Giada's forehead. In fact, he was even willing to do the same to the taxi-driver.

"It was my son, Davide, who set up the tracking device, *commissario,*" explained the taxi driver. "We can go round and see him right now if you want. He's the computer wizard in the family. I haven't a clue about how modern technology works.

Let's go and retrieve that device for you and take it round to my son. I *knew* they were up to no good, that couple," he added with self-satisfaction at his own professional astuteness.

Beppe and Giada followed the taxi driver the short distance to his son's house. Davide was a younger, scruffier version of his father, who looked as if he hardly ever left the swivel chair in front of his desk which housed a variety of gadgets and computers. But his proficiency with computers was not in doubt. A fascinated *commissario* – plus a more computer-literate Giada Costa – were soon looking at a red line which snaked its way across a map of Abruzzo, plainly heading for the Montenero Laboratory.

"That must be when they abducted..." began Giada, but was prevented from finishing the sentence by the frown on Beppe's face.

The two of them watched enthralled as the red line headed sout-eastwards towards a place called Fara San Martino. The car had made for Chieti where, they assumed, the Americans must have found a hotel. They made a return journey to Fara San Martino the following day. In the end the red line took them back to Collecorvino.

"Is there any way we can have a copy of this journey, Davide?" asked Beppe.

"Of course, *commissario,* I'll put it on to a USB device for you."

If the taxi driver's son had picked up on the word 'abducted', he gave no sign of it. Beppe and Giada took their leave with handshakes and thanks all round. Beppe felt like singing as they headed for Pescara.

"I'm sorry to drag you even further away from L'Aquila, Giada, but we simply have to take this gadget to our technicians at the *Questura* – and collect your Gianni's personal computer from them. I suspect that it will reveal nothing that we haven't subsequently discovered for ourselves."

"I hope not, *commissario*," commented Giada drily.

"If you like, I can put you on a bus to L'Aquila and that way, you won't have to hang around, Giada."

"If it's all the same to you, *commissario*, I'd prefer to tag along. I feel I am deeply involved in Donato Pisano's disappearance."

"You're welcome, Giada. I appreciated your handling of the taxi-driver and his wife. You have reserves of resourcefulness which could yet prove vital. Consider yourself engaged."

Giada gave Beppe a complicit smile and said nothing – for at least two minutes.

"May I ask you what your personal situation is, *commissario?* I noticed you are wearing *un'allianza* on your finger."

"My wife, Sonia, gave birth to our second child less than a week ago, Giada. I've been rather busy since then and have hardly seen my wife, my daughter or my newborn son – as you can well imagine."

"*Colpa mia, commissario, mi dispiace tanto,*" said Giada Costa beating her breast three times in mock contrition.

They completed the short journey to the *Questura* in record time and headed immediately down to the basement where the two technicians, Bianco Bomba and Marco Pollutri had already been warned by the *Questore* himself that they should give absolute priority to Beppe. Giada was introduced to the pair of technicians as 'an important collaborator'.

Would there be any chance that this couple could resist the temptation to keep the *commissario* in suspense – as was their well-established practice up till that point? Beppe doubted it. He usually had to endure their playful procrastinations patiently – in the certain knowledge that he would find out what he needed to know after they had kept him on tenterhooks for as long as they dared. It was their way of alleviating their boredom and isolation in this windowless basement, Beppe acknowledged.

It was to Beppe's surprise, therefore, that the usual taunts were absent. Bianca Bomba presented Beppe with Gianni Marconi's laptop, all enclosed in air-tight plastic wrapping.

"There we are, *commissario*. The *Questore* implied you might not be in the mood for our usual prevarications. So, we are sparing you the works – just on this occasion, mind you," said the voluptuous Bianca Bomba with a gleam in her eyes.

"Nothing much on this computer; that e-mail was sent via a source somewhere in the United States of America – it seems to have the hallmarks of the CIA or something similar. Apart from that, there's just a bit of soft porn on the hard drive and a few attempts at contacting a dating agency – but all of that stuff magically ceased about three months ago – I guess the *professore* must have found himself a partner..."

"Yes, he did, Bianca. The *fidanzata* in question is ME!" said Giada with asperity. She didn't seem particularly embarrassed, however.

Bianca Bomba let out a peal of trilling laughter at her own gaffe.

"I'm so sorry, Giada. I truly didn't realise."

The potentially awkward moment passed off lightly enough.

Marco Pollutri, with his usual efficiency, had slipped the USB device into a computer and double-checked the route taken by the two Americans in the rented FIAT.

"That car travelled up to L'Aquila from Collecorvino on the 13th May and then on the 15th and 16th it travelled down to Fara San Martino via Chieti. Fara San Martino seems to have been the main destination on both occasions, *commissario*. You know Fara San Martino, I suppose?"

Beppe shook his head. Something else about Abruzzo about which he was ignorant, he thought. But the positive outcome of the information he had just gleaned far out-weighed his annoyance with himself that he still had so much to learn about his new home territory.

"I'm sure we shall become very familiar with this town in the next few days, Marco..."

"It's where they make our pasta – there are two pasta factories there - De Cecco and another one whose name has slipped my mind for now, *commissario*. After that, as you can both see, the car headed back to Collecorvino – where I presume it had been hired from in the first place," concluded Marco Pollutri.

"Thank you, Marco – and you too, Bianca. Once again, you have surpassed yourselves."

Beppe and Giada climbed up from the basement clutching print-offs from the GPS device and Gianni Marconi's 'incriminating' personal laptop. Beppe did a quick round of the *Questura,* shaking hands with the officers on duty that Saturday morning and exchanging a few words about what had been going on.

"Oriana has been keeping us all very busy, *commissario,*" Giacomo D'Amico informed him, telling him briefly about the arrest of Rosa's father the night before. "Everything's under control, Beppe," said the dignified senior officer on whom Beppe relied so much.

"Come on Giada. Let's get you back to L'Aquila for now. And then it appears that we shall all be concentrating on this town, Fara San Martino. We can only assume that is where they took Professor Donato Pisano."

Beppe's mind was once again working overtime – after the brief period of euphoria on discovering the existence of the tracking device.

"Why on earth would those American agents have picked *that* particular town of all places?" he was wondering.

15:   Some localised perceptions of Time...

Lunchtime

"I don't suppose you fancy taking me for a spot of lunch, *commissario?* It's nearly one o'clock after all."

"Ah, forgive me, Giada. How remiss of me. Would you mind, for my sake, if we were joined by my two officers – the two miscreants who raided your apartment? It would save me a bit of precious time."

"Of course I don't mind. I would love to meet that nice-looking young colleague of yours – plus the mountain bear too."

"Just don't call him that to his face, Giada. *L'Orso Bruno* is the nickname he's been given by everybody in Via Pesaro. I think he's becoming a bit sensitive about it. But quiz him on anything to do with particle physics and he'll be in his element. And don't ask why Pippo walks with a slight limp – he doesn't like it being pointed out."

"Why *does* he have a limp, dare I ask, *commissario?*"

"Because he took a bullet in his kneecap which was intended for *me*. And *I* don't like being reminded of *that.*"

"*Mio dio!*" was all Giada said, looking very contrite.

The agreed meeting point was, once again, Remo Mastrodicasa's *agriturismo*.

"That way, Giada, you'll be back on home territory and my lads can drive your car there for you to pick up."

"*Perfetto, commissario! Grazie.*"

"By the way, Giada, I'll leave *you* to return this computer to your *fidanzato*," Beppe said with a wicked gleam in his eyes.

* * *

"You drove quite a long way out of town last night, *Signorina* Giada," said Pippo good-naturedly as he handed her the car keys. "It's fortunate that it's light blue in colour – or we might have missed it amongst the trees."

"Sorry, Pippo," said Beppe. "It was pitch black when we parked the car this morning."

"We filled your tank up at the local petrol station, *signorina*," added Luigi Rocco.

"Grazie ragazzi. I'm so grateful to you both."

Neither Pippo nor Luigi mentioned the fact that their *capo* had instructed them to put extra fuel into the tank of her car – in addition to the five litre can they had taken with them to get the car back on the road.

Looking at Giada properly for the first time, Pippo thought he understood precisely the reason for Beppe's generous gesture at his junior officers' expense. Later on that day, Beppe took the receipt for the fuel and refunded the fifty-odd euros they had forked out. He explained that Giada Costa was going to play a vital role in rescuing Professor Donato

211

Pisano. That, he would explain pointedly to Pippo, was the sole motive behind his generous gesture.

"I saw the look on your face earlier on, *Agente* Cafarelli," he would admonish his young colleague mildly.

When Beppe formerly introduced his colleagues in the car park of the *agriturismo*, Pippo, junior to Giada Costa by at least seven years, looked with unequivocal admiration at her and blurted out:

"You look just like that actress Sabrina Ferrilli, *Signorina* Giada. But I don't suppose I'm the first person to have told you that."

"No, Pippo, but you are the lucky prize-winner because you are number five hundred," replied the lady. "However, I thank you for what I take was intended as a compliment – although I've got another eighteen years to go before I reach her age."

Pippo, only just mature enough not to blush, nevertheless looked taken aback by the asperity of Giada's retort.

"I'm sorry, *Signorina* Giada. I only meant..." stammered Pippo.

"*I* apologise, Pippo," said Giada with a rueful smile, seeing the embarrassment on Pippos's face. "My tongue does get the better of me on occasions. *Mi perdoni.*"

Beppe, smiling knowingly, uttered what sounded like the words: 'May I introduce you to Kate?' Pippo simply looked baffled. Beppe decided it was time to put things into perspective.

"Giada has just become engaged to *Professore* Gianni Marconi," he announced.

"*Congratulazioni signora,*" said Luigi and Pippo in chorus as they went in to have lunch. Beppe noted with satisfaction that Giada had been promoted to '*signora*'. Pippo would no longer be tempted to flirt with his chief witness.

For Beppe at least, lunchtime was a simple matter of nourishment.

He told his two team members about their discovery that morning that the two American agents had visited Fara San Martino on two consecutive days.

"It must be where Professor Pisano is hidden," said Beppe. "What do you two guys think?"

"It's the only logical reason why they would go there twice, *capo*," agreed Luigi.

"But why there of all places?" asked Pippo. "Unless they are mad about pasta, of course."

"*Bravo, Pippo.* That is precisely the question I have been asking myself," said Beppe.

Giada Costa was looking very pensive as she tasted her food appreciatively – which she had not been in the mood to do the previous evening. But Beppe was sure she was mulling over an idea in her head.

"I can think of only one reason why they should choose Fara San Martino," she said. "No two – but I am fairly sure there is not a second agent like me in Abruzzo. That just leaves the one obvious answer, doesn't it, Beppe?"

The *commissario* let her slip of the tongue pass uncommented on.

"I see we are thinking along the same lines, Giada," said Beppe tantalisingly keeping Pippo in the dark. He often did this deliberately in order to force his young colleague to think laterally.

Luigi Rocco growled to himself but otherwise made no comment.

"Leave it with me," said Giada. "I should be able to find something out – but not before Monday, I fear."

They left the restaurant in a mood of heightened optimism and *camaraderie.* Beppe turned to his two colleagues and said:

"I just need to sort out something with Giada. Do you mind waiting just a couple of minutes, *ragazzi?* Then we should go and pay *la Signora* Rebecca Zannetti a visit – to let her know we've made progress in the search for her husband. Beppe got into the passenger seat of Giada's car. Their intense discussion could only be observed by Pippo and Luigi through the glass of the *Cinquecento's* closed windows.

"Pity neither of us can lip-read, Luigi," commented Pippo.

"I have a shrewd idea what they might be talking about – but it's just guesswork. Time will no doubt reveal if I'm right, *Agente* Pippo," said Luigi.

"I owe you for that bet we had, Luigi."

"No need to worry about it," replied Luigi. "I must have read it up somewhere beforehand."

The *Orso Bruno* continued to surprise Pippo at every turn.

Giada stepped out of her car and gave Beppe a *bacio* on each cheek – a gesture noted by Pippo. Their *capo* walked over to his two colleagues with an air of total nonchalance.

"*Andiamo, ragazzi,*" he said, ignoring the expression on Pippo's face.

* * *

A temporary suspension of time

Oriana Salvati was blissfully unaware of the passage of time that Saturday morning because she remained fast asleep until eleven o'clock. She had fallen into the waiting arms of her *fidanzato* on arriving home the previous evening. Exhausted, she had been too tired even to have a shower. She tumbled into bed and managed to give a garbled account of what had transpired

215

during her absence, holding on to Giovanni tightly as she spoke. Her voice trailed off and there was silence. She had fallen asleep in Giovanni's arms. He sighed – a mixture of disappointment that they had not made love and a realisation that his impulsive girlfriend had just overturned the predictable course of their lives.

When Oriana woke up late the following morning, she experienced the weird sensation that she had been robbed of the last eleven hours or so. Some invisible force had wiped out the intervening time. She could hear Giovanni pottering about in the kitchen, singing along to the radio as he often did. He had a good singing voice, thought Oriana.

She went into the kitchen in her nightdress and wrapped herself round him just to be sure he was still hers.

"What are you thinking about, *amore?*" she asked.

"That you have taken on the responsibility for these two children and that it will be quite impossible for us to ignore them from now on, Oriana," he said quietly. "I know you too well."

Oriana looked at his calm and unperturbed face. No rebuke, no jealousy, no histrionics - just a simple statement of how things were.

"But...what can we do?" she asked.

"I suppose I shall have to meet them," he said with mock resignation. "I need to know what we are letting ourselves in for."

Oriana looked longingly at Giovanni with a mixture of pure love tinged with apprehension at her own recklessness.

"*Ti amo per sempre,*" she said simply.

"For ever is a very long time, *amore mio.*"

That evening they made love in a manner that forged the final links that would bind them together for all time.

"You are unique, Giovi," she stated, not needing to go into greater detail.

"Only because I have you in my life, *mia bellissima* Oriana."

It was a two-sided coin, thought Giovanni Palena, in the certain knowledge that he could never grow tired of this woman.

* * *

Donato Pisano dispenses with the Present Time

He would simply have to get out of this cellar sooner rather than later – even if he had to set fire to it. Not that he had the means to achieve this goal – unless he could reinvent spontaneous combustion. Perhaps it would be possible to pretend he was a cigar smoker and demand they supply him with cigars and matches? He couldn't envisage the farmer falling for such a ruse.

The problem was he had written so much in his exercise book that he would need another one after only a couple more days. He was feeling inspired. There was no way he could interrupt the flow. He would have to ask that couple to go shopping for him again, which would test their willingness to help to its limits. What day was it? He had lost count of the days of the week, even if he had a firm grip on the abstract notion of time.

He had thought of feigning illness or even madness when the couple next came down to deliver his meal. The standard of the wife's cooking had been maintained. He had even had a plate of sea bass cooked with parsley on a bed of oven-roasted potatoes.

He rejected the scheme of madness and illness as it might simply precipitate his fate at the hands of the Americans. Donato lived in the vain hope that someone would succeed in working out where he was imprisoned. But he was aware this possibility was so remote as to be nigh on impossible. He sighed in resignation at his fate. At least, he assumed that his American captors wanted him alive.

He turned his attention to his blue exercise book. The next one would have to be a different colour. Yellow, he thought, since he was missing the sunlight. He began to reread what he had already written and dawdled over the passages he liked best. He had dedicated his opus to his own two children. He imagined they were six and eight years old again and he was sitting between their beds relating his story about time to his more or less captive audience. In his mind's eye, they were looking at him agog – just as they had done when he used to read them children's tales at bedtime. He was unconsciously making an effort to render his words intelligible to all who might one day read his book. He wanted them to share his passionate curiosity about the mysteries of space and time which were part and parcel of his interpretation of the Universe.

In the time it has taken me to write down this sentence in my exercise book, I have just travelled 1800 kilometres...

Yes, a good opening, he considered. It brings you up with a shock, doesn't it? He addressed this piece of information to his two children, wide-eyed with astonishment.

...Earth hurtling through space on its journey round our Sun at the incredible speed of 30 kilometres per second... Hard to believe? The truth is, our poor brains just cannot grasp the simple realities of Creation – Capital "C"? Yes, so it should be! *Imagine you are being held prisoner in a dark cellar where there is no daylight. Your captors have taken away your watch and your mobile phone. After just a few hours, you begin to lose all sense of time as you realise how much you depend on the Sun, which does not really rise in the east, telling you it's daytime. You go to school or to work and know when it's time to go to bed as the Sun doesn't really set in the west...*

Locked in an underground cellar, Donato had no difficulty in imagining the setting he was describing. He skipped a couple of paragraphs of explanation – easy to check and alter later on if needs be.

Now let me begin to explain to you about this illusion we have as to the passing of time. The clever ones amongst you... He looked hard at Sofia and Francesco who nodded at him with a look which said, '*Sì papà*, that's us!' ...*will probably have worked out something along the lines that we are all stuck in an eternal present. Well, I'm sorry to have to destroy your long-held beliefs. But things are simply not like that. Nothing, but nothing, is at it seems. The truth is that the Present lasts less than a nanosecond – in fact, the time is so brief that the human brain cannot even think that quickly. The Present Time does not really exist.*

That bit of information had his children's mouths open in astonishment, he was pleased to note. He skipped another page or so.

We all live in our own time cone. And your time cone, Sofia, works at a different rate to Francesco's. How had he managed to include his own children in his narrative? Maybe it would be a good way to present the whole book. But might it not become cumbersome and annoying to certain readers? He would have to work that one out later.

If Sofia goes to live up on the top of a mountain and Francesco lives down in Pescara at sea level, then time will slow down for Francesco and speed up for Sofia. It's a simple fact of our existence. We have clocks so accurate now that these minute differences can be measured. So Francesco will grow old more slowly than Sofia. It's all to do with gravity and being nearer or further away from its source depending on where you live.

There followed some more technical stuff in support of the argument. Donato realised that he would have to have extensive footnotes at the end of the book so that the narrative didn't get bogged down with equations and historical titbits about Einstein.

But the real shock comes when you try to come to terms with the fact that our own personal time cones are affected by space-time depending on what speed we are travelling at - relative to the speed of light. If Francesco could be magically transported to the nearest star to our solar system, Proximus B, travelling at faster than the speed of light of course, and Sofia sends her brother a Happy Birthday message on his ninth birthday, the message will arrive, so far as Earth-bound Sofia is concerned, on his thirteenth birthday – since Proximus B is four light years away. Time, as we think we know it, has simply been stood on its head by what we now understand about the nature of the universe.

That might need a bit of tidying up, he thought. He had gone on to explain how even a journey round the Earth in a jet plane - with Sofia on board leaving her brother in Pescara – would result in Sofia being 'younger' than her brother on her return.

The speed at which we travel has the real effect of slowing down our individual time cones...

Donato Pisano suddenly felt tired when he looked at the sketches of his egg timer-like light cones whose constricted middle section represented the nanosecond-long division between the past and future in space-time. He would check the clarity of this difficult concept tomorrow. What *was* he thinking? He was no longer sure when tomorrow was. He might have managed to remove the Present Time almost entirely from his calculations – but the simple fact was that his emotional self was painfully missing his wife, Rebecca, as he became increasingly desperate about his own plight.

When the farmer and his wife brought him what turned out to be his supper, he said he had run out of paper. He also discovered that it would be Sunday tomorrow – the first Sunday of his captivity it must be. On an impulse he told his captors that he wanted to be let outside and that he wanted to have lunch with them the following day.

"You have my word I shall not try to escape or warn anyone of my presence," he promised.

"*Impossibile, professore,*" he was told angrily by the farmer. His wife was looking appealingly at her husband, who was ready to dig his heels in.

"In that case, *signori*, I shall tip tomorrow's lunch into the toilet and flush it away. I shall refuse to eat or drink anything else so I may well be dead by the time *they* come back to ship me off to the States – as I suppose they plan to do."

The farmer looked perturbed. Obviously the Americans had promised him his final payment on receipt of the undamaged goods, Donato worked out.

"We'll think about it, *professore,*" muttered the farmer.

* * *

Family time

To Beppe's surprise – and possibly to Luigi Rocco's disappointment – the three police officers found Rebecca Zanetti in the company of her two grown up children.

"This is Francesco and this is Sofia," she introduced them proudly. "They have taken time off university to keep me company."

A look of secret joy appeared on her face when Beppe Stancato guardedly announced to the family that they were optimistic that they had found out whereabouts Donato was being held.

"I came to warn you, *Signora* Rebecca, that I intend to make your husband's disappearance public tomorrow with the sole aim of provoking his captors to show their hand," Beppe explained. "So you might like to watch the local TV-Tavo news bulletin tomorrow at midday. Naturally, there will be no mention of the exact location of where we believe he is being held. And, forgive me you three – I'm not going to tell you either."

"Thank you, *commissario*. I am amazed and impressed by the speed with which you have moved in the search for my husband. *La ringraziamo di cuore.*"

Her heartfelt thanks instinctively included her two children.

Back at the hotel *Bella Vista,* the husband and wife team had to resign themselves to losing their three paying guests.

"I know for a fact, *signori,*" said the *commissario,* "that accommodation is very tight at the Montenero laboratory. I am going to recommend that the administration department are told about your hotel. I think you could be sure of a steady source of income from the resident scientists. Some of them might well be glad to escape from their working environment at the end of a working day. Leave it with me to sort out over the next week or so."

The gratitude on the part of the hotel owners was quietly ecstatic.

"*Grazie di cuore, commissario,*" they chorused, echoing the words of the missing physicist's wife.

* * *

Bedtime

Sonia Leardi was overjoyed at the unexpected return of her husband that Saturday evening just as she was putting the children to sleep and thinking of following suit.

"Just as well you showed up, *amore mio*," she said in typical Sonia fashion. "I understand you've been parading around the *Questura* in Pescara with Sabrina Ferrilli in tow."

Beppe grinned sheepishly. News apparently travelled even faster than the professor's neutrinos.

"I can explain everything, *tesoro*," he said.

16:   Some Oscar-winning performances...

A grudging farmer from somewhere outside Fara San Martino led an agreeably surprised Donato Pisano into his spacious farmhouse kitchen the following day. The wife was preparing a simple tomato based pasta sauce. Three marinated fish were ready to be barbecued over an open fire. A large television set, sitting precariously on an ancient sideboard, was switched on with the sound turned down.

The pasta course was quickly devoured by husband and wife. Donato attempted to make polite and cheerful conversation, complimenting her on her *sugo.*

"Just the right touch of sugar in the sauce to offset the bitterness of the tomatoes," he said. *"Complimenti, signora."*

"Grazie, professore," she muttered, suppressing her smile of pleasure under the influence of a scolding look on her husband's face.

"What are your names?" asked the professor. "You know who I am, I suppose?"

"You don't need to know our names," barked the farmer, who could see that his wife was about to reveal hers. "All we know is that you are a scientist from that place up in the mountains. They didn't tell us anything else."

The wife stood up and placed the fish over the hot fire. The fish took minutes to cook and arrived on the table redolent of the smoke from the wood fire and the scent of the sea.

"It's delicious," said Donato, with a cheerfulness which he did not have to force. "Thank you for letting me upstairs today."

By the juxtaposition of the chairs, the wife had her back to the television and the farmer was facing towards the open kitchen. Only Donato could see the silent screen.

It was time for the TV-Tavo news bulletin. Half way through his fish, which he was eating with deliberate slowness so as to prolong his moments of freedom, he looked up to see to his surprise his own face on the screen.

"Guardate! Sono io!" he said with a broad grin on his face.

The farmer leapt up and lurched towards the television, which wobbled perilously as he jabbed at the volume slide. Donato was afraid he had been going to turn the whole thing off but the sound boomed out throughout the kitchen.

"Cazzo!" swore the farmer, at the sight of their 'guest' on the television. His wife's usually healthy outdoor complexion had blanched.

After the picture of Donato Pisano's face had faded, it was replaced by a tele-reporter, a high-ranking uniformed *Questore,* who was introduced as Dante Di Pasquale, and a good-looking younger man who was staring intently at his invisible audience as if he was attempting to mesmerise them.

"And this is *Commissario* Stancato from the police headquarters in Pescara," explained the reporter. "He wishes to make an important announcement about a very disturbing event which will cause us to question the security and freedom of our own citizens in this Peninsula of ours. *Commissario?"*

Thank you, signore. Good afternoon. We are sorry if this news item is interrupting your Sunday lunch, so I will be brief. Less than a week ago, the disappearance of the chief physicist at our mountain-top physics laboratory near L'Aquila was reported to the local police. We have since learnt from our enquiries that Professor Pisano was abducted against his will by secret agents from what I shall only describe for now as a 'friendly foreign power'. The motives for his abduction are as yet not entirely clear. We believe that he is, for now, alive and being held prisoner somewhere in Abruzzo. We have some tentative leads as to the location. Over the next few days, our search for the missing scientist will be intensified. I would remind anyone involved in the professor's abduction that this act constitutes a serious breach of the law and that the culprits will be dealt with severely. Anyone able to throw light on this incident is encouraged to contact our Questura in Pescara without delay – or, of course, you might prefer to go to your local police station. Thank you for your attention. Buona domenica and buon appetito!

"An unbelievable report which strikes at the heart of our democratic right to freedom," added the television presenter, thanking his guests. "Of course, we shall be pleased to assist our local police force should you prefer to report anything unusual directly to TV-Tavo. Our contact number will now appear at the bottom of your screens."

The farmer, with a rasping noise emerging from his throat, hit the button that switched off the television set, which wobbled precariously on its plastic base.

"That American who smelt of sweat told us the *sbirri* would never track us down. As to that other one, your brother's *fidanzata*..." the farmer snapped.

The wife was looking petrified.

Donato Pisano considered it was time to pour oil on troubled waters.

"It's obvious that *commissario* from Pescara is bluffing, *signori*. Don't let yourselves get worked up over it. He's hoping to unnerve whoever is responsible."

The scientist was smiling blithely at the couple, implying by his words that 'those responsible' for holding him prisoner were miles away in some other part of Abruzzo altogether.

He went on quietly enjoying his sea bass and sipping his white wine seemingly without a care in the world.

"Don't worry, *signori*," he continued, rubbing salt in the wound. "I shall put in a good word for you and tell the police how well you treated me."

The farmer's wife offered Donato a coffee and a *digestivo,* looking gratefully at their prisoner.

The husband hustled the professor back to the cellar as quickly as he could the minute Donato had downed the final drop of *genziana* in his glass.

"See you tomorrow at breakfast time," Donato called out with irritating good humour. "Please don't forget to get me another exercise book, if you can. A yellow one would be nice."

The cellar door was slammed and locked, leaving him in the gloom once again. But a glimmer of hope had been kindled. He had heard of this *Commissario* Stancato before – something to do with rescuing a young girl from a place in Monticchio. Yes, that was it! The media had named the investigation *'The case of the sleeping beauty'.* That was why that *agriturismo* had been called *La casa della bella addormentata.* This *commissario* had a reputation for being competent well above the call of duty, so to speak. Donato Pisano nursed the grain of optimism he felt as if it had been a candle which had burnt down to its last centimetre. He recalled the moment when he had, in desperation, turned to the CCTV cameras and mouthed the words *'Help me'* over his shoulder, just before that agent with the strong odour had deliberately blocked the line of vision as he had been hustled into their car. Maybe, someone had picked up on that. They might even have spotted the car's registration details. It was consoling to know that the outside world was aware of his plight.

The police would have been in touch with his wife too. He filled up the rest of his exercise book before bedtime.

As for black holes, he wrote before sleep got the better of him, *you should avoid them like the plague – if you can manage to resist their fatal attraction. They are dreadful places – there IS no time at all; no past, no present and no future. Nothing - not even light can escape from their grip.*

That was enough for one day. Besides which, he had only a quarter of a page left on which to write. He fell asleep and dreamt about trekking across the Gran Sasso, as a free man, in the company of Rebecca.

* * *

The following day – Monday – Giada prepared herself mentally to make her crucial Skype call to her contact in the States. It was frustrating and unnerving that she had to delay her call until three in the afternoon because of the eight hour time difference. She had sent the usual automated signal which would inform her boss, Agent Cosimo Moretto, that she needed to contact him at 7 am Boston time.

"I'm going to hand in my notice today, Gianni," she had announced proudly to her partner before he set off to the Montenero laboratory that morning. She had not tried to capitalise on her insider knowledge of her *fidanzato's* surreptitious viewing of porn on his PC - nor his search for a new partner prior to their first meeting. It was merely an indication that Gianni suffered from the usual human weaknesses – male weaknesses, of course, she added to herself.

"By the way, *amore,* the *commissario* spotted something during his second visit to the laboratory – a life-size cut out image of *il Professore* Pisano, or something. Do you know what he's referring to?"

"Yes, we use it to put outside the lecture theatre whenever Donato gives a public talk. It's amazingly lifelike. But why is the *commissario* interested in that?"

"He asked if he could borrow it, Gianni. He didn't specify why. But, if there's one thing we've learnt about Beppe Stancato, it's his ability to predict how events are going to turn out…"

Gianni Marconi had winced imperceptibly at his fiancée's use of the *commissario's* first name, but said simply:

"I guess he knows what he's doing. I'll bring the placard home with me this evening."

Giada had had to cancel all her private students 'for the next week or so' she had informed the parents. "Family matters," she had explained vaguely. The truth was, she did not intend to miss out on the action. Besides which, she might not be occupying her apartment in L'Aquila for much longer.

Finally, the crucial moment arrived. To her own annoyance, she felt her heart beat getting faster as she waited for

Agent Cosimo Moretto's face to materialise on the screen in front of her. The Skype connection seemed to be delayed for much longer than usual, which added to her anxiety. But then his unsmiling face was there. She hoped he would not go through the same ritual as before of complaining how early it was in Boston and how he needed a cup of coffee.

Giada thought that her boss looked guilty – as if he was not looking forward to the prospect of talking to her.

"How are you, Agent Costa?" he began awkwardly. "I was going to call you this week as I have some news for you. Why don't you start by telling me the reason for this call?"

Giada knew instinctively what it was her DASR chief was about to tell her. She wasn't certain whether this was going to make her task easier or harder. So she took a deep breath and began her well-rehearsed opening gambit.

"I have to inform you, Agent Moretto – Cosimo – that those two agents who arrived in Italy a couple of weeks ago have made a complete hash of what they were supposed to do."

Giada was instantly gratified to notice the look of complete astonishment on the face of her 'adversary' – the role in which she had instinctively cast her interlocutor. This announcement, pronounced in a tone of derision, was the last thing he had been expecting.

"I beg your pardon, Giada," he said attempting to bluff his way out of having to face up to what she was telling him. "You are talking about two of our most experienced operatives. I advise you to modify your language."

"Your advice is heeded, Agent Moretto, but unfortunately I have no choice but to ignore it. I have to tell you that they failed entirely to cover their tracks. In fact, Agent Attilio Lombardi, quite literally, left a trail behind him that even a poodle with sinusitis could have followed."

Apparently, Agent Moretto had also noticed the strong smell of body deodorant which the agent in question trailed behind him – since he made no comment.

"The net result is that the local police, headed by a highly experienced and very intelligent *commissario,* know more or less exactly where to go and rescue Professor Donato Pisano. If you don't act quickly, then the whole mission will have failed."

"How did you find out about all this, Giada?" he asked.

"Because I am a very good agent," she replied.

Giada paused before speaking again.

"Now, Agent Moretto, what was it that *you* had to tell *me?*"

Agent Cosimo Moretto was looking very uncomfortable but managed to utter the words which Giada had been hoping to hear.

"It has been decided to terminate your contract. In fact, you may count your time remaining on Italian soil in weeks rather than months. I'm sorry, Agent Costa, but you are being recalled to the United States..."

Giada was overjoyed. She would not have to go through the rigmarole of announcing her resignation. Her boss had virtually done it for her. Now she could act out her well-prepared theatrical scene with total confidence.

"Oh, Agent Moretto, you have no idea how happy I am to hear you say those words!"

She beamed a dazzling smile at the little spot of light that was her webcam. Agent Moretto was looking astounded and he could not conceal his relief.

"But I thought you were completely settled over there, Giada. What's changed all of a sudden?"

"Nothing has changed. I had to put a brave face on it, didn't I? I felt it was my duty. But I've been secretly dying to come back home and see my parents and family again – before I am reassigned, of course."

"Well, that's good to hear, Giada. Take your time, of course."

"I expect I shall need to go and pick up those agents again – when they come over to rescue Professor Pisano. I was hoping to go and see some relatives of mine in Sicily, Cosimo. But of course, I will cancel that trip if you want me to fetch the agents..."

"I will have to get back to you when I've spoken to...a higher authority. In the light of what you have told me, they may want to bring forward their plans."

"Will you let me know soon, Cosimo? I shall be pleased to cooperate with them again."

"Stay on line, Agente Costa...Giada. I'll call you back within the hour."

Now was the moment to ask her key question – while he was still flustered. If her guess had been wrong, there would be very little to lose at this stage.

"By the way, Cosimo, which one of those two agents is related to the people who are hiding the professor? It's Agent Lombardi, isn't it?"

"No, it was the other one, in point of fact. But how the hell did you...?" blurted out a flummoxed Agent Moretto, caught off his guard simply because he had been so relieved that he had not had to deal with Giada's expected tears and recriminations.

"I half overheard them discussing the matter – in English. They were too incompetent to realise I speak fluent English, Cosimo. Can you believe that?"

"I'll call you back as soon as I can. What you told me needs dealing with urgently – like NOW!"

Giada felt jubilant at the success of her ploy. It had been just like a game of chess. She had out-manoeuvred her boss with consummate skill. Beppe Stancato would be proud of her. She poured herself a glass of red wine and waited in a state of near euphoria for Agent Moretto to reply. Whatever was decided, it did nothing to alter her tactical victory.

He replied within the space of fifteen short minutes.

"You can go on your trip to Sicily, Giada. You won't be needed. They will be in Italy before the week is out to collect the professor."

"But surely, they will need...?" she began but was cut off brusquely.

"There will be four of them coming over – including Agent Lombardi. And it will be too far for you to drive. They are flying into some place up in the north of Italy. I repeat - your services are not required, Agent Costa."

The Skype connexion went dead. Giada needed to talk to the *commissario* to tell him what she had learnt. She felt that she had gone some way to making up for the part she had played in Donato Pisano's abduction. Now all she wanted was to be more closely involved in his rescue. If she could find a connection between the American agent, Monica Vitale, and someone living in Fara san Martino, they might be able to identify where the professor was being held. She had always enjoyed looking into people's family trees and had become adept at delving into the past. She turned on her computer and opened a site called *Dov'è piantato il mio albero genealogico?* – an Italian search tool which she had often used in the past to trace people's ancestry. Wouldn't it be good if she could phone him up in an hour or so's time with an answer to the one obstacle which remained in the way of rescuing Donato Pisano. She also wanted to ask Beppe what he had meant during the car ride to see the taxi driver in Collecorvino, when he had said something about "setting about the task of making *her* vanish?"

She was fascinated by the devious workings of his mind.

* * *

The devious mind in question was deeply engaged in wondering how to solve that self-same problem. Beppe, accompanied by Pippo and Oriana Salvati had quietly descended on the little town of Fara San Martino round about three in the afternoon. None of the police officers was in uniform. Oriana had been half relieved and half guilty that she was neglecting her two charges.

"They'll be alright for a day or two now their mother's there, Oriana. I'm sure you've given them your number if ever they need to talk to you. I need you with me and Pippo at the moment."

He had reluctantly left the *Orso Bruno* behind in the police headquarters in via Pesaro. He had had to explain as tactfully as he could to Luigi that he might be a bit conspicuous walking round the streets of Fara San Martino. He had consoled Luigi with the promise that he would be indispensable when it came to the moment when they rescued the professor. "Brave words, *commissario!*" he told himself, as he realised that the task of discovering where Donato Pisano was being held prisoner was anything but straightforward – even in a small town like Fara San Martino. Always assuming they had jumped to the right conclusion in the first place. He and Giada had both had the same thought two days ago. The unlikely choice of hiding place might well mean that either Attilio Lombardo or Monica Vitale had family connections in this town. It was the way Italians' minds worked – even if they *were* the American variety. You could always rely on your family to help you out. *I legami familiari* supplanted even the laws of the land. Besides which, it was the only lead they had to go on, thought Beppe despondently.

17: Fragments of the whole...

Beppe had despatched Oriana and Pippo to do the rounds of all the shops in the town as soon as they reopened at five o'clock. They had been charged with the nebulous task of asking all the shopkeepers if any of their regular customers had changed their purchasing habits in any way over the last week or so. It seemed a fruitless way of spending an evening but Oriana and Pippo, being good and thorough officers, had entered into the spirit of the search.

"If they ask why you want to know, tell them it's to do with the Vanishing Physicist. You can say we suspect he's being held prisoner in Fara San Martino. The whiff of a scandal might jog a few memories. *In bocca al lupo, ragazzi,*" said Beppe sending them on their way. Pippo and Oriana had decided to work the shops and mini-markets separately so as to cover more ground.

It was eight o'clock before the two officers returned to the comfortable little hotel where they had decided to stay overnight. Beppe had been suffering from the same feelings of inadequacy which always struck him at this stage of an investigation. It was the lull before the storm – or, just as likely, the point when all his efforts simply unravelled, to reveal the abyss of failure opening up at his feet.

He sat and meditated, hoping for the ray of light that would suddenly break out from behind the clouds of depression.

He phoned Sonia because she always managed to comfort him and restore his morale. The two children were brought to the phone by Pippo's *fidanzata,* Mariangela – who, Beppe commented with relief, seemed to be Sonia's constant companion during his absence.

"Yes, she's being a real treasure. We're like a couple of grieving widows without our men present," said Sonia who sounded far from being down-hearted. Beppe's daughter, Veronica, managed to gurgle something resembling *ciao papà* and Lorenzo sounded as if he was bringing up his feed. Beppe's voice must have revealed his state of mind.

"It'll be fine, *amore.* You know your instincts are always right. You'll see. By bedtime, there'll be light at the end of the tunnel."

"*Grazie, Sonia. Ti amo.* Thank you for making me believe in myself again."

Pippo and Oriana drifted back, looking as despondent as Beppe had been feeling prior to his phone call to Sonia.

"Mariangela sends you her love, Pippo. Now let's find somewhere to eat, *ragazzi.*"

Pippo and Oriana exchanged glances. The *commissario* was definitely showing signs of improvement when it came to mealtimes.

Beppe might have developed some sense that other people get hungry by eight o'clock in the evening, but he did not wait beyond the first few mouthfuls of food before asking his colleagues how they had fared in their mission.

"Nothing remotely conclusive, *capo*," began Oriana. "I went to the hairdresser's, the chemist, the butcher's and the local bars. Nobody noticed anything different. One of the guys in the bar felt he had to give me a smart answer. He said that in this town nothing ever changes until someone dies – and even then it doesn't cause too much of a stir, seeing as most of the population is over seventy."

Beppe was beginning to feel despondent again.

"The only place where anyone noticed a change in customer behaviour was the greengrocer's. He said that one of his regular customers had started buying double the amount of vegetables in the last week. She even bought three kilos of broad beans."

Beppe looked alert for the first time in the last hour or so.

"Does this lady have a name?" asked Beppe.

"The greengrocer said her name was Maria – he couldn't recall her surname," replied Oriana apologetically, not wanting to disappoint her boss. "I'm sorry, *capo*..."

The *commissario* looked at Oriana and said quietly:

"It is possible you don't realise the *professore* is a vegetarian, Oriana. It could possibly mean something..."

"It's strange though, *capo*" Pippo interrupted, "because the only shop I went into where I got any reaction was the town's *cancelleria*. The shop-owner, a middle-aged lady, mentioned a woman called Maria – who came in a couple of days ago and bought an exercise book and pens. As far as she knew, this woman could barely write. She went to school with her and this Maria was the subject of all kinds of unkind jokes – because she was always the dunce at the bottom of every class..."

Pippo had fallen silent at the transformation of expression on his chief's face.

"Is there something wrong, *capo?*"

"Did you say this Maria bought an exercise book?"

"That's right, *capo,* but why do you...?

"What colour was the exercise book?"

"I'm sorry, *capo,* It didn't occur to me to ask what colour it was. Should I....?"

"Go back to the shop, Pippo... now! Find the woman who sold the exercise book and ask her what colour it was."

"But my dinner, *capo...*" protested Pippo. "Can't I just...?"

"They'll keep your dinner warm for you, *Agente* Cafarelli. This can't wait."

Oriana, out of pure sympathy for her hunger-inflicted colleague, offered to accompany Pippo back to the shop, leaving Beppe sitting on his own, his veal cutlet barely touched.

Pippo and Oriana were back within ten minutes, having found the little shop still open.

"Well?" snapped Beppe unable to supress his impatience. "It was a blue one, wasn't it?"

"Yes," replied Pippo and Oriana in chorus.

"But how did you know, *capo?*" asked Oriana.

"It's the Archbishop of Pescara, Don Emanuele. He's done it again!" said Beppe without enlightening them further.

"This same woman, Maria, came in again today since Pippo spoke to her earlier on, *capo.* She bought another exercise book. It was a yellow one this time," said Pippo.

"Yes, *capo,*" added Oriana, speaking with her usual bell-like clarity. She suspected she was about to utter the words which would change the course of events. "Her exact words were: *The professore insisted he wanted a yellow one this time.*"

The mood turned festive and Beppe found his appetite again.

"At least we know we are in the right town, *ragazzi,*" sighed Beppe with satisfaction. He deigned to fill his colleagues in on Don Emanuele's remarkable revelation. "It would appear that Donato Pisano is exploiting his time in captivity by writing a book."

Beppe would have to tell his colleague, *l'Orso Bruno,* about this seemingly miraculous manifestation. During the course of some 'casual' conversation he had had with Luigi during their days together in L'Aquila, Luigi had tried to explain to his chief that, at quantum level, it was theoretically plausible for information to be transferred from the future back to the past. "It's all to do with the true nature of quantum space-time, *capo,*" Luigi had explained to Beppe – who was forced to admit to himself that he had been motivated to bring up the subject of science purely because of his usual aversion to knowing less about any given subject than the people who worked with him.

"It's totally counter-intuitive stuff, *capo.* Our imagination can't cope with the quantum world," Luigi had added unnecessarily.

Apparently, the Archbishop of Pescara's mind *could* cope with the quantum world, thought the *commissario.*

The three police officers wandered back to the hotel in good spirits and sat in the hotel lounge where the television was switched on. Pippo and Oriana became involved in a mystery drama called *Sorelle,* which they had both been following over the past couple of weeks. Beppe sat there, oblivious to his surroundings, working out the various ways in which he could trace a woman called Maria.

That was the moment when Giada decided to phone Beppe. He mouthed an apology in the direction of his colleagues – which went unheeded - and walked out of the lounge into the reception area to take the call.

"*Pronto, Giada.*"

"*Buona sera, caro commissario.* I hope you aren't going to be angry with me."

"Why should I be angry with you – *cara* Giada?" replied Beppe, deliberately imitating the mock familiarity in her tone of voice.

"Because I probably should have phoned you several hours ago."

"It doesn't matter, Giada. I've been feeling anxious about our lack of progress and not very receptive. You should know that I am in Fara San Martino, as we speak. Now please tell me why you think you should have phoned me beforehand."

"Well, *commissario*... Are you sure I can't call you Beppe?"

"*Sicurissimo, Signora* Giada! When we have found the professor, we might review the situation."

Giada was under the impression the *commissario* was smiling as he spoke these words, judging by the modulation of his voice. But she couldn't be entirely sure.

"Well, *commissario,*" she began again, relating every detail of her verbal exchange with Agent Cosimo Moretto.

"So it would appear that we only have a maximum of three days left in which to rescue the professor," said Beppe. "We've got to find out where he's being held first."

"Ah, I haven't told you the best bit yet, *commissario*. It's the reason why I didn't phone you immediately after talking to Agent Moretto. I've managed to trace back the American agent's connection with the family in Fara San Martino..."

Beppe Stancato felt the thrill of excitement coursing through his body. He had been right to trust this woman.

"Giada - please tell me her first name is Maria," he said with bated breath.

"How in the name of all that's sacred did you know *that?*" asked Giada, feeling deflated. "I know – you just came up with the most common first name in the whole of Italy, on the chance it would be right," she ventured.

"Giada... don't be upset. We found out her first name purely by chance. We haven't a clue about her surname, nor where she lives – which is the all-important factor."

"Well, I can tell you her name is Maria De Amicis and she's married to a man called Benedetto Cavallo. Maria's brother must be related to Monica Vitale in some way. I hope that information is enough to track them down."

"Giada, you have worked miracles. I cannot thank you or praise your talents enough," said Beppe effusively.

"You can thank me in person, *commissario*. I'm going to join you tomorrow in Fara San Martino. I've got that item you asked for from the laboratory. It looks amazingly lifelike."

Beppe could hardly exclude her at this point so he gave her the name of the hotel where the three of them were staying. After all, thought the *commissario,* unbeknown to Giada, she still had a vital role to play in a sinister game of make-believe he was intending to stage.

"A domani, commissario."

"See you tomorrow, *Agente* Costa. Make sure you've got enough fuel in your tank. I can't afford the manpower to come and rescue you a second time."

Giada's burst of rippling laughter rang pleasantly in his ears.

* * *

In a wine cellar beneath a farm house just outside Fara San Martino, a robust lady called Maria De Amicis placed a tray of food and a yellow exercise book on the table. Her husband was standing guard at the other end of the cellar.

"I don't think you will have long to wait now, *professore*," she whispered furtively.

"Sbrigati, Maria!" growled her husband rudely from where he was standing. "You're always dawdling, woman."

They must have been told about the return of the American agents, thought Donato Pisano. He took little comfort from her words. But out of courtesy to her, he said *'Grazie, Maria'* under his breath.

She started at the mention of her name coming from the lips of their captive professor.

* * *

Beppe returned to the lounge where Oriana and Pippo were still glued to the screen.

The drama was set in an ancient-looking town which Beppe did not recognise. He asked them for enlightenment.

"Matera, *capo*," they replied together, without taking their eyes off the screen. Beppe decided they deserved a break. His two young colleagues were right – it was an extraordinary production. Bit by bit, Beppe got drawn into the plot, which revolved around the mystery of a missing mother of three children and her sister - who found herself inevitably caught up in events through the need to care for her two nephews and her vulnerable but alarmingly outspoken thirteen-year-old niece. Beppe began to appreciate that the film must strike a chord with Oriana too, who seemed to be reliving her intense emotional experience with her own two 'adopted' children back in Pescara.

When the episode came to an end, he vowed to watch the next *puntata* at the same time the following week. He hoped it would be in Sonia's company by that time. He wondered if Sonia and Mariangela had been watching the same programme up there in Atri. It was likely, he reckoned - especially as one of the characters was a sharp lady *ispettore,* who reminded Beppe of Sonia. There was a striking physical likeness between the actress and his wife. The police woman in the film was heavily pregnant and had refused to give up her job whilst still involved in tracking down the missing sister.

As soon as the episode came to an end, Beppe deliberately switched the television off, to ensure that his two colleagues could concentrate on their own unfolding drama. He related everything that Giada had told him, finishing up with the news that the American agents were due to return in a matter of days. When Beppe relayed the significant fact that they were arriving at, and presumably leaving from, an unspecified airport 'somewhere in the north of the country', Pippo turned to his chief and said:

"You know what *this* means, don't you, *capo?*"

"No, honestly, Pippo, I don't know what to make of it."

"It means they're taking no chances. My guess would be that the agents will be landing at that big American military base outside Vicenza – where they won't need to show any form of identification."

Beppe smacked his forehead with the flat of his palm.

"Bravo, Pippo! Of course, I had completely forgotten about that place. You're right - they mean business. They would equally be able to smuggle the professor out of the country without opposition. *Che bastardi!* It also means we shall have to move very fast. We probably have only two clear days left at the most. We shall be paying a visit to the *comune* first thing tomorrow morning, *ragazzi.*"

Armed with the names furnished by Giada, it should be a simple task to find out from the town hall where the professor's presumed jailers lived, Beppe hoped.

The last thing Beppe did before retiring for the night was to phone Luigi Rocco.

"Make your way down to Fara San Martino as early as you can tomorrow morning, Luigi. We urgently need you here with us now – in uniform."

"Agli ordini, capo," was Luigi's only response.

18:   The incredulity of Professor Donato Pisano...

After all the drama and tension which the hunt for the vanishing physicist had engendered, his rescue turned out to be a subdued – even comical – event.

Luigi Rocco had arrived at the hotel where Beppe and company were staying shortly after five o'clock in the morning.

"You did tell me to arrive as early as possible, *capo*," said the *Orso Bruno,* plaintively stating the simple truth.

Even Giada Costa made the journey from Monticchio to Fara San Martino without incident. She presented herself cheerfully to the gathered team of police officers at breakfast time, sat down and ordered an extra *brioche* and a coffee.

"I brought the cut-out of Donato Pisano with me, *commissario.* I left it in my car – covered with a large sheet. I had to lower the rear seat to get it in," she explained. "It's very heavy – I had to ask Gianni to help me."

"Leave it where it is for now, Giada," suggested Beppe. "We'll deal with it after we've been to the town hall."

An unwilling, middle-aged lady clerk, reluctantly supplied Beppe with the information they needed concerning the whereabouts of what turned out to be a smallholding a couple of kilometres outside Fara San Martino. The lady then had to suffer the indignity of accompanying the police officers to the farm in her own car – on the pretext that she would act as their guide. The *commissario's* real reason for keeping her with them was to make sure she did not make any telephone calls to friends or family to give them a lurid account about how she had been visited by the police. In a community as intimate as that of Fara San Martino, the temptation might have been too great. When, after half an hour, the lady from the town hall asked fearfully if she was allowed to go back to Fara San Martino, Beppe went through his usual ritual of implying her whole career and that of her family would be in ruins if she breathed a word to anyone. The lady was by now in awe of this *commissario* from Pescara. She promised not to tell a soul.

"And that includes your husband," added Beppe.

"I'm not married, *commissario*," she assured him – as if her status was a guarantee against any indiscretion on her part. Beppe wondered how long it would be before the temptation to gossip became irresistible. Long enough, he hoped, for it not to matter.

A man and a woman, purporting to be trekkers, knocked at the door of a farmhouse, asking for a glass of water. The stockily-built woman who opened the door eyed them suspiciously before informing them that her husband was out milking the sheep.

"We only want a glass of water, *signora*," said the woman, who reminded the farmer's wife of a well-known Italian actress whose name she could not recall. She looked at the man and her brow wrinkled for a moment while her memory cells got into working order.

"Where have I seen you before, *signore?*" she asked, before the light dawned.

Beppe realised that she must have watched the previous day's TV-Tavo report and recognised his face.

Her reaction, however, took both Beppe and Giada off guard.

"You've come to rescue that nice professor, haven't you?" she stated smiling with evident delight. She might not be able to read or write, thought Beppe, but there's not much wrong with her compassion for her fellow men.

"Come in, come in," the woman said, opening the door which led directly into the kitchen. "You're only just in time, officers," she added. "Those Americans are coming to kidnap him on Thursday evening – after dark. My husband was talking to them only yesterday evening."

"And what will your husband say when he discovers that the Italian police have arrived on your doorstep and beaten the Americans to it?" asked Giada, happy to play out her newly acquired role as unofficial police woman.

The farmer's wife was busy fetching them glasses of water, not quite bright enough to cotton on to the idea that the request had merely been a pretext to gain admittance. However, there was a fire burning slowly in the grate which raised the room temperature up to mid-summer temperatures, so Beppe and Giada took sips of natural spring water from two not-very-clean glasses before replacing them on the table.

At the mention of her husband, the woman's features had darkened.

"He'll probably kill me," she answered fearfully, as if the consequences of her generous act of hospitality had only just occurred to her. "I told him we were doing wrong," she added.

"Maybe you would like to take us to where you are holding the professor, *signora?*" suggested Beppe.

She nodded, waddled over to the other side of the kitchen and unhooked an old iron key from a board.

"He's in the wine cellar, *commissario,*" she explained guiltily. "We made it as comfortable as we could..."

The first surprise when the metal door was opened was that the captive professor did not charge at them in a bid for freedom, thought Giada. The second surprise was that there appeared to be nobody inside the cellar, which was plunged into gloom.

"He really has vanished," whispered Giada to Beppe.

It was a disturbing experience, admitted Beppe to himself.

But a muffled voice from within could be heard defiantly proclaiming that he was stark naked and absolutely refused to be shipped off to America by a bunch of semi-criminal political state lackeys. Donato Pisano was surprised to hear an amused burst of female laughter – which certainly had not emanated from the mouth of the farmer's wife.

"*Professore* Pisano. We are the Italian police. We have come to rescue you," said Beppe. "I am *Commissario* Stancato from Pescara."

The dim lights went on because the farmer's wife had found the switch in the darkness. The comic sight of Donato Pisano's head peering at them from round the edge of an old plastic shower curtain brought a smile to Beppe's face. He really *had* taken his clothes off.

"We'll go out and let you get dressed, *professore,*" said Beppe.

The professor's face broke into a grin.

"It really *is* you, isn't it, *commissario!* I recognise you from the television."

"It's time to go home, *professore.* Even Rebecca doesn't know about your rescue, so it'll be a lovely surprise for her."

Donato Pisano was looking embarrassed.

"You don't understand, *commissario.* This good lady told me that I wouldn't have long to wait. I assumed she meant before the American agents came back to take me away – or whatever their plan was. I managed to tear all my clothes up into shreds. I just wanted to make it difficult for those American thugs..."

The lady was looking even more guilty than the professor looked embarrassed.

"I'm sorry *professore.* I couldn't say much because my husband was there. But when I went back to buy your yellow exercise book, the lady in the shop – Cinzia – told me that the police had been there enquiring about a missing professor. I was sure she was talking about you…"

Beppe felt a surge of sympathy for this unlikely-looking heroine, obviously in total awe of her husband. And yet, she had come out on the side of righteousness. He placed a kindly hand on Maria's shoulder and asked her to sort out some old clothing for Donato. She scurried off nervously. Another person who would need protecting, thought Beppe. How complicated human relationships could become, he thought, multiplied exponentially with almost every new person who came on to the scene.

Thus Donato Pisano, dressed in an old pair of khaki trousers hitched up by a length of string, a tatty cowboy-style check shirt and a pair of open-toed sandals, was ready to be driven home by *Agenti* Luigi Rocco and Oriana Salvati.

"I think you've forgotten to pick up your blue exercise book, *professore,*" Beppe said with studied casualness.

"Of course! In the excitement I'd completely…"

Donato Pisano stopped mid-sentence and looked at this *commissario* with an expression of bewilderment on his face.

"How in the name of goodness did you know about that book? Even what colour it is," exclaimed Donato.

"Do you know Don Emanuele, the Archbishop of Pescara, *professore?*"

"Not personally, no. But I've heard about his reputation, of course…"

"I suggest you go and pay him a visit one day. If it hadn't been for him, we might never have found you in time," was all Beppe deigned to say.

"I will, *commissario.* I promise."

Donato Pisano was ensconced in the back of the police car when Beppe had an idea.

"Pippo, would you mind taking Luigi's place and drive the professor home. You know where he lives."

Oriana looked secretly relieved. Luigi looked guardedly disappointed about the change of plan – for very un-police like reasons, Beppe was certain.

"Luigi, I'm sorry. But I need you and Giada with me. We need to discuss the next stage in this operation – which is likely to be very complex and possibly risky."

"You mean we haven't finished, *capo?*" asked Pippo in surprise. "I assumed rescuing the professor was enough to be going on with."

"No, believe me, *Agente* Cafarelli, that was the easy part. In fact, we have very little time left - so no loitering on the way back, you two – not even for lunch." Beppe added pointedly.

The farmer, Benedetto Cavallo, returned whilst Beppe, Giada and Luigi had just sat down round the kitchen table. Maria was sent off to another part of the house. The farmer recognised the police inspector from the television the previous day. He realised he was in deep trouble with the Italian law. He was about to make a run for it, but was halted in his tracks by a man who looked the size of a mountain who had swiftly moved to block his exit.

"Benedetto Cavallo, I am placing you under arrest for aiding and abetting the abduction and imprisonment of a free Italian citizen. You may get away with house arrest if you do exactly as I tell you. Am I making myself clear to you so far, *Signor* Cavallo?" said Beppe.

The farmer nodded, looking guilty and overwhelmed by this unexpected reversal of his fortunes. The prospect of receiving several thousand American dollars had just gone up in smoke.

"You will both stay here until the Americans arrive – and you will act normally when they arrive. Give them the key to the cellar when they ask you for it," continued Beppe. "Meanwhile, you will treat your wife with the respect she deserves. If you fail to help us or communicate any of this to an outsider, I will have you locked up for at least five years in the most overcrowded jail I can find – probably in Milano. Are you quite clear about all that?" Beppe thundered.

The farmer looked cowed by the wrath of this terrifyingly determined police officer.

"*Sì commissario. Grazie commissario,*" he added meekly.

Beppe had deliberately avoided mentioning anything about the Americans contacting him. It was very unlikely, he considered, and even more improbable that Benedetto Cavallo had the means to contact them.

The truth was, Beppe knew, he was severely under-staffed at this point of time. He needed to talk to Giada and Luigi urgently while the three of them were on their own. They went to sit in Beppe's car as being the best and most comfortable place to talk without the risk of being overheard. He drove the car inside the little courtyard so as to make the farmer aware there was still a police presence there.

"The plan I am about to outline to you both is totally between us three and must *never* be divulged to anyone – even people you can trust. You will have to tell your *fidanzato,* Giada – but not until after the event. Luigi, I have seen a side to you that I never knew existed before and I trust you entirely. I cannot carry out what I intend to pull off without your help. We shall be doing this entirely for the sake of Giada here to guarantee she can spend the rest of her life happily on Italian soil. I can think of no other way of achieving this goal."

Beppe gave them the outline of his plan. Giada's mouth was open in shock most of the time. The *Orso Bruno* remained impassive and, when Beppe had finally finished talking, he said simply:

"*Bravissimo, capo!*"

"Why are you doing all this for me?" asked Giada Costa, her eyes alight with amusement, curiosity – and more than a modicum of apprehension.

"Because you deserve it, *Agente* Costa, and I really am determined to nail those legalised gangsters who think they can stroll around our country indulging in their own form of political terrorism just to save the face of the United States of America – all on *our* patch furthermore."

"*Grazie,* Beppe," she said simply without reflecting.

On this occasion too, the *commissario* let her use of his first name go. After all, the professor had been rescued...

19:   *The collapse of Giada's time cone...*

"How does it feel to be marrying a woman who is not called Giada?" Simona Gambino asked Professor Gianni Marconi mischievously after a particularly intimate coupling, during which the duvet had been impatiently kicked to the floor to give her room for greater freedom of expression.

"I don't believe Giada did half the things to my body that you have just done," replied Gianni.

"Ah! A bit more inhibited than I am in bed, maybe?" asked Simona.

"Decidedly, *amore mio.*"

"Well, I hope you spared a thought for Giada before you abandoned her to her fate," said Simona aggrieved by the ease with which Giada had been cast aside.

"I can hardly forget her altogether. After all, she was the one who led me to you," said Gianni, holding Simona in his arms and forcing her on to her back as he lay on top of her – the first time during those timeless moments when he had found himself in this position.

"I'm so happy we're together at last," she sighed contentedly, "even if you're holding me prisoner in your beautiful house."

"I'm happy too, Simona, without a shadow of doubt. We should try to put the memory of Giada out of our minds," said Gianni Marconi. "For *her* sake, of course."

* * *

A crescent moon shone over the tranquil Abruzzo countryside, casting a pallid silvery light on the slopes of the distant Maiella mountain range and creating eerie silhouettes out of trees and farm outhouse buildings. The moonlight transformed the smoke from the farm house, rising lazily into the night sky, into a wraith escaping the pull of Earth's gravity. Inside the ancient stone dwelling, Maria De Amicis and Benedetto Cavallo were sitting nervously under the watchful eye of Luigi Rocco.

It was only 10 o'clock on that Thursday night.

Beppe had been phenomenally busy for the past forty-eight hours. He had spoken at length to his boss, the *Questore,* Dante Di Pasquale, who had turned to his colleague with a knowing look in his eyes and asked simply: "Are you perhaps being a little frugal with the truth, *caro commissario?* I suspect there is an ulterior motive hidden behind the encounter you are proposing."

Beppe smiled at his chief but declined to add anything other than a slight shrug of his shoulders.

"I trust your judgement entirely, Beppe. But let us not create an international incident out of this affair – if possible," added the *Questore* with a sigh of resignation.

His next visit was to his *Carabiniere* colleague, *Colonnello* Riccardo Grimaldi, from whom he extracted the promise of help when the situation arose. He then stopped off at the main hospital in Pescara, where he had enlisted the help of his associate, the chief toxicologist, Bruno Esposito. He had been obliged to go into much greater detail with Bruno than he had dared to with the two senior officers, Dante Di Pasquale and Riccardo Grimaldi, constrained by the nature of the favour he was requesting.

"I thank you for the chance to alleviate the tedium of my routine existence, Beppe," Bruno had reassured him, intrigued by the complexity and deviousness of Beppe's intended plan. "But how can you be sure you'll get the right reaction from this Lombardi character?" Bruno had asked Beppe.

"Just leave that side of things to me, Bruno," Beppe had replied evasively.

He had spent the rest of Tuesday afternoon and evening visiting Pescara's *Teatro Massimo,* where he had held detailed discussions with various experts in their specialised fields of theatrical knowledge. It was a couple of the theatre's technicians – a young man and an even younger looking woman who provided him with an ingenious way of putting his scheme into practice – reducing the risk of injury or death to certain members of his team.

"I never knew such a device even existed!" Beppe had told his two new allies.

"There seem to be no bounds to what science can do these days, *commissario*," the young man said.

"We'll supply the transport for you and your equipment, *ragazzi*," the *commissario* reassured them. "And meals and accommodation are on us."

His final visit had been to the technicians in the basement, Marco Pollutri and Bianca Bomba, whom he had to bribe with the promise that he would tell them all about his latest escapade as soon as he returned - before they would agree to supply him with the equipment he needed.

"You do realise, don't you, *commissario*, we shall have to neglect our families and work through the night to get the thing completed?" pointed out Bianca Bomba with glee.

"I shall be for ever beholden to you both," said the *commissario*.

"Even more than usual, I would imagine," added Marco Pollutri pointedly.

He called Sonia from his office at nearly eleven o'clock that night and then fell asleep at his desk with his head resting on his arms until it was five o'clock on Wednesday morning. He forced himself to find a bar that was open to have a coffee and a couple of *brioches*. It might well be the last thing he ate until late that evening – in the company of his makeshift team.

The morning was taken up transporting the two extra members of the team whom he would need with him – Danilo Simone and Gino Martelli. Oriana was happy enough to stay in Pescara since she felt she had neglected Rosa and Steffi, who had phoned her to tell her they missed their new 'best friend in life'. She felt her heart-strings being tugged.

Beppe, Danilo and Gino, drove down with the two helpers from the theatre plus their equipment in the police van. Gino and Danilo plied their *capo* with questions to which they never received a clear answer. It was obvious the young man and the girl from the *Teatro Massimo* knew far more than they dared let on. They had both been sworn to absolute secrecy by Beppe.

"Let's just say you two guys are part of a reception committee for a group of undesirable Americans," was all Beppe would reveal to Gino and Danilo.

They rejoined Giada, Luigi Rocco and Pippo at the farmhouse outside Fara San Martino after an hour's steady drive down south through the province of Chieti. At one point late that day as darkness was falling, Beppe informed Pippo, Gino and Danilo that they should go back into town and find somewhere to have a meal.

"We'll join you later, *ragazzi,*" Beppe had told them, furnishing them with no further explanation.

Thursday, 24.00 hours.

It was Danilo, hidden at a vantage point some two hundred metres down the road, who phoned Beppe at around midnight.

"There's a car coming up the road now, *capo*. It must be doing eighty at least."

"OK, *ragazzi*. This is it," said Beppe tersely. "Get into your positions."

'Getting into position' meant disappearing into the shadows – or in Luigi Rocco's case climbing halfway up the farmhouse staircase, as it was assumed that the farmhouse itself would be the first port of call to collect the key to the cellar. Giada herself, alongside the young couple from the theatre, were already concealed in the cellar. The lighting in the cellar was very subdued since Beppe had ordered the removal of every single light bulb. The cars in which the police team had arrived were parked in a field above the farmhouse. They were all as ready as they ever could be. The peace of the countryside was, no doubt, about to be disrupted by the rude intrusion of the Americans.

A Chrysler Jeep roared into the space in front of the farmhouse, did a complete circle without slowing down and ended up pointing back downhill the way it had come.

From where Beppe was standing in the black shadows of the encroaching trees, he could make out the driver who remained where he was with the engine still running. Three men leapt out with what appeared to be turbo-charged energy. The man who got out of the front passenger seat was instantly recognisable as Attilio Lombardi. His appearance recalled that of one of the many *mafiosi* gangsters he had encountered back in his native Calabria. The two others followed their leader as he headed for the farmhouse door.

Following Beppe's instructions, the farmer opened the door with the key already in his hand. But this did not prevent Attilio Lombardi pushing him aside and entering the kitchen, a silver revolver in his right hand. He prayed that the *Orso Bruno* was really out of sight. As Beppe had predicted, the leader of the group would check to see that there were no 'intruders' inside the house. He was worried about being ambushed, having been warned that the local police might have discovered the farmhouse. All he saw was the quivering figure of Maria standing fearfully behind the table.

"You had any strangers visiting you?" snarled Attilio Lombardi, looking daggers at Maria and Benedetto in turn.

They shook their heads without replying.

"Get the cellar door open, you!" shouted Attilio at the shaking farmer. As he inserted the key into the lock of the metal door, Beppe was gratified to hear the farmer saying, in a plaintive voice constrained by fear, "What about the rest of my money?" Benedetto was doing his best to play his prearranged role.

"You'll get it after we've got the professor out of the country," snarled Attilio. "You, wait back inside the car, Franky. You, Manny, stand in the doorway and be ready to help me."

"*Sì capo,*" replied the two lackeys. Beppe could detect even from where he was standing, the clear trace of an American-Italian accent during the course of a further brief exchange of words between the three invaders – as Beppe thought of them.

The first hint Attilio Lombardi had that all was not quite as it should be was the sight, some twenty-five metres away, of his prey apparently standing passively behind a table at the other end of the cellar. He seemed to have a fixed smile on his face. The professor was so dimly lit that Attilio Lombardi could not quite decipher the scene.

"Come on, *professore,* it's time to go on a long journey. Let's get on with it," said Attilio Lombardi impatiently beginning to walk down the empty cellar towards the table where the professor was standing. He still could not believe what he was looking at. The face of Donato Pisano was clearly recognisable but he was still smiling fixedly in Attilio's direction.

The rage which he felt when he saw how he been duped was alarming. He picked up the wooden image of the professor and hurled it on to the stone floor with a force that snapped it in two.

"Cazzo!" he snarled into the darkness. "Manny, haven't you got a torch on you, you imbecile?"

"No, boss, you told us we wouldn't need torches," was the military-style reply, whose tone went some way to concealing his scorn for his superior.

"You, *Signor* Cavallo – turn the lights on. You know where the switch is."

Benedetto, the farmer, groped for the switch but nothing happened. He made his way outside, fearing the wrathful outburst that would ensue.

But the next thing that occurred caused Attilio Lombardi to freeze in his tracks because it seemed so utterly surreal. *"Che cazzo...?"* he began again.

"Buona sera, Signor Lombardi," said the voice of Giada Costa. "How unpleasant it is to see you again. I should listen very carefully if I were you, because when I tell them back in Boston just how incompetent you have been in your handling of this business, you simply won't survive in our organisation. Have I got your full attention, Attilio?"

"You two-faced little bitch..."

"Good, I thought you would be interested," continued Giada mockingly. "By the way, Attilio, you didn't even bother to find out if I spoke English. If you like, I can switch to English – just so you know how stupid and unprofessional you've been."

Giada did just that, continuing to lambast the man in fluent English.

"I'm bilingual – just like you. Are you aware how many times you spoke to Agent Vitale in English - arrogantly assuming I didn't understand what you were saying? You gave so much away. And by the way, that white Punto you rented *did* have a tracking device fitted to it. That's how the Italian police tracked down the professor - that, plus the smell of your vile deodorant, which left a trail all over Abruzzo. By the way Attilio, Professor Pisano was rescued two days ago. I advise you to get out now while you still can."

Giada rounded off her tirade of words with a mocking burst of laughter. Attilio Lombardi felt a powerless rage as he strode towards the entrance to the wine cellar where he could clearly make out the figure of his henchman, Manny, silhouetted by the moonlight as he stood in the doorway. Attilio was clutching his silver revolver in his right hand. He wanted to spray the whole cellar with bullets.

Outside, he shouted at his colleague to get back in the car, whilst looking round in the darkness for the sight of any moving target he could shoot at. Nothing! Just shadows as far as he could make out.

"*Cazzo, cazzo, cazzo...*" he swore, reverting to Italian.

He was back in the front seat of the Jeep, still too angry to give the order to drive off. He was debating with himself whether he would be justified in going back into the farmhouse to shoot the farmer – and his fat bitch of a wife. He was seething inside with an anger that he could not control.

"Look, *capo,*" said his driver, pointing out of the car window. No more than twenty metres away, he could see Giada Costa – somehow illuminated more than she should have been from the moonlight alone – standing outside the cellar from where he had just emerged. She was wearing some white woolly jumper which bore the image of a huge red heart on the front. The bitch was waving goodbye mockingly in his direction, her left arm raised cheerily. She had an insolent grin on her face.

He heard what he assumed to be one of his two cronies in the back seat saying to him:

"Take her out, Attilio. She's a treacherous little slut."

He did just that, leaning across his driver and resting the revolver on the door panel. He aimed a single shot as he gripped his revolver in both hands. He was gratified to see the figure of Giada Costa jerk backwards in a final twist of agony as she was flung to the ground, before the scene was plunged inexplicably into darkness. The moon must have passed behind a cloud, Attilio assumed. Afterwards, Attilio could not remember whether those provocative words which he had rashly acted upon had been spoken in English or Italian.

All hell was let loose ten seconds later just as Attilio Lombardi was opening the door of the Jeep with the intention of going over to inspect his handy-work. Unseen marksmen were letting off rounds of bullets which struck their vehicle with a series of metallic twangs.

"DRIVE, for Christ's sake!" yelled Attilio. The Jeep shot off down the hill, the tyres spinning for a second as they sought a grip on the rough gravel road.

The invisible police officers and the young man and woman from the theatre appeared on the scene from the various positions where they had been concealed. Beppe headed for the spot where Giada was lying motionless on the ground. It was the *Orso Bruno* who arrived first, kneeling down by Giada's side. He took one look at her face and shook his head as Beppe approached – with Pippo, Danilo and Gino several metres behind him. The young couple from the theatre appeared to be carrying something back inside the cellar. They made no move towards the motionless figure of Giada.

Beppe took one look at Giada's face and let out a wail of grief which filled the cool night air with its lament. There was a neat round bullet hole in the centre of her forehead. Her eyes were staring up at the skies in frozen horror. He knelt down by Giada's side and wept.

"I've killed her," he cried. "I should never have allowed her to take this risk."

Pippo arrived next. One brief glance was enough to tell him that the shot must have been fatal. Danilo and Gino were still unfamiliar enough with sudden death to be deeply shocked by the scene – especially in one so young and attractive. They hung back a few metres away from the motionless body.

"Cover her up," Beppe said tersely, the words sticking in his throat.

Luigi placed a piece of material over Giada's face and upper body and rose painfully to his feet.

"I'm so sorry, *capo,*" he said to Beppe. He went over to his chief and put his arms round his chief's body in a hug of consolation. "You mustn't blame yourself, *capo.* It was Giada's decision to expose herself to danger."

Beppe, out of sheer habit in such circumstances, took out his *cellulare* and made a phone call.

In what Pippo had the impression was in record time, an ambulance arrived on the scene. Giada was carried away on a stretcher, under a sheet which covered her from head to toe. The ambulance drove off into the night under the sliver of the crescent moon. Its siren was switched off.

Only Pippo was looking hard at his chief with a deep frown on his face, still not daring to interrupt his grief.

"I need to be on my own, *ragazzi,*" he said to them all. "Luigi, perhaps you could take the two theatre kids back to Pescara with their bits and pieces. Pippo – and you two," he said looking at Gino and Danilo, "there's no point in your hanging around. I'll catch up with you tomorrow."

Beppe went up to the young man and woman from the *Teatro Massimo* and shook them by the hand.

"Thank you for trying so hard," he said. "I don't suppose you will forget this night in a hurry."

"Indeed we won't, *commissario,*" said the girl meaningfully.

When he was on his own, Beppe made one more urgent phone call before sitting on a cold stone bench outside the darkened farmhouse. He wished he was still a smoker at this moment in time. A cigarette would have been so soothing. He sighed deeply, wondering how deep a hole he had dug for himself with this latest attempt at carrying out justice as he perceived it. He was certain his chief, the *Questore,* would not whole-heartedly condone his excesses on this occasion.

"Ah, well," he said resignedly to himself, "at least Giada will be remaining on Italian soil – just as she had wanted. He had an image in his mind's eye of the funeral service that would have to be held – a further complication which he had not entirely thought through.

* * *

On the way back to Pescara, Gino turned to Pippo and asked quietly:

"What did you make of all that, Pippo? I've never seen our chief crying before. It was very disturbing, wasn't it?"

What Pippo thought, he kept to himself. If his instinct was correct, then his friend and colleague, the *commissario,* had very sound reasons for acting the way he had. 'Acting', he realised, was probably a most appropriate choice of words. He chose his *own* words carefully before answering Gino.

"The *commissario* had a very soft spot for Giada Costa, Gino. They bonded over the last few days like true friends. It's natural that he should be upset by such a violent departure from this life. He feels responsible for her death."

The rest of the journey back to Pescara proceeded in meditative silence.

"I bet that young couple from the theatre know a lot more than we do," Pippo thought, determined to play along with what he sincerely hoped was a complex game of charades on Beppe's part. Only at that point did a somewhat aggrieved Pippo Cafarelli realise that his imposing colleague, the *Orso Bruno,* sitting passively in the driver's seat, must also have been 'in the know'. A sharp-eyed Pippo had been struck at the time by the fact that Luigi Rocco had had a blanket or something to hand to cover the face and chest of Giada Costa – before any of the others could get a closer or a more prolonged look. His chief had left him in the dark. Pippo could only console himself that he had managed to see through the convincing subterfuge – as he prayed fervently it was.

* * *

A black Chrysler Jeep was driving north along the slower coastal road following the Adriatic coast between Pescara and Ancona. Attilio Lombardi was deeply regretting his fatal loss of self-control in eliminating Agent Costa less than an hour ago. His instinct for self-preservation was stronger than any sense of remorse at taking another human life. If anybody back at the farm had taken down the details of the number plate on the Jeep, there could be Italian police on the lookout all the way up and down the length of the A14 *autostrada.* He had ordered the driver to take minor roads. The atmosphere inside the Jeep was charged with silent hostility and suppressed retribution.

Finally, Manny from the back seat of the Jeep, could contain his disgust no longer.

"You murdered that young woman, chief. I don't care how you dress it up. You shot her in cold blood."

"She betrayed us. She was our agent and she deliberately sabotaged the whole operation," yelled Attilio Lombardi from the front seat.

"And we'll all get the blame for your f***ing sadistic desire for vengeance," shouted the one called Francesco.

"You just hold on there," shouted Agent Lombardi. "Which of you two was it who told me to 'take the bitch out'? You're as much part of this shit as I am."

The two men in the back seat remembered hearing the words clearly. At the time, while they were concentrating on the woman in the farmyard, they had each assumed it was the other one who had uttered the words. Now they looked at each other with a wordless question mark on their faces. Each of them replied with a brief shake of the head. They knew each other too well to doubt the other's integrity.

"It wasn't either of us, chief," stated the one called Manfredo quietly.

"*Cazzo...*" muttered Attilio, realising that he had somehow allowed himself to be manipulated by some unknown person. He took one look at his driver but dismissed that possibility outright. The white jumper with the big red heart on it – it had been like a deliberate provocation to shoot. And then Attilio Lombardi recalled the figure of that Costa woman insolently waving goodbye – with her left arm. He was sure he would have spotted her left-handedness during his first visit. It was all very puzzling.

"Just get us back to Vicenza as soon as you can," he said to the driver. "We'll sort this mess out when we're out of this f***ing country."

*　*　*

Beppe's final phone call that night had been to his friend, Riccardo Grimaldi, the *Carabinieri* colonel in Pescara. It was a very succinct message which said simply:

"They're on their way, *colonnello.* It happened just the way I said. I'm texting you a photo of the number plate. It's a dark-coloured Chrysler Jeep."

Riccardo Grimaldi had already prepared the ground the previous day by contacting a colleague in Vicenza. He had been put through to a high ranking *Generale,* who had expressed his delight at the prospect of having an excuse to intercept even a single one of those arrogant American military *bastardi,* who considered it their birthright to drive round Vicenza at whatever speed they wished, on whatever 'mission' they saw fit to pursue with total impunity. Riccardo Grimaldi had felt bound to point out that the Americans in question most certainly belonged to a more covert organisation than the United States' armed forces.

"So much the better!" the *Generale* in Vicenza had roared with gusty laughter. "What are the bastards being accused of?"

"If I have understood my colleague, *Commissario* Stancato correctly, it is likely to be on a charge of the murder of a young and beautiful Italian woman who bears a striking resemblance to Sabrina Ferilli, *mio Generale.*"

Riccardo Grimaldi could swear he had heard the general rubbing his hands in glee.

"Phone me directly on this line as soon as your *commissario* gets in touch, *Colonnello* – whatever the time of day or night," the *Generale* had concluded.

Riccardo Grimaldi made his phone call to Vicenza as soon as Beppe had contacted him – despite the late hour. After all, it was what the *Generale* had wanted him to do.

20: *Varying degrees of job satisfaction...*

The occupants of the black Chrysler breathed an audible sigh of relief as they joined the road that skirted the military base outside Vicenza. It was nearly dawn but the lights on the vast campus revealed aeroplanes standing like huge alien birds of prey on the tarmac. One of them would be taking them back home. Their sense of relief was short-lived. The blue flashing lights seemed to be right outside where the entrance to the base was situated. Attilio Lombardi counted four police cars set at various angles to block the deserted road. This could only mean trouble. As the Americans came nearer, it was clear that the police cars all belonged to the *Carabinieri* rather than the ordinary police. Now they were waving the Jeep to a standstill just before the entrance to the US base. They were still on Italian soil.

"*Cazzo...*" Attilio muttered under his breath, a hint of foreboding creeping into his voice.

The entrance to the base appeared to be blocked by two FIAT cars battered and crumpled by a violent collision.

A senior officer strode over towards the Jeep making a circular gesture with his hand to indicate that Attilio should wind the window down. Attilio feared the worst because the senior *Carabiniere* officer had ignored the driver and headed directly for the passenger side of the vehicle.

"What seems to be the trouble, euh...*colonnello?*" asked the American.

"*Generale,*" corrected the police officer curtly. "As you can see, *signori,* two of our fellow countrymen have managed to crash their cars immediately outside your base."

The four Americans could see their fellow countrymen scuttling around like hens the other side of the barrier, busy phoning to communicate with sleeping senior military personnel that there was a major crisis going on just outside their territory.

"How long do you think it will be before the cars are cleared...*Generale?*" Attilio Lombardi asked, correcting the rank and trying his best to sound ingratiating.

The *Generale* smiled at the speaker's feeble attempt at evasion. He was enjoying the moment immensely. He had hit on the idea of retrieving two cars from the knacker's yard and arranging them outside the US base - just as if he had been setting up a Hollywood film set. A pity he could not savour this moment a little longer. Never mind, he could still look forward to the interrogation of his main suspect.

"As long as it takes me to arrest you for the murder of one, Giada Costa, *Signor* Lombardi," said the *Generale* with a cheerful grin.

There was a collective groan from the three other Americans inside the Jeep. The ones called Manfredo and Francesco looked at each other and mutually decided that they would save their own skins and leave Attilio Lombardi to his fate at the hands of the Italian police. They would simply shop their disagreeable colleague without compunction – anything to avoid having to share their living space with the pervasive smell of his particularly ill-chosen deodorant. The three of them wanted to return home as soon as they were allowed to. The D.A.S.R lawyers would soon sort out the matter of their release.

It became clear why there had been four cars as each of the Americans were carted off in separate police cars. The number 112 would be emblazoned on Attilio's mind for the rest of his life. A truck equipped with a crane was already removing the two wrecks from the scene as the four Americans were frog-marched towards the cars. The *Generale* accompanied Attilio in the back seat of the lead car. He was still grinning like a smart schoolboy who had just outwitted a tyrannical teacher. It was, considered the *Generale,* easy to dislike this man Lombardi – he looked exactly like a mafia gangster from his native Sicily.

The four Americans suffered the indignity of being locked up in police cells while the *Generale* went home to get some well-earned sleep. He did not reappear until after lunchtime the following day, by which time Manfredo, Francesco and the Jeep driver - a young soldier of low rank – were even more willing to disown their leader. This high ranking officer embodied their preconceived notions of how an Italian law-enforcer would react to any attempt at simply denying their own culpability. Being of

Italian origin themselves, they reckoned they possessed an inherent understanding of how a policeman's mind worked.

It was, therefore, in a spirit of complete surrender that they asked to speak to the *Generale,* without Attilio Lombardi being present, as soon as this redoubtable officer arrived after lunch.

The imposing figure of the *Carabiniere* General announced his name as Gaetano Molè – a good old Sicilian surname, he announced proudly to the three Americans.

"I gather you are ready to denounce your colleague's actions without reservation?" he stated with a sardonic smile.

"Sì signor Generale!" they replied smartly.

"In that case, I shall get the three of you to write out your depositions in the presence of one of my senior officers," stated Gaetano Molè. He still had a mischievous glint in his eyes as he got up and left them in the presence of a *colonnello.*

Two hours later, he came back and read the three depositions, taking at least ten minutes on each one, before getting them to sign the official documents in turn.

"May we go now, *Signor Generale?"* asked the man called Francesco.

The *Generale* smiled broadly at them and replied, savouring every word:

"Yes, you may go. Our penitentiary colleagues will drive you down to Pescara in Abruzzo, where a very able police officer called *Commissario* Stancato, is conducting a murder enquiry. I'm sure your lawyers will get you released in no time at all, gentlemen – *after* you have told the *commissario* your side of the story," the *Generale* concluded with malicious delight at his parting shot.

"What have you got against us Americans?" Manfredo asked angrily – and very unwisely. Gaetano Molè made as if to re-read his deposition but placed both hands at the top of the official document as if he was about to tear it in two down the middle.

"How would you feel if a bunch of Italian soldiers turned up in your town, gave themselves diplomatic immunity and proceeded to come and go as they wished – as if they owned the place? But if you really want to know the truth..."

Generale Molè was delighted to be able to deliver his homily as his parting shot to his 'guests'. It was an unlooked for bonus.

"... my father was a *Carabiniere* general in Sicily at the end of the war. Thanks to Mussolini, we had just about got the nascent mafia clans under control. Then along came the Americans to liberate us! And what do they do? Appoint officials who were in the pocket of the local Mafioso clans and put them in control of my homeland. My father fought them all the way – and got himself assassinated by some mobster. I was only a boy of fifteen at the time."

The three Americans were looking suitably contrite and apologetic.

"We're sorry, *Generale*. We're too young to realise what..." began Manfredo. But he was talking to the departing back of this formidable man as he left the room without a backward glance.

Attilio Lombardi was dismissed in peremptory manner by the *Carabiniere* General.

"Your three colleagues have denounced you, so you don't have a leg to stand on, *Signor* Lombardi. You can face the consequences of your cowardly killing of this young woman, Giada Costa. I'm sending all four of you back down to Abruzzo where the investigation into her murder is being officially conducted."

Attilio Lombardi looked as if he was about to attack him, even with two other officers present. Ah, that would have been too much to hope for, sighed the General.

* * *

"I wish to thank you three for your cooperation in coming all the way back to Abruzzo to help us wind up this sad business. My name is *Commissario* Stancato and this is my colleague, *Agente* Cafarelli. This interview is being monitored and recorded on our internal television system."

What a contrast to the *Carabiniere* General in Vicenza, thought the three Americans – who were being kept separated from Attilio Lombardi. This *commissario* was so relaxed – bland almost, concluded the one called Francesco. The *commissario's* companion was too young to pose a threat, he considered, although he felt under scrutiny from this young man, as if he was attempting to catch them out in the smallest divergence from the facts.

The joy of this interrogation from the perspective of the interviewing police officers was, of course, that the four men – including Lombardi, still in his cell down below – had absolutely no idea that both of these officers had witnessed the whole scene at the farmhouse. This was Beppe's ultimate trump card.

Beppe's apparently relaxed stance was deceptive – he had been extraordinarily busy in the intervening day, in ways that would have astounded the three men sitting in front of him.

Beppe was looking at their written depositions one after the other with a disconcerting frown on his face.

"Are there any details of your accounts you would like to alter in any way at all?" asked the *commissario.* He had fixed Manfredo and Francesco with his well-known unblinking stare. "What you have written will be used in evidence at the trial of your colleague, Attilio Lombardi. You have all unequivocally and very effectively consigned him to a lifetime in an Italian jail..."

Manfredo was becoming painfully aware that this inoffensive-looking *commissario* was infinitely more dangerous than their interrogator up north. He was attempting to undermine their position. Did he suspect that their betrayal of their senior colleague was too neat? Was he trying to implicate them in the murder of this woman, Giada Costa?

"It seems to me, gentlemen," continued Beppe quietly, "that the only unexplained element in your lucid accounts is the matter of this voice urging *Agente* Lombardi to 'take out' *Agente* Costa. What do you say, young man?" said Beppe suddenly turning on the driver of the Jeep.

The junior army officer started in shock and stammered his reply.

"I heard the voice clearly, *commissario*. It came from behind me, so I just assumed it was one of these two. It sounded just like..." His voice petered out.

"Thank you Private Johnson. You see what I'm getting at, don't you gentlemen?"

They did see – only too well. They were being accused of collusion.

Manfredo considered it was time to scotch this suspicion. After all, both he and Francesco knew they were telling the truth on this occasion. The 'voice' had smacked of the supernatural as far as they could tell.

"*Commissario,* we are as puzzled as you are as to who spoke those words – but it was neither of us, I can assure you. We shall stick to this assertion through thick and thin – simply because it happens to be true."

Pippo Cafarelli, sitting by his chief's side, was fully aware of what was going on. He knew *exactly* whose voice the Americans had heard that night. Of those present, only Pippo knew of Beppe's consummate skill at mimicking accents. He understood that his *capo's* line of questioning was designed solely to guarantee that his 'ventriloquist trick' would never be unmasked.

"Well, gentlemen," smiled Beppe. "I think that concludes this interview - unless you have anything relevant to add?"

"We would like to know when we shall be released, *commissario,*" said the agent called Manfredo in hopeful tones.

The *commissario's* reply dispelled any impression they might still be harbouring that they were dealing with a simple local cop.

"Ah yes, *signori,* I nearly forgot to tell you. I've been speaking to your contact in Boston – Agente Cosimo Moretto. Two D.A.S.R lawyers are on their way as we speak – one for you two – and of course a separate lawyer for Agent Lombardi. Cosimo Moretto was deeply shocked to hear about the death of Giada Costa. I think he was quite fond of her..."

"How the hell did you manage to get in touch with…?" began the agent called Francesco. He was silenced by a stern look from his colleague.

"You, Private Johnson, are free to return to Vicenza. You two will, I regret to say, have to remain here in Pescara until your lawyer arrives. I am sure he will have the necessary extradition papers for you," Beppe reassured them.

Attilio Lombardi was summonsed and informed of his rights by Beppe and Pippo. He imperiously demanded the presence of his own lawyer, refusing to cooperate until he was present.

"Your lawyer, Diego Manduria, is on his way from the States right now, *Agente* Lombardi. *Agente* Cosimo Moretto – your D.A.S.R contact in Boston – has been duly informed of your crime," Beppe told him calmly.

"How the f*** did you…?" began Attilio Lombardi but thought it best to conceal his shock that his supposedly covert presence on Italian soil had been so easily uncovered. "That bitch, Giada Costa!" he concluded muttering the words under his breath.

"*Agente* Giada Costa betrayed her Republican heritage. She didn't deserve to be an agent with us," stated Lombardi, revealing his extreme right wing beliefs in all their horrific nakedness, reminiscent of Negro slavery and the Klu Klux Klan.

"*Ex* Agent Giada Costa," Beppe spat out in anger. "My talks with Giada would suggest she was a decent woman irrespective of her politics – far more decent than you could ever aspire to being," said Beppe in disdain. "She was a good woman who enjoyed life to the full in a country she loved – *our* country - before you saw fit to murder her in cold blood."

The venom in his voice was undisguised and was obviously heartfelt.

Beppe and Pippo outlined the course of events at the farmhouse near Fara San Martino in graphic detail.

"Sounds a very interesting story, *agenti,*" sneered Attilio Lombardi. "You'll have a harder job proving what really happened – anyone could have shot that Costa woman!"

"Oh, we have witnesses, *Agente* Lombardi. Your three henchmen for starters," stated *Commissario* Stancato calmly. "And you are obviously unaware of the fact that both myself and *Agente* Cafarelli were also present. The case against you is clear cut."

"Everything that happened at that farmhouse was a mirage, *commissario!* A set-up," said Lombardi aggressively, "including that image of Professor Pisano that you put in the cellar. Giada Costa was not left-handed, you see – that's what gave the game away for me."

"She was ambidextrous, Agent Lombardi. She was proud of the fact that she could write with either hand – and she could play the guitar right-handed or left-handed," Beppe explained with an innocent smile on his face. He had been forced to cover up his shock at Lombardi's words with the first excuse that came into his head. He had to be honest with himself – the particular effect of a mirror image reversing left and right had never occurred to him. He had to admit grudgingly to himself that Attilio Lombardi must be acutely observant and intelligent despite looking like a low-life mobster. Interesting, thought Beppe, how astuteness and criminality so often go hand in hand.

But Beppe had anticipated the eventuality of Agent Lombardi suspecting that things might not have been quite as they appeared in the farm yard. He unfurled a copy of a well-respected national newspaper and passed it over to the American. Even the headline was stark. *Italian woman of thirty-five murdered by American secret agent,* it stated.

"I don't think even your lawyer will attempt to argue with this level of proof - plus the testimony of your three underlings. The television coverage was even more graphic. The most you can hope for, Agent Lombardi, is extradition."

Beppe had spoken the words calmly. He was feeling a lot less self-assured inside.

Attilio Lombardi was dismissed and taken back, seething with frustrated anger, to his cell.

"I think he must have run out of deodorant, *capo,*" commented Pippo, relieved they could breathe normally again.

"You *knew,* didn't you, *Agente* Cafarelli?" said Beppe quietly to Pippo when they were sure they were far from any recording device.

"Yes, *capo* - you took a huge risk, didn't you?"

Beppe shrugged.

"I trust it will all prove to have been worthwhile once the dust has settled," he said simply.

"So Giada is alive. You would never have provoked Attilio Lombardi into shooting at her unless you had been totally sure of her safety."

"Giada Costa is dead, Pippo. And don't you forget it! But the phoenix may well rise from the ashes one day soon..."

"You could have trusted me enough to tell me beforehand, *capo,*" Pippo said despite himself.

"I'm sorry, Pippo. You're right, of course. Now please forget this conversation. I have to go and see the *Questore* now. I have a feeling that I am going to be hauled over the coals."

"In bocca al lupo, capo!"

"Crepi!" replied the *commissario,* who was convinced that the 'wolf' was going to eat him alive on this occasion.

Chapter 21: The Questore is not amused...

The *Questore,* Dante Di Pasquale, did not get up from behind his desk to shake Beppe's hand warmly as he usually did. This was a bad sign. He gestured to his second-in-command to sit down.

"Congratulazioni, commissario," he said. It hadn't sounded at all sarcastic, so Beppe did not know what was coming next. He raised a quizzical eyebrow in his chief's direction.

"You have succeeded where absolutely no other officer under my command has ever succeeded before," began Beppe's chief amiably enough.

"Capo?" said Beppe, cautiously optimistic that he was not going to receive the expected verbal drubbing.

"You have managed to carry out a whole police operation whilst I have been kept entirely in the dark."

Beppe knew from that moment on that he was in for a rough ride. He would need to summon up all his powers of verbal persuasion if he was to convince his chief that he had been justified in setting up his elaborate *sceneggiatura,* without consultation and all at public expense.

"I expect you would like me to explain everything that happened prior to our discovery as to the whereabouts of *Professore* Donato Pisano – and his successful release," began Beppe, pointedly reminding his chief that the main purpose of their mission had been successfully accomplished.

The *Questore* managed a crooked smile despite himself.

"I am rather more concerned, *commissario,* at trying to understand what was going through your devious mind *after* your rescue of the professor."

"You need to understand, *capo,* we would never have discovered where Donato Pisano was being held in captivity without the intervention of Giada Costa. Her contribution was vital. And, as far as she was concerned, she was putting her own livelihood and personal freedom at risk for the rest of her life as soon as she decided to help us track down the professor. Once her contacts in the USA realised she had 'changed sides' and scuppered their attempt at abducting Donato Pisano, she would have been extradited to America and put on some mission in some godforsaken part of the world until her dying day. That is a fact of American secret service life about which she managed to convince me quite unequivocally. Freedom of choice would be totally denied her - even to the extent that vetting her sexual partners would form a permanent part of her life. I truly believed that we, as Italians, could not abandon her to this fate after what she did to help us. She wanted to stop her covert spying on our country, but she knew that, while she lived, her employers would never let her go. She also intended to marry one of the other scientists at the Montenero laboratory, a man called Gianni Marconi. In fact, Giada had already moved in with him."

Beppe continued in like vein for the next five minutes or so without a pause, relieved to note that his chief was listening intently.

"So you allowed this woman to take part in the scenario you had dreamt up to entrap the American agents who came back to Italy to abduct Professor Pisano. Is that about right, *commissario?*"

Beppe nodded, waiting with bated breath for the *Questore's* next words.

"But it all went wrong, didn't it? You have brought about the death of an innocent civilian involved in an unofficial police operation. You do understand, don't you, *commissario,* that I am the one who will be blamed for Giada's death. A public scandal will be inevitable, with me on the receiving end. I have already been contacted by the *Ministro dell'interno* – demanding to know how I ever allowed this situation to get so out of hand."

Beppe was looking suitably contrite. But inside, he was feeling jubilant. Those of his team who were in the know – including the couple from the theatre - had kept faith. The *Questore* was unaware of the real circumstances.

"Excuse me, *capo.* I fear I am about to muddy the waters a little. There is something important which you are still unaware of. A fact that hardly simplifies your life, I'm sorry to say, but which alters the perspective of the problem entirely."

"*O Dio!* Now what are you going to tell me, *commissario?* I do hope I am not, after such a happy partnership between us, going to rue the day I ever appointed you as *commissario...*"

"I'm not sure, *capo.* But you do need to know that Giada Costa is still alive."

"You mean, she survived her bullet wound, *commissario?*"

"No, *capo,* I mean the bullet never touched her. It was all a *mise en scène* – an illusion for the benefit of Attilio Lombardi and the other three in the Jeep."

Dante Di Pasquale simply closed his eyes and kept them shut for the space of thirty long seconds. He sighed deeply but did not utter a word.

He opened his eyes again. Beppe read a hint of relief in them. But evidently, his chief was not ready to let him off the hook so easily. Beppe was meditating on the nature of true leadership. Had he not respected the *Questore* so deeply, he might have attempted to argue his case more aggressively. Respect, thought Beppe is truly a quality which has to be earned. It has nothing at all to do with rank. Thus, he waited patiently, humbly almost, until Dante Di Pasquale had digested the implications of what he, Beppe, had just told him. However, the next words uttered by the *Questore* were devastating.

"*Commissario* Stancato, I am suspending you – without pay – for a period of three months. What we save by not paying you a salary will go some way to recuperating the cost of your unofficial act of total irresponsibility. You may choose when your period of suspension begins – as long as it starts before this year is out. This time should be spent considering whether you wish to continue in this post under my command. I could, if you prefer, have you transferred back to Calabria."

Beppe was reeling under the mental shock to his system. But his chief had not finished. He continued his assault on the most vulnerable aspect of Beppe's life.

"This period of three months will also give you the opportunity to help Sonia raise your young family without your embarking on hazardous ventures which run the risk of depriving your offspring of their father if they go unchecked."

Beppe stood up to attention, saluted his chief with respect, said the words *'Grazie, capo'* in total sincerity, turned round smartly and headed for the door with tears in his eyes.

"Excuse me, *commissario*," Dante Di Pasquale said with quiet dignity. "I don't remember dismissing you. We now need to have a very urgent discussion as to how we are going to protect this Giada Costa and ensure that she remains officially dead. You are really going to need my help to achieve this. We need first of all to decide what name to give her in her new life in Italy. Have you already spoken to her about her new identity?"

Beppe had to turn round and wipe the tears from his eyes before he returned, smiling like a son chastised and forgiven by a loving father, to his seat in front of the *Questore's* desk.

"She has her heart set on the name Simona, *capo*. I suggested Gambino as a suitably uncomplicated surname."

"Where is she, by the way, Beppe?"

"Safe and sound and out of the public eye. She's in Gianni Marconi's house – her *fidanzato* and the physicist who is standing in for Professor Donato Pisano. She's a virtual prisoner in the house and has been told to stay in the back rooms which are not overlooked by neighbours. But she has access to a secluded garden."

"I shall have to see her in person, Beppe. We're going to have to set up a kind of 'witness protection' programme for her. It shouldn't be too difficult. You will need to get her to Via Pesaro under the cover of darkness, disguised as far as possible – but such a feat shouldn't overtax a man of your ingenuity," said Dante Di Pasquale without the hint of a smile on his face.

Beppe bowed his head in acknowledgement of the irony – and the instructions received.

"How about the apartment where she lived, Beppe?" continued the *Questore*. "I imagine it was only rented – and probably contains some expensive equipment to communicate with the USA."

"All taken care of, *capo*. The equipment is here in Via Pesaro for now. I spoke to Giada Costa's 'controller' in Boston – Giada herself set that up for me without his knowledge. I informed him of her death at the hands of one of his own agents.

I told him he could pick up his equipment from us. Bianca Bomba and Marco Pollutri are having a good look at it before the Americans send someone to collect it. We also informed Giada's landlady in L'Aquila about her death – no details. But we did leave a little notice on the entrance door with Giada's photo on it, announcing her death 'by the hand of an assassin' – for the sake of the private students whom she was teaching guitar and maths to. I hope you don't consider I went too far, *capo...*"

For the first time during their emotionally charged exchange, the *Questore* let out a guffaw of unrestrained laughter.

"*Commissario,*" said Dante Di Pasquale, "thank you for lightening the tone of this dreadful and unnatural interview, whose necessity I deeply regret on all levels. The truth is, you *always* go too far. The posting of an obituary notice on Giada's apartment door seems trivial by comparison with the rest."

Beppe looked relieved. He had been fearing an extension of his sentence beyond the prescribed three month period.

"We need to set up local and national television interviews to make this affair very public throughout Italy," stated the *Questore*. "For this fiasco you have managed to create, the whole of Italy has got to believe that Agent Giada Costa is the victim of American aggression. She has Italian nationality already, I understand?"

Beppe nodded.

"I am very willing to appear on television, *capo,*" said Beppe. "If you need to disassociate yourself from my..."

"*Commissario* Stancato, let me make one thing absolutely clear. If I find you anywhere within one hundred metres of a reporter or a television camera in the next few days, your suspension will become a fully-fledged dismissal from the police force. I shall need to work hand in glove with the *Ministro dell'interno* – it will simplify matters no end that Giada Costa is already an Italian citizen. But it will be ME and not you who will take care of everything else from now on – including television interviews. Need I say more, Beppe?"

"*Nossignore!*" replied a contrite Beppe Stancato. "What about Attilio Lombardo, *capo?*"

"His lawyer will arrive in two days' time – armed with an extradition order so that he can be tried in the United States. We have already agreed at ministerial level that we will go along with his extradition. Naturally, I shall make noises of protest to his lawyer – but just for appearance's sake. You are welcome to be present at the meeting with the lawyer, *commissario* – unless, of course, you have decided to begin your three months of exile by then," rounded off the *Questore.*

Beppe made a non-committal gesture indicating he would not be leaving while the consequences of his actions were still being played out. He stood up to leave, wondering if he should hold out his hand to his exceptional leader. He did not need to make the decision.

"Sit down, Beppe. You haven't yet told me how you managed to pull off this little stunt which you staged."

Beppe could not help smiling at the *Questore's* boyish eagerness to satisfy his curiosity despite his official condemnation of his second-in-command's irregular conduct.

"We practised it over and over again the previous evening until it looked and sounded convincing. It was just me, the two young technicians from the theatre – an amazing couple – Giada herself plus *Agente* Rocco. He, by the way, has been simply astounding throughout the whole investigation, *capo.*"

"I had the feeling he would prove to be worth his weight in gold when I interviewed him," said the *Questore* with a touch of pride.

"The theatre couple set up a microphone behind the scenes and a loudspeaker in the cellar so that Attilio Lombardi would hear Giada's voice. We had a subtly illuminated wooden cut-out board with Professor Pisano's image on it just to entice Lombardi inside. The rest of the illusion was really down to our own technicians in the basement and some special effects by the girl and the boy from the *Teatro Massimo.* They supplied us with some very advanced theatrical equipment – very easy to use – which ironically enough has been developed by an American company specialising in scientifically advanced special effects.

It's a programme linked up to a virtually invisible 'cloud' of ionised molecules on to which the computer image is generated. The result is a lifelike three dimensional hologram. They were very keen to try it out in a real life environment. It works perfectly at a distance but becomes progressively fragmented if you get too close.

We made a film of Giada waving a mocking 'farewell' to Agent Lombardi, wearing her white jumper with a big red heart on it, and a separate film of her hurling herself on to a mattress to coincide with the gunshot. We took the precaution of making her wear a bullet proof jacket underneath her jumper. But we overlooked the fact that it was a mirror image that got projected on to the screen – so she appeared to be left-handed. The American spotted this discrepancy, which gave me a nasty moment while I was interviewing him here. The couple from the theatre could operate the images from a computer some distance away, linked by some super-conducting cable... I didn't really understand the technical stuff myself, *capo,*" added Beppe on seeing the mystified look on his chief's face.

"Finally, we had some new-fangled transparent bullet-proof screen behind the hologram image from our own technicians, so the bullet wouldn't hit the building behind. The bullet just loses its energy on striking this material and doesn't ricochet at all. The noise it would have made ricocheting off the stone wall could easily have wrecked the illusion – and been potentially lethal to Giada Costa, who had already taken up her 'dead' position on the ground outside the cellar. I believe our two technicians were quite excited about trying out their new technology too..."

"But Giada looked convincingly dead, I gather," asked the *Questore.*

"Make-up, *capo* - the girl from the theatre was a professional make-up artist. She made Giada's face as white as death and stuck on a ready-made moulded plastic bullet hole on her forehead. It only needed to be momentarily convincing before Luigi Rocco was on the scene with a cover ready to throw over Giada's face and chest. The ambulance team, including Bruno Esposito, took photos of her 'dead' body when they were safely on their way so we had 'proof' of her death. The ambulance took her back to Monticchio – alive and kicking."

"But how did you manage to keep Pippo Cafarelli, Gino and Danilo at bay?"

"I told them not to emerge until they heard shots – that was me shooting at the back of the Jeep. Pippo emerged a bit too soon and saw Giada on the ground – but it was good because he reacted convincingly for the sake of Gino and Danilo. Pippo was only temporarily fooled by the theatricals, because he's a very smart young man."

"And now we come to the matter of the voice telling Lombardi to shoot at the image of Giada Costa. Or would you rather not comment on that aspect of this bit of play-acting?"

Beppe smiled sheepishly.

"I would prefer not to go into too much detail, *capo.*"

"But couldn't you just have arrested the four Americans before they drove off?" asked the *Questore* – even though he could see the flaws in his own argument.

"Attilio Lombardi had to leave with the conviction that he had committed a murder. He would quickly have picked up on the fact that there had been no crime committed by the way we reacted. We're not *that* convincing as actors, *capo.*"

"Besides which, you had already set up a far more dramatic scenario outside the military base in Vicenza, I am told," concluded the *Questore.*

Beppe shrugged his shoulders in acknowledgement of the *fait accompli.*

Dante di Pasquale stood up and came round to Beppe's side of the desk. To Beppe's shock, he hugged his junior colleague briefly but warmly and said:

"Now get out of my office, *commissario,* I have a lot to do. You are an almighty pain in the backside, by the way."

Beppe headed for the door without further ado.

"No hard feelings about your suspension, I hope," he heard the *Questore* say as he had his hand on the door knob.

"Nossignore!" said Beppe as he left the room, filled with a renewed and profound respect for the man whose quiet authority he had unwisely attempted to bypass.

22:   *Entropy at work...*

"Sono incinta," stated Oriana as if she had been announcing some misdemeanour on her part.

"Whose fault is *that,* Oriana?" smiled her new friend.

"My *fidanzato's,* I suppose," replied Oriana – who was not smiling, but whose eyes expressed a hint of wild excitement. "I'm not sure why I'm telling *you* this, though."

"Because we're friends, Oriana," replied Rosa simply. "Why shouldn't you tell us? What's his name, by the way?" asked Rosa.

"I don't even know if it's a boy or a girl yet!" snapped Oriana without thinking.

"I mean your *fidanzato's* name, *scema!"* replied Rosa equally as tartly.

"Giovanni," replied Oriana, embarrassed that her first thought had been for the tiny beginnings of a human being inside of her, rather than its father.

"Have you told Giovanni yet?" asked Rosa.

Oriana shook her head.

"Why not?" asked Rosa, in genuine astonishment. "You love him, don't you?"

"Yes, of course I do!" replied Oriana.

Rosa looked reprovingly at her new 'best friend'.

"You must tell him today, Oriana. I'm sure he'll be over the moon."

It was amazing how this twelve year old girl – coming up thirteen - had grown up in the last few days. Instead of acting like a wayward street urchin, she took care of her appearance, she dressed differently – partly because Oriana had taken Rosa and her little brother on a shopping spree two days ago – and she talked as if she was enjoying life. Rosa had been inordinately proud of the fact that Oriana had bought her her first bra. Steffi had simply stood there with his eyes wide open in disbelief at the necessity of this inexplicable purchase for his own, once-familiar sister. He had been perfectly content with his new football top – an acquisition which did not open the doors to some unfamiliar world.

"I suppose I told you first, Rosa – and you too Steffi – because I won't be able to throw myself around teaching you judo and karate moves for much longer."

They had just emerged from the gymnasium, usually frequented by the local police force, and were standing outside on the pavement.

"And then... Giovanni and I were talking about the possibility of you two coming to live with us," said Oriana hesitantly, not knowing what the children's reaction would be. "Giovanni would love to meet you two. I've told him all about you. Now, being pregnant, I'm not sure how that will change things. I suppose that's why I told you two first."

In the next instance, the little group of three merged into a single entity as Rosa and Steffi hugged Oriana tightly. It was Oriana's eyes which were watering. "I'm getting soft in my old age," said the twenty-four-year-old police woman in alarm, more renowned for her scathing tongue than for having to suppress unbidden tears.

"We've still got to look after our mum, Oriana," said Steffi softly.

"Now *papà* is in jail, she's only got us to take care of her – which works in *mamma's* favour. She's been working full time in a local supermarket for the last few days," explained Rosa. "And you'll never guess who found her the job, Oriana."

"It was that other lady policewoman who used to boss us about," said Steffi. "She's nice to us now."

"I think it's because she's got someone else to nag now – *cioè,* our mum," said Rosa.

Oriana smiled at the perception of Rosa's observation. She had obviously sussed out the character of her police woman colleague, Lina Rapino.

"Well, we'll see what happens, *ragazzi.* But Giovanni and I want to take you for a trek into the mountains next weekend - if you would like that? We'll have lunch at a little *trattoria* near a big lake."

Rosa and Steffi were beaming, their eyes alive with excitement.

"Will we see bears and wolves up there?" asked Steffi.

"Not too close up, I hope," said Rosa, who could not imagine that her newly acquired martial arts' skills would be sufficient if faced with a real life *orso bruno*.

* * *

Beppe and Sonia were lying in bed locked in a warm, post love-making embrace – a first cautious attempt since the birth of Lorenzo, he realised. Sonia had forgotten to 'take steps' but was sure it wouldn't matter this time.

"Good job you came home when you did, *amore mio*. Another few days and I'd have been scouring the streets of Atri for a substitute lover," stated Sonia. Beppe took this revelation in the spirit in which it was intended.

He then enthralled his lifelong partner by narrating every single thing that had happened since his last homecoming. She laughed at the details of the vanishing physicist's rescue. The event as related on TV-Tavo had failed to mention the comical details of Donato Pisano's destruction of his own clothes before taking refuge in the shower cubicle.

If the account of Donato Pisano's rescue had amused her, she remained astounded by the night time episode at the farmhouse, as well as by the behaviour of the *Carabiniere*

General in Vicenza – the details of which Beppe had gleaned from his friend Riccardo Grimaldi, the *colonnello* in Pescara.

"You *have* been a busy boy, *commissario!* I believe you have even surpassed your previous record of allowing yourself to be imprisoned by the mushroom poisoner. And all this for the sake of Sabrina Ferilli - she really *must* have made an impression on you, Beppe Stancato!"

"You would have liked her very much," protested Beppe weakly.

"Why the past tense, *amore?* I assume Sabrina Ferilli is alive and kicking."

"*È vero,* Sonia. I have got into the habit of convincing myself that she is dead."

"There's another confession I have to make, Sonia...*amore,*" began Beppe reluctantly. But he noticed halfway through the account of his meeting with the *Questore* that Sonia had fallen asleep.

The following morning, still in bed, he told her about his 'punishment'. Sonia was overjoyed and kissed her partner all over in delight.

"God bless the *Questore!*" she said. "I love that man. You'll be able to change all Lorenzo's nappies for the whole three month period – and talk endlessly to Veronica to make sure she's a precocious speaker – which is obviously what she's striving to achieve on a daily basis."

Beppe was simply relieved that she had not censored his waywardness. She had brushed aside any concerns about the shortfall in their income.

"And harking back to your narrative of last night, Beppe, I suppose there's no need to ask whose voice it was which incited that American to shoot at Giada Costa," whispered Sonia slyly – just before Lorenzo began wailing for his next feed.

* * *

Dante Di Pasquale had surpassed himself. In the space of only two days, the news of *Professore* Donato Pisano's abduction, his rescue from the American secret service and the arrest of one Atillio Lombardi for the murder of an innocent Italian woman had spread faster than a forest fire throughout the whole of the Italian Peninsula. The public outrage was tangible wherever you went.

Rai 1 was the first to scoop the story on television, followed closely by La 7 – both channels interviewing the *Questore* in person. The newspaper, *Il Corriere della Sera,* had immediately sent a reporter and a photographer down from Milano, so seriously did they take the story. The other national newspapers soon followed suite, having to content themselves with a Skype interview with the *Questore* from Pescara.

In the *Questore's* spacious office on the top floor of the police headquarters, *Commissario* Stancato, sworn to silence unless directly invited to comment, was sitting on the *Questore's* left side. *Agente* Luigi Rocco was seated on his right. They were facing Atillio Lombardi – trying his best to look contrite on the orders of his lawyer. The aforementioned lawyer, Diego Manduria, had been brusquely efficient, slapping the extradition order on the *Questore's* desk as soon as he had sat down, as if to say: "There – you try arguing with *that!*"

Dante Di Pasquale, however, was quite prepared to do just that.

"It is strange, is it not, *avvocato,* how we Italians are expected to leap to attention and hand over prisoners at the sight of a piece of paper issued by you – whereas a mere foreign prisoner can languish in an American jail for years before an extradition order is respected."

"It's the advantage we have of being the most powerful nation in the world, *signore,*" sneered Attilio Lombardi's lawyer, who showed his scorn by omitting to use the *Questore's* proper title.

The *Questore* kept his counsel with difficulty. Beppe was seething in silence and the *Orso Bruno* remained inscrutable.

"I shall have to send this extradition order to the *Ministro dell'interno* in Rome by registered post and await the Minister's approval before I release this prisoner into your custody,

Avvocato. It's the advantage we Italians have of being the most artful procrastinators in the world," said the *Questore* evenly, staring directly into the eyes of the lawyer, Diego Manduria.

It was Attilio Lombardi's turn to seethe. He failed to control his temper.

"You can't hold me here any longer. You're just ordinary policemen. I refuse to stay in that cell for another single night – on the strength of some trumped up charge concocted by *this* officer. I was tricked into shooting that woman. There's no proof the Costa woman's even dead," roared Attilio Lombardi.

Attilio Lombardi was jabbing his finger in Beppe's direction.

"What do you say to this accusation, *Agente* Rocco?" asked the Questore quietly.

"It's simply offensive," replied the *Orso Bruno*. "You are forgetting, *Signor* Lombardi, that we witnessed the whole scene. We had to suffer the grief of watching the death of a decent woman whose life you extinguished in a moment of rage."

Luigi had finished talking. Beppe wanted to applaud him but the *Questore* turned his attention to Beppe and asked:

"Anything to add, *Commissario?*"

"Have you seen the newspapers, *Signor* Lombardi? Have you watched the Italian news on television recently? The whole country knows about the crime you committed. I feel sorry for you, Attilio. If your only defence is that you were framed, then you are unlikely to be let off by *any* court in the world – least of all in the United States."

Attilio Lombardi leapt to his feet, ignoring his lawyer's restraining hand on his arm. He had murder in his eyes again. The reason why the *Questore* had selected the *Orso Bruno* to be present at this interrogation became instantly apparent.

* * *

How pleasurable by contrast the *Questore's* job had been when faced with a smiling Giada Costa that same evening. Beppe ushered her into his chief's office after dark, when only a sleepy officer on duty at the desk downstairs had saluted his *capo* automatically but had paid scant attention to the woman with him.

For the sake of avoiding any risk of an accidental encounter, Attilio Lombardi had been transferred to a single cell in Pescara's jail. His lawyer had promised he would 'make waves the size of a tsunami' to get him extradited within days. He succeeded in achieving this, but only because this had been the behind-the-scenes agreement reached between the Italian *Ministro dell'interno* and Dante Di Pasquale beforehand. The prison staff voluntarily went and bought three spray cans of 'Ocean Mist' in an attempt to make the cell habitable again after Attilio Lombardi's departure.

The *Questore* stood up and shook Giada Costa's hand warmly as she entered his upstairs office.

"I cannot comment on your famed similarity with Sabrina Ferilli, Giada, because I never saw you before you changed your appearance."

It had been a clandestine visit to the young woman from the *Teatro Massimo* who had so convincingly made Giada look dead that had brought about the transformation of Giada Costa into her new persona.

The three of them discussed Giada's future in minute detail until well past midnight.

"We must all get into the habit of thinking of you as Simona Gambino from now on," said the *Questore*. "I've heard so much about your contribution to Professor Donato's rescue that it occurs to me that the career move which we must organise on your behalf becomes self-evident...Simona."

Dante Di Pasquale outlined his idea to 'Simona'. She smiled, delighted by his solution to the problem. Beppe nodded in total agreement.

"Getting your identity changed should not take more than a week, Simona. Meanwhile, you must make a binding promise to remain inside your *fidanzato's* house in Monticchio until I tell you it is safe to emerge – with your new documents."

"Don't worry, *Signor Questore.* If it means I shall be free for the rest of my life, then I am sure I can put up with being imprisoned for a few more days," she reassured him gaily.

"There only remains the question of your funeral," continued the *Questore.* "But I feel sure your *fidanzato* and Beppe here can cope admirably with the necessary arrangements to provide Giada Costa with a fitting departure from this life.

* * *

The two couples who were destined to make a lifelong commitment to each other managed to agree on only one thing: the reception should be held at Remo Mastrodicasa's *agriturismo, 'La casa della bella addormentata',* just outside L'Aquila.

Both separately and together, their ideas on matrimony as opposed to simply living together were debated endlessly. The 'discussion' resembled more a game of mixed doubles in tennis – with the advantage constantly fluctuating between the two teams. There were even moments when it appeared that an individual player would change allegiance and seemed to be playing for the opposite team.

It was Oriana Salvati who publically resisted the notion of marriage more than anyone else.

"It's not that I don't love you totally, Giovi," she told him in private. "It's just that the actual act of signing that piece of paper is like a life sentence. There is something about getting married that spoils the spontaneity and joy of living together. Suddenly, the future weighs heavily on the mind and you begin to think of old age and the grave."

At a later stage, when Donato Pisano's book entitled *'Dov'è sparito il tempo?' (Where has time gone?)* was finally published, she might have read about entropy and realised that she was suffering from a lack of perception about the true nature of passing time – thereby saving herself the pain of the current dilemma.

Pippo's *fidanzata,* Mariangela, was adamant that she would only accept the state of matrimony over cohabitation. She even threatened to go back to her father's restaurant in Penne to serve customers with *porchetta* for the remainder of her days if Pippo procrastinated any longer.

In the end, matrimony was deemed to be the only practical solution – out of respect for the traditional values of their parents and the arrival of children on the scene.

Then began the debate about whether they should be married in church or simply at the town hall – the latter alternative winning the day quite easily. It was Beppe, when consulted, who suggested that his friend and ally the Archbishop of Pescara could bless their union. "God gets a look in that way, *ragazzi,"* he said, thinking that the younger generation had lost so much of its cultural heritage and beliefs in the course of the early twenty-first century.

Only when agreement had been reached did Oriana, in her own characteristically blunt manner, turn to her *fidanzato* and announce defiantly:

"I'm pregnant, by the way, Giovi. I hope you don't mind."

She was deeply relieved and moved by Giovanni's reaction to the news.

"I really wanted to be married to you properly all along," she confessed, spontaneously performing a complete *volta face.*

"I know you did," replied her partner gently. Giovanni Palena was probably the only man in Italy able to cope with the vagaries of his impulsive lover and partner without ever becoming ruffled. Oriana put her arms round Giovanni and hugged him.

23:   A near miss, an encounter of giants - and two happy families...

Giada's funeral was a deeply moving experience for all concerned – except for Simona Gambino, as she was now officially renamed, fully equipped with the documents to prove it. Beppe had had to forcibly stop her attending her own funeral. He had threatened to gag her and shackle her to a radiator in Gianni's house before she acknowledged that the risk of being recognised was too great – despite her valiant attempts at altering her appearance.

"Besides which, the Rai Uno and TV-Tavo cameras will be outside the church – on our invitation. We have to convince the whole world that Giada Costa no longer exists," Beppe explained.

The parish priest attached to the little country church in Monticchio had no inkling that the coffin, resting on two stands in the main isle, was weighted down with sand. The flowers placed on the lid of the coffin radiated their colour and scent all around the interior of the packed church.

Beppe, not the parish priest, delivered an emotional tribute to a 'beautiful, lively young woman who enjoyed every minute of her life to the full.' There were few dry eyes by the time he had stopped talking, including his own.

Beppe was feeling deeply guilty about the deception being practised on Holy Mother Church, but he had convinced himself that the hoax was for the greater good. When he had hatched the whole scheme a couple of weeks previously, he had not thought through all the practical implications involved in staging a funeral for Giada Costa, who was to be buried in an obscure rural cemetery just outside Monticchio – in full view of the media. The 'celebratory' wake was held in Remo's *agriturismo* – entirely at Gianni Marconi's expense. He thought of his new partner, languishing in solitary confinement behind the walls of his house less than one kilometre away.

The whole carefully staged subterfuge might have come unstuck had it not been for an uncanny event in Beppe's life only a week before the funeral.

'Simona Gambino' had been ordered to destroy her old mobile phone and was issued with a completely new one. It would be too risky for 'Giada' to contact her parents on an easily traceable mobile phone number. Thus, Beppe himself had spoken to Giada's mother and father, using a land line, explaining in the most covert terms possible that their daughter was 'at risk' and had been forced to change her identity – for her own safety. He decided not to mention the fake funeral at all because of the unnecessary anguish this would cause them.

But during the night following his phone call to the Costa parents, Beppe had a vivid dream. He could clearly see the parents – whose photo had adorned the mantelpiece in Giada's apartment in L'Aquila – and their American farmhouse sitting in a shallow valley surrounded by hills. Behind a tree up on the hillside, he saw a black car with a man inside it who was clearly Attilio Lombardi.

Beppe woke up with a start. Of course! What would the American agent have done on returning to his headquarters in Boston? He would have told his bosses that the whole scenario of Giada Costa's death was make-believe. Being a very smart man, he would have understood that, had the death of Giada Costa been genuine, the parents were bound to make the journey to Italy to attend her funeral. If they didn't go, then his assumption that her death had been a clever bit of trickery would be well-founded.

Beppe forgot about the time difference. As soon as he was back at the *Questura* at seven o'clock that morning, he talked to Dante Di Pasquale about his 'dream' and the conclusion that he had come to.

"The parents must make the journey to Italy, Beppe," said the *Questore*. "Otherwise, this whole *sceneggiatura* of yours might well crumble to pieces around us."

Signor Costa and his wife had gone to bed and were fast asleep at midnight. Beppe spoke urgently to a now alert farmer.

"You must come and attend your daughter's funeral," he said, without going into details as to the exact consequences of their failure to be there. He was worried about the risk of eavesdroppers if their land line had been tapped. This fear hampered his efforts to explain the situation to Giada's parents in clear terms. But he felt that the father had grasped the issues involved. "We'll foot your travel expenses if necessary," said Beppe.

"We wouldn't dream of taking your money, *commissario*. We have enough money to travel to Italy – in fact we wouldn't miss the chance to say farewell to our daughter for all the worlds. Strange though," added Giada's father as an afterthought, "we've noticed a black limousine up on the hillside for the last couple of days, and I'm sure I saw flashes of light like the reflexion off a spyglass or a camera lens. And we've been receiving unusual phone calls purporting to be from travel agencies offering us cheap flights to Europe and various people asking if they could speak to Giada..."

If the line was bugged, any listener would understand that suspicions had been aroused – despite *Signor* Costa's careful choice of words.

Only after he had replaced the receiver on its cradle, did the utter weirdness of his dream strike him forcibly.

Giada's parents arrived in Italy and were picked up by Gianni Marconi from Fiumicino airport. They failed to recognise their own daughter when they first saw her in Gianni's house. But to Beppe's relief, they put on a perfect display of grief and tears at the funeral for the benefit of the TV cameras, once Beppe had explained the complex reasons behind the subterfuge.

When, later on, Beppe told the Archbishop about his dream, Don Emanuele simply looked at him intensely, shrugged his shoulders and said:

"What did you expect the Holy Spirit to do, Beppe? Ignore you?"

* * *

Beppe and Sonia, sitting on their sofa holding hands, switched the television on at nine o'clock one evening, some days after the funeral. They selected the TV-Tavo channel. There was to be an encounter between Don Emanuele and the now renowned Italian physicist, Professor Donato Pisano. This meeting of minds had been heavily billed for days – and it was to be broadcast *in diretta,* the viewing public had been assured.

The luckless young man who had been assigned the task of preparing and conducting the live discussion was called Andrea Massi – officially the local TV channel's expert on scientific and religious affairs. He had completed a degree in physics which he had passed by only a narrow margin and had considered at some point entering holy orders.

"You're just the right man for this interview," the director of TV-Tavo studios reassured Andrea Massi.

Don Emanuele and Donato Pisano had struck up a friendship as soon as they had met in the presbytery of San

Cetteo cathedral. Keeping his promise to Beppe, the physicist had made an appointment with the Archbishop to tell him about the blue exercise book and the part it had played in his rescue. Once the idea of the TV interview had been proposed and after they had made the acquaintance of the pleasant but overawed young journalist who was to interview them, Donato and Don Emanuele reckoned that their diverse viewpoints on life would make for entertaining viewing. Andrea Massi appeared on the screen, looking surprisingly serene, thought those who knew him as a young man who did not brim over with self-confidence. Before the programme had begun, the Archbishop of Pescara had blessed him and the Professor had shaken his hand warmly.

"Don't you worry about a thing, young man," Donato Pisano had told him. "We'll help you get through this interview unscathed. Here's an idea we came up with to get the interview off to a flying start..."

Three, two, one – ON AIR, signalled the producer.

A.M.   This evening, cari telespettatori, we are privileged to have with us two remarkable men from two very diverse walks of life - the Archbishop of Pescara, Don Emanuele, whom most of you have certainly heard of at some stage – if only because of his famous Sunday sermons. The other man, whom until recently, you may be forgiven for never having heard of, is Professor Donato Pisano, the chief physicist in Abruzzo's mountain top particle physics

325

laboratory. Since the laboratory is buried beneath the Gran Sasso itself, you may have good reason for being unfamiliar with him.

Professor Pisano sprang to instant fame a few weeks ago under mysterious circumstances – he simply VANISHED into thin air. It is now common knowledge that he was shamefully abducted by two American agents who held him in captivity until such time as they could transport him in secret back to the United States - an attempt ably thwarted by our own Commissario Stancato of the Pescara police force.

May I first ask you a personal question? Do you believe in God?

A close-up of Andrea Massi's face had posed the question. The physicist appeared on the screen, full face. But it was the voice of the Archbishop which the viewers heard answering the question.

D.E.   *Well, I do have my off days. But generally speaking, yes I do!*

The camera focussing on Don Emanuele was immediately selected, so that it was a mischievously smiling Archbishop whom the viewers saw.

"He's up to his old tricks again," Beppe whispered to Sonia.

"He just can't resist it, can he?" added Sonia.

The amused – if somewhat bemused - face of Andrea Massi turned to Don Emanuele.

A.M.   *Some viewers may be deeply shocked by that statement, Don Emanuele. Could you explain to us where you are coming from?*

D.E.   *It's very simple, Andrea. I am, contrary to public opinion, just an ordinary mortal. We tend to forget that Jesus himself was as mortal as we are – which is why he should be an example, a comfort and a hero to us all. Even Jesus on his cross cried out to his father: 'Why hast though forsaken me?' Looking round the world today, it can be difficult to believe in a merciful God. But the base line is still the same – life is the most mysterious and inexplicable gift we possess.   In the end, I always come up against this unavoidable barrier to my disbelief – we can only know him as God.*

A.M.   *Thank you, Don Emanuele, for your candour – and for the unconventional manner in which you express your faith. May I ask you the same question, professore?*

D.P.   *Certainly, Andrea – even though Don Emanuele has taken the very words out of my mouth.* (Twinkle in the grey eyes of the scientist) *But I suppose I approach the subject of God from a very different angle, but I arrive at a similar conclusion. I am unlike so many of my scientific colleagues who always act as if they are on the brink of coming to a complete understanding of our presence in the universe – which may soon be proved to be multiple universes. They firmly believe they are only one step away from revealing the true nature of matter and life. Fortunately, there are a growing number of us who are wise enough and humble enough to see the simple fact that the more we appear to discover the deeper the mystery of our existence becomes. Take my favourite particles – neutrinos, for example. Millions of these practically massless little things are passing through our bodies every second. We detect them with great difficulty, but as to why they exist, we are eons away from understanding the role they play. I always come up against the same barrier to disbelief as Don Emanuele.*

A.M.   But do you still believe that your neutrinos arrived from Geneva travelling at faster than the speed of light, professore?

Andrea Massi's producer took one look at the script they had prepared in advance – and simply confined it to the rubbish bin. His protégé was sailing away under his own steam.

D.P.   Yes, I do – which is why I probably won't be allowed to continue in my post in the Montenero laboratory. I checked and re-checked our results a thousand times before I published my controversial findings. I was forced by my abductors to write a letter denying my conclusions. What's more, I believe the Americans are afraid I might be right – otherwise why would they have gone to so much trouble to abduct me?

A.M.   That is a fascinating insight you have given us, professore. But you are flying in the face of accepted beliefs. How do feel about that?

D.P.   Imagine you were interviewing Galileo some centuries ago, Andrea. You would be saying to him: 'Professore Galileo, you surely don't expect us to believe that the Earth is a sphere and that we are travelling round the sun?' May I misquote Shakespeare – who spoke these famous words through the mouth of Hamlet, Andrea? 'Ci sono più cose in cielo e in terra che non sogni la tua filosofia.'

A.M.   Point taken, professore, and thank you for your totally frank reply. Do you believe that things can travel faster than the speed of light, Don Emanuele?

D.E.   (Long pause for thought) Yes, I do. If it were not true, then we would be able to see the Holy Spirit – and that does seem to be quite out of character!

A.M. That is a fascinating notion, Don Emanuele. Do you really believe that it's true?

D.E. I'm not sure, Andrea. I've only just thought of it. (Broad grin on face of archbishop)

Andrea Massi suggested that the viewers would be fascinated to know more about Donato Pisano's abduction and rescue. The Professor obliged, telling them everything – including the kindness of his 'hostess', Maria De Amicis, whilst imprisoned and his rescue which had hinged on a blue exercise book. He told the viewers that he was writing a book about time to be published before the year was out. He added that he was scheduled to appear on Rai Tre's intellectual chat show, *Che tempo che fa,* as soon as his book *'Where has time gone?'* was published.

A.M. Is there any aspect of your adventure that you would describe as negative, professore?

"This is the bit I asked them to insert," Beppe told Sonia. Andrea Massi's producer was tapping the face of his watch impatiently. Andrea simply ignored him.

D.P. Yes, I understand from Commissario Stancato, of the Pescara police force, that my rescue was successful mainly thanks to a courageous young woman called Giada Costa – herself a former agent belonging to the American secret services. During the apprehension of the agents who tried to abduct me, she was shot and killed by one Attilio Lombardi – who belongs to the self-same secret agency. I shall go to my grave remembering that my good fortune was only achieved at the expense of an innocent woman's life. The world has lost a good and beautiful young life – and my colleague, Gianni, at the Montenero laboratory has lost a wonderful fidanzata.

Andrea Massi brought the interview to a close in his own good time. The broadcast overran by twenty minutes.

A.M.   *"One final question to each of you; what message would you give to our viewers that they should take away from this programme? Don Emanuele?"*

D.E.   *"Live your life believing that every second that goes by is merely part of your eternal existence. You are accountable to God and his creation for everything you do, say and think."*

A.M.   *And you, professore?*

D.P.   *"Remember that every cat, every dog, every tree, every flower and every pebble on the beach are made up of the same invisible particles as you and I are. You'll never cease to wonder at the mysteries of our existence – and you will never experience boredom again."*

Afterwards, Andrea Massi told Don Emanuele and Donato Pisano that he had never been so sure of himself in his whole life.

"It felt as if I had been cured of an illness," he explained to Don Emanuele.

"You must draw your own conclusions, Andrea," said Don Emanuele with a kindly smile. The studio lights shone on the Archbishop's shiny bald head. Andrea Massi could not help thinking it must be Don Emanuele's halo.

* * *

Oriana Salvati was staring at a photo which a passer-by had been recruited into taking of her, Giovanni, Rosa and Steffi standing on the shores of Lake Scanno.

"But you surely don't want me to take the photo with the camera facing the sun, do you?" asked the passer-by.

"Yes, I do," snapped Oriana, settling any argument instantly.

It captured and encapsulated for ever one second of her new life. Against the backdrop of shimmering water and blue mountains, the silhouette of all four figures, with their backs to the camera, were standing hand-in-hand with arms raised high to salute the setting sun.

It was already the third time that the two kids had taken the bus to L'Aquila to be met by Oriana and Giovanni. The couple had abandoned their rented apartment in Loreto Aprutino and were living in the spacious country house – renovated after the 2009 earthquake – which they shared with Giovanni's parents and which Giovanni would inherit some day in the future.

"Just like Beppe and me with my parents in Atri," Sonia had commented to Oriana during one of their increasingly regular phone calls to each other. "It gives an amazing feeling of *solidarietà familiare,* doesn't it?"

The four of them had spent three days by the lakeside during the school summer holidays. They had trekked up mountains, swum in the lake, shrieking with delight as the cool waters shocked their sun-drenched skins, taken out a rowing boat and tried fishing and eaten in family-run *trattorie* whenever they felt hungry. They had made the northwards drive back to L'Aquila, arguing and laughing like any family. Back in Giovanni's house, it had been Oriana who badgered the children into having showers and going to bed – not usually before eleven o'clock at night.

Oriana drove them back reluctantly to Pescara – because she was still officially working in Via Pesaro, knowing that she would have to transfer to the police station in L'Aquila before too long. At least, she could still take them to their judo classes. What joy there had been when Rosa achieved her yellow belt status – even if she had to be very adult about accepting that Steffi had achieved his orange belt in the same length of time.

"You have changed our lives, Oriana," confided Rosa. "We are so happy when we come and visit you and Giovanni. He's great and just perfect for you. But Steffi still misses his mum and we need to be at home to make sure she doesn't stray into prostitution again."

Oriana was amazed to hear these blunt words emerging from the lips of a now thirteen-year-old adult, but it was obvious that she, Rosa, was now firmly in charge of bringing up the family.

"Besides which, I am starting up at the *Liceo Scientifico* in Pescara next September," Rosa explained with undisguised pride at her own achievement.

If ever Oriana had doubts about her involvement with Rosa and Steffi, they were dispelled by comments from two sources. The head teacher from the kids' school spotted her one day as she walked to school with Oriana and Steffi.

"Congratulations, *Agente* Salvati," said the lady. "You have turned these two children's lives around. I have rarely seen such a rapid transformation. It's heart-warming to see."

Even *Agente* Lina Rapino approached Oriana and made peace with her colleague.

"I've learnt such a lot from you, Oriana," the severe police woman confessed.

Oriana stifled her desire to make some cutting comment. It must have cost *Agente* Rapino a great loss of pride to admit such a thing to a woman so much younger than herself.

"Grazie, Lina," she said simply.

It was always Oriana who felt sad when she had to leave Rosa and Steffi. She reminded herself that, when she had her own child, the same feelings of joy and sadness in equal measure would be repeated throughout her life.

She sighed with a mixture of secret happiness and a feeling of nostalgia for her recent past.

* * *

Commissario Stancato convened a meeting of all his team members. They were gathered in the main assembly room, curious to know the motive behind their *capo's* summons. It had been weeks since they had all met together. It had to be something significant, they assumed. Their curiosity changed to shock when Beppe announced that he was taking three months leave. Pippo was more shocked than anybody; he usually managed to get a hint from his chief but this time he was simply bewildered by this uncharacteristic announcement. For a time, nobody spoke.

"Should we be alarmed, *commissario?*" asked Giacomo D'Amico after a good fifteen seconds silence.

"Not at all, Giacomo. The *Questore* was acting on a request from me that I should be allowed to spend time with Sonia and my two children. I also have family matters to attend to back in Calabria. Now there seems to be a pause in our lives after the Vanishing Physicist affair, I felt that it was the right time to put in this request for temporary leave of absence."

It was the massive form of Luigi Rocco who rose up like the *Orso Bruno* he was supposed to be and growled a few words to the gathered assembly:

"Your loyalty to the *Questore* is admirable, *signor commissario.* But if I suspected that your three month absence has anything to do with our settling a score with those American crooks who came over to abduct the *professore,* I would feel duty bound to put in a similar request for leave of absence for myself."

The former atmosphere of surprise became a stunned silence at Luigi Rocco's words.

The silence was broken by Pippo who had begun to clap his hands together in a gesture of appreciative applause. He was soon joined by other members of the team. It was Oriana who cried out the words *Bravo, Luigi!* In an instant, everybody was on their feet joining in the applause. The 'brown bear' was finally part of the team.

The last matter that Beppe had had to deal with in recent days was a rumour initiated by a lower ranking member of the team that Luigi frequented prostitutes in his time off. Beppe had summoned Luigi in private to his office and, with great sympathy, broached the delicate subject. Luigi had simply smiled and said:

"But *capo*, it's a half truth. With my size, I put most women off. This lady is an intimate friend of mine – who also happens to earn a living as a *ragazza squillo.* I count myself lucky to know her."

Beppe had complimented Luigi and lavished praise on him for his courage, intelligence and loyalty over the last few weeks – bringing a distinct blush to his officer's cheeks.

When the applause in the meeting had died down, Beppe resumed speaking. He looked appreciatively at Pippo, whose act in initiating the applause had relieved the growing tension.

"Rest assured, all of you," he said. "The *Questore* has acted solely in my best interests in the only way he could. Let's leave matters there! Now, I have one further announcement to make. Our dear colleague, Oriana Salvati, is expecting a child – much to her own surprise, I believe. She has put in a request to be transferred to L'Aquila – which has been accepted."

There were sympathetic sounds of surprise and sorrow at the news.

"I should also like to mention the remarkable transformation Oriana has made to the lives of two children in Pescara – I am sure you all know what I am talking about. *Brava, Oriana!* What you did showed initiative, kindness and bravery – and you have certainly prevented one girl from falling into a life of crime."

There was another standing ovation before Beppe finally managed to drag himself away from his colleagues and go home to his family.

* * *

Sonia was right – as always. Spending three months with his family created bonds between them all that would have never been forged at such a vital moment in their family life had he been working. Beppe became adept at changing nappies and his daughter, Veronica, had managed to enunciate at least ten new words by the end of his leave. Sonia convinced him that Veronica was noticeably more interested in life and smiled more often since he began living with them for twenty-four hours at a time. He had no desire to doubt the truth of what Sonia claimed.

Beppe and Sonia's love-life gradually resumed – although Sonia tactfully suggested that the decision about a third child should be delayed for a while.

"Don't you feel you've got your hands full even with two children to look after, *amore?*" she asked.

"I have just begun to realise, Sonia, just how great a responsibility is laid upon women in this life. I am so fortunate to be sharing my life with you, *amore mio.*"

They decided that one month spent in Calabria would be all they could stand. Beppe's doting mother had apparently fainted and collapsed on to a sofa when her absentee son had announced their intention of travelling down to Calabria – for only the second time since their marriage.

"Oh Beppe! I shall be able to spend time with my very own grand-daughter, Imelda," she cried.

"*Mamma,*" Beppe sighed in resignation, instantly having doubts about their rash decision to travel down south to Calabria. "She's called Veronica."

His mother seemed to have forgotten that she also had a grandson from Sonia. At least, Beppe could console himself with the knowledge he could spend time with his beloved father and his sister, Valentina – also mother to two children by then. She had elected to live in a neighbouring village rather than share her two boys with their over-attentive grandmother.

After a couple of days back home in Calabria, out of simple courtesy to his former *capo* at Catanzaro's police station, Beppe plucked up the courage to enter its hallowed precincts – with a strange feeling of dread at the troubled memories it brought back. His former chief – looking much older – hugged Beppe. He had tears in his eyes. They went to find a bar near the police station.

"We miss you, Beppe," said his former *capo.* "I'm dealing with a strange case at the moment. Someone – or something – is going round starting up small fires all over the place - just little ones - for no apparent reason. The *vigili del fuoco* always seem to arrive in the nick of time. I don't suppose you would be able to help me out while you're down here, would you, Beppe?" said his ex-chief, a desperate look of appeal in his eyes.

"I don't think I would dare, Massimo," he replied, thinking of Sonia's reaction. But there was a gleam in his eyes which he had no means of controlling.

Epilogo

A hotel in L'Aquila called La Bella Vista found that it's trade was picking up, so much so that la signora began cooking meals for her very normal seeming clientele – who were happy to take refuge from their laboratory up in the mountains. The proprietors said a silent prayer of thanks to that Commissario from Pescara, who had saved them from destitution.

Attilio Lombardi's lawyer succeeded in convincing a jury that there was insufficient evidence to convict him of Giada Costa's murder. Nevertheless, the D.A.S.R., sensing that his impulsive use of a weapon cast sufficient doubts on his sense of moral judgement, dispatched him to Venezuela. He swore he would get even with 'that bastardo commissario' in Pescara one day. After a confrontation with some undesirable elements in the drug world, he was shot dead in a back street of Caracas.

Transferred to the police station in L'Aquila, Oriana Salvati replaced a young female officer called Valentina Ianni who had specifically requested to be moved to Pescara 'to work under that nice commissario Stancato'. Valentina Ianni had been immensely disappointed to discover that the aforementioned commissario was only one week into a three month leave of absence.

The L'Aquila team under Ispettore Fabrizio De Sanctis, was informed by Dante Di Pasquale to expect a new female recruit who *would take up a position in the following few days. It was Oriana Salvati who was assigned the task of looking after her on her first day. She was an attractive, vivacious lady in her thirties who announced herself as Simona Gambino. Oriana took to her instantly but could not escape the sensation that she had met her somewhere before. The face was vaguely familiar and her voice too... But it could not be who she was thinking of. That person had been murdered. Nevertheless, Oriana's sharp mind finally led her to draw her own conclusion, which she kept firmly to herself.*

On meeting the newcomer, Ispettore Fabrizio De Sanctis just stopped himself from telling his new team member that she bore a slight resemblance to an Italian actress – whose name he could not recall.

All weddings were postponed until the Stancato family returned to Pescara. Beppe had promised to be Pippo's best man before his departure. Don Emanuele undertook to give his blessing to the future couples – as long as he was invited to the reception at the Agriturismo della Bella Addormentata, where he would gladly carry out his spiritual duties. Pippo and Giovanni Palena were informed by Remo Mastrodicasa that they had a room set aside in the agriturismo where the local official could legally carry out marriage ceremonies. Both couples decided to kill two birds with one stone. The two clans would simply have to head for Monticchio and sleep there overnight.

Beppe himself spent an agreeable 'holiday' in Calabria, which was extended to a tentative five weeks, on Beppe's mother's insistence. His father was quietly content to be with his son a little longer. They would sit together, drink together, fish together and talk about life sitting on the quayside. It was Beppe's father's role to curb Imelda's desire to take over her grandchildren completely. "They aren't your children, amore. Let Sonia deal with them and leave everyone in peace, for heaven's sake," he would reiterate at salient points throughout the day.

Guiltily using his trips with his father beyond the confines of the home, Beppe managed to help his chief solve the case of the illegal fires. He conceived an instant mistrust of one of the junior officers in his chief's charge. He looked too shifty. Beppe was convinced that this officer was in some way connected to some scam with the firemen. Beppe was given a push in the right direction simply because he had heard of a similar case in neighbouring Sicily. It transpired that the firemen in the town waited for a phone call from Agente X, the shifty 'sbirro'. He would phone his mates just after he had located a suitable spot to set fire to – usually during the hours of darkness. They arrived minutes after the phone call to extinguish the fire and could then claim the additional bonuses they were entitled to from the comune *every time they successfully extinguished a blaze.*

Beppe felt saddened by the petty dishonesty of the scam and left his grateful chief to administer justice as he saw fit. But the incident helped him gather up the courage to make the necessary move to drive up north again towards Pescara when the appointed day arrived. He experienced the same sense of nostalgia as he had felt that day – so many years ago – when he had set off for Pescara in his boat, leaving his father on the quayside on that grey dawn morning. Only Sonia spotted the stray tear on his cheek as they drove out of Catanzaro. She placed her left hand on his thigh and left it there for several kilometres. Veronica and Lorenzo soon settled down, soothed by the motion of the car.

"We can come down here and live if you really want, amore," she said.

"No way, Sonia! My tears are for Calabria – not for myself."

Professor Donato Pisano is waiting for the scientific world to catch up with his unconventional convictions regarding the true nature of the universe, which he is convinced will only be a matter of time - as he ironically puts it. He is content to stay at home and write books and articles – venturing forth to give the occasional lecture in various European universities. An advanced physics laboratory in Bern is angling for his attention...

Glossary of Italian terms and cultural notes

Chapter 1

Il mondo scientifico
The Scientific World – a fictitious publication

accidente!
A mild expletive, meaning Bother! What a nuisance!

capo
Used throughout the story: it means 'chief' (lit. 'head')

Non ti preoccupare
Don't worry. Don't be concerned.

Che palle!
Lit: What balls! We would say "What a pain in the backside!"

Chapter 2

la Questura
police headquarters

un cellulare
a cellular / mobile phone

Chapter 3

Con permesso?
May we come in?

un bacio */batcho/*
a kiss on the cheek

Il Questore
The senior officer i/c of a Questura

Mi dica tutto
Tell me all

Vero capo?
True boss?

carta bianca
carte blanche

l'Orso Bruno
the Brown Bear – the nickname given to Officer Luigi Rocco because of his physical bulk. Brown bears were deliberately reintroduced to Abruzzo's mountains last century.

fidanzata
girlfriend / fiancée

Agli ordini!
Yes sir!

un palazzo
a block of apartments / a palace

ragazzi
lads – and lasses, if women are present.

Liceo Scientifico
A scientifically orientated high school

Chapter 4

una masseria
a farmhouse in Puglia

Sei mai stata sulla luna?
Apologies to you, readers – I am using a bit of poetic licence! This is a recent film made after the events in this novel supposedly took place. I allowed myself the anachronism simply because the film is so delightfully entertaining. If you understand Italian reasonably well, I would recommend you buy the DVD. There are subtitles because much of the dialogue is spoken in Salento dialect.

una festa
a party : a street festival

la Pizzica
a dance peculiar to the Salento region of Puglia – cf My first novel "Dancing to the Pizzica"

L'hotel Bella Vista
'Beautiful View' – ironic since the hotel is located opposite an earthquake damaged 'palazzo'

Chapter 5

In quale senso?
In what sense?

una lacuna
a gap : a lacuna – a commonly used word in Italian, being Latin based.

Chapter 6

La faccio strada
I'll show you the way – when the speaker walks in front of the 'guest' because the 'street' is unfamiliar.

Chapter 7

Che bell'uomo!
'What a good-looking man!' says the secretary. Beppe modestly assumes the compliment is not directed at him.

The 'mock gesture involving thumb, index and middle fingers pressed together'
A very common gesture in Italy – implying a host of ironic meanings. 'You're kidding yourself, right?"
In bocca al lupo
Best of luck! (Lit: in the mouth of the wolf)

Chapter 8

più simpatico
nicer : friendlier

appunto
precisely : exactly

un agriturismo
a restaurant-cum-farmhouse where the proprietors are legally bound to source about 50% of the food from their own estate. A splendid Italian institution!

un abbraccio
a hug

La bella addormentata
The Sleeping Beauty – the restaurant name has a connection with Beppe's first case.

cacio e uova
a typical dish from Abruzzo – as described. Recipe can be found on the internet – of course.

un prezzo d'amico
a friend's price – a reduced price just for a friend.

"La cucina è eccezionale"
The food is exceptional

La Vestina
A trattoria in Penne belonging to Pippo's fidanzata's father – where the couple first met in "A Close Encounter with Mushrooms" – the second novel in this series.

il comune
the town hall

Mi manchi un sacco
I miss you lots

Chapter 9

mille grazie / grazie mille
Lit: a thousand thanks

un bacione
a big kiss

scuola media
middle school

grazie di cuore
thanks from the heart

Calcio Pescara
Pescara football team - 'un calcio' literally means 'a kick' so it has come to mean football. The Dolphin is the symbol of the Pescara team.

la prego
I beg you

Pasta all'Amatriciana
A pasta dish with chillies, tomato sauce and pancetta – from the town of Amatrice, destroyed by the earthquake of 2016.

Oriana defending herself
We know from The Case of the Sleeping Beauty that Oriana Salvati is a martial arts expert

Chapter 10

Sono d'accordo
I agree

Chapter 11

porchetta
hog roast – very popular in central Italy

Chapter 12

Ci dia ancora un attimo per cortesia
Could you give us a moment longer please

Senti, Remo
Listen, Remo

Arrivo subito
I'm on my way

Io ti amo / Ti voglio bene
I love you (emotional, physical) / I love you (to a family member etc)

Marta
Remo Mastrodicasa's partner from the previous novels.

genziana
a liqueur from Abruzzo – flavoured with the gentian flower

La notte porta consiglio
The night brings us counsel i.e. Let's sleep on it

Chapter 13

Ti vogliamo bene
We love you = we are very fond of you (Says Rosa to Oriana)

al fresco
An idiomatic expression meaning prison. Lit: In the open – a reference to out of town jails

L'eredità
A very popular daily quiz on Rai 1

Che cazzo fai qui?
What the f..k are you doing here? The vulgarity of Rosa and Steffi's father is made even more evident since he uses the familiar 'tu' form to Oriana.

Chi sei tu?
Who are YOU?

Mio Dio!
Good heavens!

stronzo
A very strong word used by Oriana – equivalent to saying 'You piece of s..t"

Chapter 14

Eccolo
There he is

un'allianza
a wedding ring

colpa mia
my fault

mi dispiace tanto
I'm so sorry

Chapter 15

Mi perdoni
Forgive me : Pardon me

tesoro
treasure – term of endearment

Chapter 16

Il sugo
(tomato) sauce

Guardate! Sono io!
Look! It's me! calls out Professor Pisano.

cazzo
f..k

Buona domenica. Buon appetito.
Have a good Sunday and enjoy your meal.

uno sbirro : due sbirri etc
one cop : two cops

un digestivo
an after dinner alcoholic drink

Dov'è piantato il mio albero genealogico?
Where is my family tree planted? (My fictitious name for an ancestral website)

i legami familiari
family ties

Chapter 17

una cancelleria
a stationery shop

"Sorelle"
Sisters – a Rai 1 production – and, I must confess, another anachronism. This outstanding TV drama was first broadcast in March 2017.

Sbrigati!
Get a move on!

The American military base near Vicenza
Not an invention on my part! There is, in fact, more than one such base in northern Italy. But I did not wish to over-complicate the plot.

Chapter 18

l'autostrada A14
The motorway which follows the Adriatic coast.

Chapter 19

the number 112
- the emergency phone number stencilled on every Carabinieri police car.

Chapter 21

sceneggiatura
a scenario

Chapter 22

Sono incinta

I'm pregnant

scema */shayma/*
silly!

'imprisoned by the mushroom poisoner'
A reference to events in the previous novel, 'A Close Encounter with Mushrooms'

Sabrina Ferilli
A prominent Italian actress

È vero
It's true

Rai 1 : La 7
Two TV Channels – the first is the national channel, the second a respected independent channel.

Il corriere della sera
A renowned independent national daily – based in Milan

avvocato
advocate = lawyer

Chapter 23

in diretta
live – a live broadcast

cari telespettatori
dear viewers

Ci sono più cose in cielo...
Quite obviously, THAT quote from Hamlet... 'There are more things in heaven and earth than are dreamt of in your philosophy.'

Il Lago di Scanno
Lake Scanno - a well-known beauty spot in the southern part of Abruzzo

solidarietà familiare
Family solidarity

ragazza squillo
call girl

Epilogo

The firemen who started their own fires
Yes, this really did happen in Sicily

About the author

Richard Walmsley lived, loved and worked for eight life-changing years in Puglia – the 'heel' of Italy. From 2002 until 2005, he taught English at the University of Salento in Lecce until he reached the age of sixty-five when he reluctantly retired from teaching and began instead to write novels.

The first three novels were inspired by his vivid experiences in this fascinating and contradictory region of Italy.

The second series of novels, of which this is the third, are set in the little known and largely unspoilt region of Abruzzo – half way down Italy on the Adriatic side of the Peninsula.

The author finds the current confusion caused by Brexit deeply disturbing. He fervently hopes that the bonds formed with other European countries over the past forty years will not be broken by this political divide.

August 2017

nonno-riccardo publications
richard_s_walmsley@hotmail.com

86042428R00199

Made in the USA
Middletown, DE
28 August 2018